THE END

OF THE

BEGINNING

To Susan

Tim Styled

THE END OF THE BEGINNING

A NOVEL

BY TIM STAFFORD

Franklin Park Press
Copyright © 2023 Tim Stafford
ISBN 979-8-8508-8819-0

Visit the author's website at timstafford.wordpress.com

2005

1

VERITY IS DEAD

Despite their many years of friendship, Mindy had never attended a service at Verity's church, St. Chrysostom. Verity had never invited her, which was strange, since the church was so important to her and the two of them were very close.

The building, when Mindy found it, surprised her with its ordinariness. The dome was unusual, but the parking lot—already half full—suggested conventional suburban life. She thought to herself that nothing said normalcy like the asphalt grit of a parking lot. Walking toward the church entrance in the heels she so seldom wore, Mindy felt sure she was in for a long, dull service. It distressed her to think so. Verity was extraordinary, like diamonds hidden in a paper bag. Mindy longed to honor her, who had received so little honor in her life.

Inside the church doors, light flooded down from a cupola high above, illuminating ranks of supersized saints on the walls and pillars. Every surface was figured with shimmering design and strange, staring faces. It was a dream environment, crowded with brilliant, enigmatic beauty—a treasure box glittering with gold.

Dazzled, Mindy stood still to take it in. She had never seen a church like this: radiant, foreign, and dominated by inscrutable faces. Mesmerized by the brilliancy, she only gradually realized that the room had pews holding scattered worshipers. Far up at the front was a plain casket. Verity, she thought, and felt the idea grab her like a vise grip. Her perception of ornamental glory fell away, and she longed to see her friend inside the box. Just as powerfully, she felt terrified. She had never seen a dead person.

Prying her eyes off the casket, she was able to take a seat. Scattered around her were older, gray-haired, somberly dressed people. They did not move or speak to each other but appeared as stolid as mushrooms.

Cautiously twisting to see who sat behind her, Mindy was utterly surprised to glimpse Leslie in the back. Leslie saw her in the same moment and gave a bright smile.

Mindy had called all the old Mount of Olives camp friends, telling them the news, but she hadn't expected them to come. Least of all Leslie. She was as sleek and well-dressed as ever, poured into a black sheath. Just behind her sat Howard and Julie, the glamorous couple, who always seemed like movie stars to Mindy.

She had imagined complete anonymity at the service, or nearly so. Now she realized it would not be possible to grieve Verity in solitude. Her friends would compete for her attention. It made her anxious; it was as though she were already neglecting her friend.

The service began with deep male voices chanting the words of an antique liturgy—words that she assumed would be beautiful if she could stop them long enough to savor them. Mindy was accustomed to a service that approximated a town hall meeting. How could she describe this? She might be in a mountain village in Greece.

Through the long service, Mindy thought of Verity. It was surely impossible for her to be gone. She was too real, too earthy. How, Mindy wondered, was she going to live without that scratchy voice on the phone?

When the service was done, the choir continued singing while a procession of people made their way to the coffin. Some crossed themselves as they reached their destination, and many leaned over into the coffin, putting their heads right down inside.

Mindy edged her way to the central aisle. The line slowly inched ahead, and she felt her heart racing out of control as she neared the front. People leaning over the body were kissing it, she saw. This made her nauseous, and she would have stepped out of line and fled if it were not for the fact that she wanted to see her friend—to see her in the flesh.

To distract herself, Mindy looked up, away from the line of people and away from the plain brown casket to the golden, glittering icons. Not understanding them, not even liking them, she nevertheless could feel them, like spirits made visible above and around her. Stepping forward when her turn came, she looked down on Verity.

She thought someone had made an awful mistake. This was not her friend. Then, swiftly, she saw that the corpse was modeled closely on Verity, that Verity's features were there as though stamped on a form. Yet everything was off. The body in the casket had her hair permed and spread out over the white silk, which Verity would never have done with her straight, black hair. The body wore eye makeup and its lips were a coral pink, whereas Mindy's friend wore no makeup at all. Staring, Mindy came to realize the greatest difference of all: the body was dead. It was possible to imagine Verity's soul filling a shape like this one, but it clearly did not: whatever had once lived there was gone. It went beyond utter stillness; here was no life at all. This was a dead, dead thing.

Then, in an instant—for these reactions came very quickly, flipped like a shuffled deck of cards—she realized that this flesh was dear for what it had been. It had held the soul of a beautiful person. Mindy instinctively leaned forward to touch. Then she saw, placed over Verity's heart, an icon—a small red-and-black image of a saint rendered in the peculiar Orthodox tradition. People were kissing that, Mindy realized; it was placed over the heart for exactly that reason. She lowered her head, so far down, and put her lips to it. There was nothing to kiss, mere cold cardboard.

As she raised her head again, she thought she felt a fleeting ghost of life, Verity's presence, just for an instant. Without warning, tears came, flooding her eyes. She knew, profoundly, that she would never see Verity again. That funny, awkward girl she missed so much was gone for good.

2

OLD FRIENDS

Outside, wiping her eyes, Mindy was embarrassed to find all her Mount of Olive friends waiting in the courtyard. She couldn't believe they had come. Sam and his wife, Cynthia, and Brian had made the trip from Kansas City. (Not together, surely—Mindy didn't know whether Sam and Brian were speaking after what had happened to Sam's church.) That they had cared enough amazed her.

The day was windy and brisk—fall weather. At the gravesite she spotted Verity's daughter, Ivy, dressed in Goth: her eyes clotted with black, lace-up boots on her feet, a scowl on her face. Watching her during the graveside service, Mindy saw no hint of emotion. She never raised her eyes to look at anyone but glowered at the casket as though it were loaded with explosives and about to go off.

The service was brief and when it was complete, they were offered pink carnations to drop on the casket. Mindy watched Ivy carefully. She didn't take a flower. After observing a few mourners deposit theirs, she turned to walk away.

"Ivy!" Mindy called.

She turned, evidently surprised but not in a friendly way.

"I'm a friend of your mom's," Mindy said. "Mindy. She was a dear, dear friend."

Ivy said nothing.

"Do you need anything?" Mindy asked. "Do you have a place to stay?"

Ivy set her teeth as though the question were an affront. "I'm fine."

"Look," Mindy said, "I want to give you my phone number. This is for your mom, whom I loved so much. I know she would want me to. If you ever, ever get stuck, for anything, call me. I'll help. No questions. Just whatever help you need. Money, food, doctors. Okay?" Before Ivy could answer, Mindy pulled a small pad of paper out of her purse and carefully wrote her name and phone number on a page. "Here," she said, tearing it off. "Don't lose it."

Ivy stuck it in the pocket of her black jeans. "Thanks," she said, shrugging her shoulders, and walked away.

A huddle of Mount of Olives friends stood in the cemetery road, saying goodbye. Once Mindy would have unhesitatingly claimed this group as her best friends in the world. But it had been years, and did she even know them now? There were hugs and promises to call, but when Leslie said, "Let's go somewhere and get a drink," she had everyone's attention.

"They have a meal back at the church," Mindy offered. "We could go there." Her spirits were raised by the thought of more time. Looking at these friends, she remembered how attached she had once been.

Howard said, "I'd rather drink." That gave Mindy a small shock of surprise. When they were young, none of them drank, and Howard had been their leader.

Howard led them to Tony's in a caravan of cars. The room was low and dark, the tables battle-scarred, and their waitress chewed gum. She made no pretense of writing anything down as she worked her way around their table, and of course she confused their orders. For some reason this loosened the mourners; they were already gabbing in multiple conversations before their drinks came, and while straightening out who had ordered what, they began laughing.

"Hold on, hold on," Mindy said over the hilarity and the tangled conversations. "Could we go one at a time around the table? That way nobody has to repeat themselves. Is that okay? I'm really wanting to catch up on everybody. Let's start with Randy, and when he's done, we'll go to Candy and then to Julie and so on. Does that make sense? And you can ask any question you want."

It was her natural role—the den mother. She had chosen Randy to start because she thought his life was probably the least complicated of any of them, except herself.

Randy surprised her by telling the group that he worried how the money he made would affect his kids. They were growing up rich, and he couldn't honestly tell them there was anything too expensive to buy. He wanted them to learn to be generous, but even their generosity, he said with a grimace, was easy. It wasn't sacrificial. He didn't know what to do about that.

It went like that all around the table. Each person opened a crack of vulnerability, even Leslie. She was on her second drink before Randy finished talking, and by the time the circle came round to her, her consonants were sloppy and her beautiful dark hair was coming apart. She admitted that she'd thought her dairy cow greeting cards would keep on selling indefinitely. "It's just confounded me," she said. "The damn things. I'm furious with the distributors. I think they're screwing me, and I've yelled at them and threatened, and it doesn't do a lick of good. It's made me wonder—just what is the point of it all?"

Howard built on that and admitted he had lost faith in people. "I've always been the optimist, the guy who sees the good in others, but lately, leading this fast-growing church, I've found people are terribly selfish. They don't want to do anything that isn't in their interest."

"Like what?" Brian said. "Give me an example." That was typical of Brian—, always a very concrete thinker. He was the shortest of the group, built like a pit bull, and sometimes he acted like one.

Howard puckered up his mouth and thought for a minute. You wanted to believe in Howard, Mindy thought. He no longer had the long, golden hair of their youth, but his handsome face still communicated simplicity and sincerity.

"Well, I could give you dozens of examples," Howard said carefully, "but a lot of it comes down to money. We need money to buy things, money for airtime, money for equipment and staff, and when you ask people if they will help, they just come up with these excuses. 'Our company operates on a quarterly basis, and I can't do anything before August.' 'All our charitable giving goes through our foundation, and here's an application.'"

"Maybe it's the time of life we're in," Sam suggested. The years had not been kind to him. He had never been particularly handsome in Mindy's eyes, and now his face looked stretched and tired. "When we were kids, we had no money but so much faith. Now there's so much disappointment."

When Mindy's turn came, she told how she had come to work at Randy's company, and funnily, how similar it was to her previous job teaching preschool. "Whether they are three years old or thirty, people need help in cleaning up messes, and they want to know that you're going to take care of them, and then they're fine."

"Mindy is incredible," Randy said. "She's the best thing that ever happened to our company."

Mindy smiled and thanked him. "As some of you know, Randy's company has done extremely well, and so the question somebody asked him applies to me. How has all the money changed you? I understand how people are curious about that, but the truth is, I don't think it has changed me at all. The money is nice, don't get me wrong, but it's not nearly as important as people think. I'm just not that interested in it. I live exactly the way I did before. I don't have kids, so I don't have to worry about them the way Randy does."

She expected a wash of feedback, because that was what she'd experienced when she tried to say the same thing to her family. Before anybody could start on that, however, Julie spoke up. "Can you tell us about Scott? About how that's affected you?"

"How do you mean?"

"I know you were close. I heard he asked you to marry him. How did his death affect you?"

For half a minute she sat in silence, and then came tears—the second time in the day, and she was someone who never cried. "That was the end for me," she said, and instantly wondered where that answer had come from, for she had never consciously thought it before. "He didn't actually ask me to marry him. I thought maybe he was going to, and I even tried to think about what my answer would be. I didn't really know him all that well. We went out for over a year, and you would think that was plenty of time, but I don't know—it was not so deep." She let her eyes travel around the table. "When he died, and I found out he had AIDS, I was totally shocked, but in some ways not utterly surprised. I guess I felt something in him that wasn't completely open."

"Did you feel betrayed?" Leslie asked.

Mindy nodded. "Yeah, I felt some anger, but I think the deepest feeling was relief, that I'd never gotten entangled. Mostly I just thought, *My God, what if I'd married him?*"

She stopped there, aware that she had opened a crack that could become a canyon. Part of her wanted that. She had held these thoughts in long enough. For a moment, she poised on the brink of saying more, spilling it before these friends. Then she remembered Verity. She had come today for Verity.

"Has everybody given us an update now?" she asked. "Could we talk about Verity? I'd love to hear your memories. She became my dearest friend, but she didn't like to talk about herself, and there's a lot I don't know. I thought if we put our memories together, it would be meaningful."

They were suddenly quiet, remembering. Mindy thought how uncanny it was that Verity, of all people, had brought them together again. On the surface she had appeared to be the least charismatic personality imaginable. Her face was plain, her speech sputtered, she moved awkwardly, and yet she was so utterly honest. Something about her simplicity made you feel safe and home. At least that was the case for Mindy.

"Do you remember when she had the seizure?" Howard asked. "I think it was the first night of camp. She fell on top of somebody, remember? Was it you, Leslie?"

Leslie said it was and smiled her beautiful, mysterious smile that had once so beguiled them all. "It was so embarrassing for her. We were all thrilled to be there, you remember? And she was scared out of her mind. I didn't think she'd ever come back after she got out of the hospital."

"But she did," Mindy said softly. "She had a lot of courage."

"And then Howard—you got her to stop taking her medicine." Leslie had a gleam in her eye as she reminded Howard of his youthful zeal. "You told her if she had faith, she wouldn't need drugs. God would heal her. Remember that?"

"She did have faith," Julie said. "But then her mother told her that she had to take her meds or she would make her come home. So, she took them. She was terrified that we would all condemn her for it."

"Did she take medications for the rest of her life?" Leslie asked.

"I don't know," Mindy said. "She never said anything about it to me, but then, she wasn't very interested in that kind of thing. Verity was interested in what she was interested in."

"Who was that girl you were talking to after the burial?" Julie wanted to know.

"That was her daughter."

"Born of a virgin," Howard said and chortled. "Boy, was that a story."

"It's funny," Mindy said, "but Verity never seemed embarrassed about it. It wasn't like she'd bring it up, but when it came up, she would laugh."

"What are we talking about?" Randy asked.

"Oh, sorry, Randy; maybe you missed it." If they had to talk about that episode, Mindy wanted to keep the discussion factual and dignified. "Verity was married—you know that, right? To Cass. But they couldn't consummate the marriage. They kept trying and trying, and Verity wouldn't go to the doctor because it embarrassed her. Somehow, she got pregnant. Nobody could explain it. Technically, she was still a virgin. That was Ivy."

Mindy braced herself for questions and maybe wisecracks, but only Randy responded. "Ivy looked unhappy," he said, and Mindy could have blessed him for moving the conversation off the virgin birth.

"Yeah, Verity told me Ivy was having a hard time. She and Cass don't get along. I gave her my phone number and told her to call if she needed anything, but I doubt she will. I don't know how she's going to manage. Cass is her only family now."

"What was Verity like as a mom?" Cynthia asked. She had stayed on the sideline, conscious that she wasn't one of the original group. Verity interested her, however, even though she had barely met her.

"She was very dedicated," Mindy said. "Very permissive, too. She let Ivy do whatever she wanted to do. I guess she was reacting to her own mom, who was so strict. You know, when we knew Verity at camp, her mother terrorized her. She hated to think she would be that way to her own daughter, and I think she took it a little far. But who am I to say? So, Ivy got into the Goth thing, and she missed school more than she made it. I don't know how much drugs came into it."

"How did Ivy relate to her mom's church?" Sam asked.

Mindy gave a short, explosive laugh. "Not very well, I guess. Early on, when she was little, I think she loved church. That was when Verity was Pentecostal. Ivy liked to dance, and she would go up on stage during worship time. She got quite a reputation as a dancer, Verity told me. But later, Ivy stopped going, and Verity never made a big thing out of it, as far as I know. Of course, Cass stopped going, too, so it would have been hard to fight."

"That's the truth," Cynthia said. "If the dad won't go, the kids won't go either." Everybody knew she was talking about Sam. Cynthia was the least known of the group; she had married Sam years after college. She was extremely thin, and she stared so intently at someone she was talking to that it was hard to meet her gaze. Mindy was very curious about her.

"And then when she became Orthodox, that was it, Ivy wanted nothing to do with it," Mindy said.

"You can't blame her for that," Brian said. "That is some weird stuff."

"I wonder what Verity saw in it," Howard said.

"She loved it," Mindy said. "She was so focused on that church and her little community there. I sincerely believe all her woes, like her divorce from Cass and Ivy's rebellion, didn't get to her because she was in love with her church. Other things washed off her."

"I never understood it," Howard said, shaking his head. "Verity was smart, you know. She started out a solid evangelical, and then during that Pentecostal stage she seriously wanted to raise people from the dead. Those stories about angel feathers falling out of the church ceiling—she believed them. Then she took a U-turn and became Orthodox, with all that chanting and ritual and those icons they pray to. She wasn't like some people who are always searching. Verity was always finding. She didn't even see the contradictions when she went from one to the next."

Mindy felt her face burning. She admired Howard, but how could he speak that way? "She was pure," Mindy said. "Pure in a way I just haven't seen in anyone else. I mean, she could be silly, and she had terrible judgment. I had to talk her out of this real estate scheme—a scam, really. It would have left her on the hook for huge debts. She could go off in the wildest ways and have no idea she'd done anything stupid. But she loved her church, and she could get lost in it, 'lost in wonder.'" In that last phrase Mindy caught herself becoming quite emotional and stopped.

"We won't see her like again," Howard said grandly. "She was one of a kind."

"What was it about that summer?" Sam asked after a pause. "It always stands out, but I don't know why. We were just dumb kids who thought we knew so much. I'm sure we said a lot of ridiculous things that would embarrass us now. But it was quite a summer."

"That's why we're here now," Mindy said. "Because it was amazing."

"But what made it so amazing?"

"We were young," Julie said.

"Yes, we were young," Mindy said with a sigh. "And we believed we were doing incredibly important work. We were going to change lives. At eighteen."

"What a trip that was," Leslie said. Mindy couldn't tell whether she meant it or spoke sarcastically.

3

CHASING MEMORIES

They had been at the bar for nearly two hours when Randy and Candy stood and said they had to go.

"Oh, do we have to leave?" Leslie asked. "I feel like we just got here."

"The rest of us can stay," Howard said expansively. "Do you want to order some food?" Leslie had been drinking non-stop.

"Why don't we go somewhere?" she said. "Why don't we drive up to Mount of Olives?" She looked over the six of them who were left. "C'mon, it would be fun, don't you think? For old times' sake."

"We could go to dinner up there," Brian said. "What was the name of that restaurant?"

"Trantoni's," both Julie and Sam said simultaneously. All that summer, they had gone there after a Saturday afternoon at the beach.

"That's it," Brian said. "Trantoni's. That would be fun. Assuming it's still there."

Howard slammed his fist on the table, making the glasses rattle. "It has to be there! They wouldn't dare change anything from our magical summer!"

Mindy invited Leslie to drive with her and was thankful when Leslie said yes. It wasn't a road for a sloshed driver. Mindy invited Brian, too, but he had changed his mind and said he wasn't coming.

The highway was narrow, crowded with fast traffic. They passed a lake in the grassy foothills and soon entered deep redwood forests. The road ascended in wide, swooping curves. Mindy had to concentrate. She didn't have brain space for talk.

Yet right away, Leslie started in on Scott. "Let me ask you," she said, "did you ever sleep together?"

Mindy was shocked. "No!" she said. "We barely kissed."

"Well, that makes sense, if he was as gay as I think he was. But you dated, right? He asked you out. What do you think he was trying to do?"

"Maybe he just wanted a friend," Mindy said, though she didn't fully believe it.

"But you thought he was going to ask you to marry him. Didn't you say that? You must have thought there was more going on if you were waiting for him to pop the question. Didn't you? If he never touched you, that must have confused the heck out of you. Right? What on earth did you think? It must have been quite a shock when you found out."

"It was," Mindy admitted. She didn't want to discuss this with anybody, let alone Leslie, but she had thought again and again about Scott.

Gripping the wheel and leaning toward the windshield, she said, "I wonder if he was trying to figure things out. Trying to see whether he could live a normal life with a woman. He must have been so miserable, carrying his secrets."

"So he was using you like a test case?"

Mindy didn't like the phrasing, but it was more or less what she meant. "Sort of. He liked me, I'm sure. I don't know whether he loved me."

"But if you want to test, you have to get physical, right? You have to try out the equipment. Otherwise, what do you know?"

"I think it's more complicated than that," Mindy said.

In answer, Leslie began laughing—a sloppy, drunk laugh. She got so wrapped up in her hilarity she couldn't stop. "Well, what do you know?" she said when she got control. "You've never been married, have you? I bet you're still a virgin. Am I right? You don't have to answer that—I know it's obnoxious. I've been married three times, but I couldn't begin to guess what turns on somebody like Scott. I've known some gay men at work, but I've never gone out with one. Can't imagine what that's like."

Her volubility stopped at that point, and she was quiet the rest of the way up the hill. The silence felt intolerable to Mindy, but she had no idea what to say. The ride couldn't be over soon enough.

* *

First to arrive at Mount of Olives were Howard and Julie, with Sam and Cynthia pulling up just behind them. Howard had not been to the camp since college, and his first thought was that nothing had changed at all. The buildings—all single-story wood construction—were scattered haphazardly on the side of a hill, some old and weatherworn, some bright and newly painted. As a young person, Howard had never thought about the way the camp looked; it just *was*. He thought now that it seemed to have grown without a master plan. It had the sleepy serenity of a site that had spread organically over the years.

"Where should we go?" Julie asked. Her face was pink and bright. "I can't believe we're here again. Do you remember the day we first arrived?"

Cynthia wanted to see their cabins, so the four of them puffed their way up the hill to where Howard and Sam had spent their summer shepherding fourteen-year-olds. They were summer cabins, uninhabited at present, so they could poke their heads in the door to see the bunk beds. It seemed smaller and shabbier than they remembered. With the electricity off, the dim rooms seemed profoundly empty, like mining cabins on an old dig.

Outside, Sam pointed out two battered picnic tables. "That's where we sat, isn't it?" He spoke to Cynthia. "After the kids were asleep, we would come out here and talk. Howard had us all mesmerized, explaining the Bible to us. We thought he was brilliant."

Howard waved off the compliment. He found it strange to see Sam's worn and lined face, so changed while the camp stood unaltered. To Howard, Sam would always be that slender, quiet, intense boy he had met that summer. It was sad, how his life had gone.

"You could say this is where Howard began," Julie said, as though awestruck at the thought.

"Began what?" Cynthia asked. Sam was immediately alert; he recognized her tone.

"Began teaching," Julie said fondly. "That's really what it is. People call it preaching, but it's really teaching."

"So, Howard," Cynthia said. "Today you were complaining that nobody wants to help. Nobody is willing to sacrifice for the good of all. Yes? So, I wanted to ask you, what do you sacrifice for anybody else's good?"

Howard hardly knew Cynthia, so he wasn't sure where her question led. "I try to help people," he said lightly. "I try. Maybe I need to try harder. Is that what you think?" He smiled at Cynthia.

"Where do you perceive the sacrifice?" she asked.

"Pardon?"

"You were saying that nobody wants to make sacrifices for the good of your church. What's your sacrifice?"

He was tongue-tied, a rare thing with Howard, but Julie jumped to his defense. "Howard is very sick," she said. "Don't you know that? He has a lung disease. The doctors say he could die of it."

"*Will* die of it," Howard inserted.

"*Will* die of it. It's amazing he can do what he does. I'm very proud of him."

Cynthia raised her eyebrows. "I'm glad. I'm just sick of hearing preachers who think they get special credit. If you want to be a preacher, good for you. But don't go around asking other people to do what you're not willing to do."

Stunned, Sam and Julie waited for Howard's retort. It did not come. Howard acted like he had not heard. Sam thought that what Cynthia said was true; everybody knew that Howard thought the world revolved around him. What Cynthia didn't understand—and how could she?—was what Howard had been for them. Sam's faith wouldn't have survived college without Howard.

Julie hung on to Howard's arm as they went back down the hill. They poked their heads into the dining hall and Julie, trying her best to forgive Cynthia, told her about the skits they put on. "And the singing," she said. "The singing was really fun."

"Was Verity part of that?" Cynthia asked. She knew she had upset the others, and she wanted to make up for it without issuing an apology.

"No, Verity worked in the kitchen. She wasn't program staff."

"She took part in the evening programs," Sam said. "Remember when she was the human Veg-o-matic?"

He explained the skit for Cynthia. "And Brian stuck a big hunk of potato in her mouth and nearly suffocated her. It was scary for a moment, but Verity felt proud of it. Proud to be included, I guess. She was the star that night."

"I wish I had known her," Cynthia said. "She obviously had something, or you wouldn't all be here."

"Yes," Howard said. "She was a rare kid. Very sincere."

They wandered across the road to look at Victory Circle, a wooden amphitheater with a fire pit in the middle. The camp had met there every Thursday for the week's most sober moment. One at a time, the counselors put a stick on the fire and told how they had given their lives to Christ, urging campers to make the same commitment.

The amphitheater looked much smaller than Sam remembered it. He couldn't see how the whole camp had fit on the risers. It triggered a feeling of deep melancholy. He wondered where those high school kids were now, and whether they still believed. How many of the counselors still believed?

Mindy and Leslie appeared at the top of the risers, calling *hello*. "Oh, hi!" Sam cried, waving back, glad for a diversion. "I didn't know you were coming. Did you just arrive?"

"God, it looks so small!" Leslie said. "It's like a toy land! Wasn't it just enormous in our day?"

"And yet," Howard said, "with great consequences! Lives were changed in this circle."

"Oh, for heaven's sake, Howard," Leslie said.

"What?" he asked. He was still feeling the smart from Cynthia's takedown.

"Don't be so melodramatic."

"I'm not being melodramatic. Kids made decisions about their lives here."

"Ah! They were just kids. We were kids, too. We made decisions then, we've made decisions since; what does it amount to?"

"What it amounts to," Howard said, "is a change of direction. Even if it was just a change of one degree, it makes the difference of a thousand miles if you carry it out far enough."

"Sure, if you go straight. But who goes straight? We zigzag. You zigzag yourself. Look, you started out to be a movie guy. That was your plan, remember? You were going to make life-changing movies. God knows we all heard about it. And now look at you. You're a preacher, just like your father."

"The medium may have changed, but the direction didn't. I'm still telling stories to change people's lives."

"Fine," Leslie said. "If you say so." She wasn't going to argue with Howard. She remembered him too well.

After a few moments of quiet, Mindy spoke up. "This is the thing I've been thinking about. Who goes in a straight line? In her own funny way, Verity did. We didn't necessarily see it because she didn't explain herself. And she didn't follow any regular pathway, so it looked like she was in a zigzag, like you said, Leslie. Her change of churches, or her marriage, or her way of raising children seemed pretty erratic. For her, though, those weren't the main thing. Underneath, at the core, she wanted what she wanted, and she went straight for it."

"Which was?" Sam asked.

"What we were saying in the bar. She wanted God, and she didn't care if she looked foolish. I wish I had seen it more clearly. I wish I could ask her questions, but it's too late for that, isn't it?"

* *

The next morning, Howard and Julie headed south on the I-5 with Julie driving, as she usually did since Howard had gotten sick. On their right were the tawny hills of the Coast Range. Nearer to hand the grass looked lifeless and colorless, the long, rainless summer and fall having beaten it to trash. Howard was unusually still. Ordinarily, he fiddled with the radio, impatiently changing stations.

"Am I really selfish?" he asked.

Julie threw him a glance. "What?" She knew exactly what he had said and what it referred to, but she wasn't ready to give a straight answer.

"Like Sam's wife said. I noticed that nobody answered her."

"I did. I said that you were very sick, and that everything you did in the church was a sacrifice."

"OK, but nobody else said a word defending me."

Julie considered her options. She knew, as few other people did, that Howard was fragile. Still, much as she loved him, it would do him good to recognize that he wasn't the only character onstage.

"I'd say you are single-minded," she said. "That's one reason you are so great. You have such focus. But sometimes other people feel left out."

"Left out?"

"Yes."

He was silent, and Julie hoped he had moved on. The topic was a sure loser for her.

"What can I do?" Howard asked.

For a moment, she pondered her response. She did not believe Howard had the capacity to escape himself. Putting out a hand, she said, "Don't do anything. Just be yourself."

1973

4

MOUNT OF OLIVES

The printed directions put the camp on Mt. Olive Road, but when Verity and her mother turned down a strip of asphalt they thought was correct, they drove miles through redwood-shrouded hills without seeing a sign. Verity knew they were lost. Her mother, who would never swear in English, exploded with Polish expressions that Verity did not know. Verity said nothing. Shrinking in her seat, she tried to disappear. She felt helpless and tiny—a baby.

When they reached a wide space in the road by a sand quarry, Verity's mother threw a looping U-turn and started back the way they had come. Firecrackers kept popping out of her mouth while Verity looked straight ahead, imagining that she was watching a driver's training movie. *Keep your eyes ahead, sweeping from point to point; do not fasten your gaze on one object.* What she saw was a landscape utterly unfamiliar: deeply forested mountains, with signs of human habitation only in occasional roadside businesses—a Stihl chainsaw vendor, a liquor store, and a home with hand-lettered signs advertising "eggs" and "succulents."

At the intersection where they had first turned, Verity's mother veered into a gas station. Pulling up to a pump, she pointed into the store. "Go ask."

Verity walked as though she were hoping to vanish. She shuffled pigeon-toed, with thin shoulders and scrawny arms bent inward as though to part the curtains of air and find a safe and secret pocket inside. The day was bright and breezy, and she blinked when she got into the shadowy store. A man, bored, threw out the answer like a playing card. "You gotta go way past the quarry. At least a mile. You can't miss it, on your left."

Her mother doubted and complained, but they went back again, past the quarry. At an intersection for the Roustabout Logging Train, Verity spotted the sign, carved into a half-log with a red arrow pointing left: "Mount Olive Campground." She pointed and her mother turned, accepting without a word that Verity had been right, though she would never admit it.

Up the hill on a narrow road without any shoulder, they came to another larger sign fronting a small parking lot and a post office. "Here," Verity said, and her mother pulled in and parked. "There," Verity said, pointing at a sign that read *Dining Hall*. Before she could be corrected, she was out of the car and heading up the path.

The dining hall was an old wooden building painted cream white, with a wide porch in front. Verity went through the double doors into a large room crammed with round wooden tables and empty chairs. On the far side, five or six people about her age were looking at Verity as though she had interrupted their conversation. Taking them in, she was suddenly filled with anxiety. In the drama of getting lost, she had put aside her chief worry. It came rushing back. Nobody at this camp knew her—not one soul.

After a moment's hesitation, Verity set out across the room toward the group of strangers. When she was still ten or twenty feet away, a boy called out, "Whatcha need?" His voice reverberated in the empty room. He had dark, watchful eyes and a small head that reminded her of one of the aliens in her favorite film.

Verity stopped short. Her heart was pounding. "I'm here for the kitchen," she said.

"The kitchen's closed," he said. "We start tomorrow."

She nearly turned around and left, but her mother was somewhere back there. Forward was her only choice. "I mean, I'm here for the summer. I'm on the work crew." She blurted it out, hoping beyond hope someone could help her.

Another boy flipped a backhand cuff at the first young man, and what sounded like a good-natured razzing rose from the group. "Are you Verity?" asked a pretty girl, small and lithe with long auburn hair. She stood up and smiled. "We wondered when you would get here."

"Yeah, well, we got a little lost." Verity grabbed on to the sign of welcome: she was expected.

Just then the doors crashed open behind her, and her mother appeared. "That's my mom," Verity said. "She drove me."

One by one the group staggered to their feet and came toward Verity, smiling, extending handshakes, introducing themselves and then moving toward her mother, who instantly became a bobbing, grinning, middle-aged Polish mother, capable and gracious.

"You got your stuff?" one of the boys asked when the commotion simmered down.

"It's in the car," Verity said.

"Let's go get it," said the pretty girl, "and I'll show you your cabin."

* *

She was the loveliest thing to look at: neat, with dark eyes like polished stones. Leslie talked easily as they climbed the path to Bethsaida cabin, carrying Verity's sleeping bag. "Isn't this amazing?" she asked, flinging a hand across the sky and redwoods. "I just love it here. I think it's the most beautiful place I've ever been."

Verity watched Leslie out of the side of her eyes. To be with such a pretty girl was difficult, considering that Verity knew she was plain and flat, ugly from all sides. She had sometimes tried to simulate a mysterious Eastern European, but her body did not cooperate, let alone her mind. She was a peasant with a watchful eye who could sometimes disappear but never shine. She was skinny but not sinuous, angular without grace. Her long, black hair was her one special feature. Smart, yes, but her brains meant nothing to her. She would give up all her grades for one minute of belonging to that effortless, happy group she had just met. How could they be so relaxed and friendly? Automatically, she suspected some motive, some unsavory secret that pushed them to treat her like a friend they already knew. She didn't trust it, but she was drawn toward it.

"So, have you been to Mount of Olives a hundred times?" Leslie asked. She had on blue jeans and a plaid men's shirt—simple clothes that fit perfectly.

"No. This is the first time ever."

"I can't believe that we get to spend the whole summer. I've been coming every year since I was in the fourth grade, but this is the first time I've ever worked here. It's like heaven."

"Are you in the kitchen?"

"No, I'm a counselor. But don't worry—we'll have plenty of time together."

Verity noted that Leslie wanted to reassure her that they would get time together. Had such a thing ever before been said to her? She had lived surrounded by people who hardly noticed her existence.

The cabin was set on the side of the hill—a rustic shack made of unpainted redwood, with a plain white door and "Bethsaida" stenciled on it. Apart from the thick trunks of trees, there were no plants around—only the brown duff of fifty years of dropped needles. The cabin's interior was a dark hole with one small window, four bunk beds, and four cubbies with hooks and shelves. It smelled of mildew and mice, of old gym clothes and sawdust. That didn't bother Verity; her preferred place at college was the deep library stacks, with their low ceiling and smell of moldy books. Leslie told her she could pick whether she wanted to be upstairs or down, since the other two girls had yet to arrive. "Julie's got the top bunk here," she indicated. Then she remembered that Verity didn't know anyone. "You'll meet her," she said. "She's in the kitchen with you."

"I better take the bunk underneath," Verity said. "Close to the ground." That prompted a small giggle from Leslie.

"Hey," she said, "we better get back down so you can say goodbye to your mom."

Verity had forgotten all about her mother. Following Leslie out of the cabin, she tried all the way down the hill to think of something to say. Just as they arrived back at the parking lot, she managed to ask, "Is everybody here a Christian?" It had only just now crossed her mind that a Christian camp was different from Girl Scout camp. The application had asked about her church affiliation and her journey of faith, but she couldn't remember what she had said. It had not registered as significant.

"Sure," Leslie said. "I think so. Didn't it say that on the application?"

Verity was a Christian, but she harbored doubts, and the possibility that people at the camp might want to probe those doubts made her suddenly, intensely upset.

To Verity's surprise, her mother, who was not one to wait, was still standing by the car. Even more remarkably, she was talking to three of the staff, looking happy and relaxed. The loveliness of the scene threw Verity off stride: the small, quiet parking lot; the easy conversation; the high trees all around, holding them in, sheltering them.

What could they be talking about? When she got close enough to hear, Verity found that it was the weather in Santa Cruz. The redwoods that sucked in the overnight fog. The hot, sunny afternoons. They were chatting about nothing as though they had known each other all their lives. It upset Verity. They made it seem so easy. *It's not easy*, she thought. Her mother was the last person in the universe for whom it should seem easy.

Verity caught her mother's eye. "You better go," she said.

A glint of annoyance crossed her mother's face. "Why are you so quick to get rid of me?" She said it in a teasing way, but her displeasure leaked through.

That was normal for her mother, but Verity saw that the group noticed.

"I thought you were worried about traffic," Verity said.

Her mother straightened herself, as she always did when she made ready to move. "You're right," she said. "I better go. You work hard. Make me proud." She leaned forward to give the least involved hug possible, then turned to say goodbye to the others.

"Don't worry about her!" one of the staff said. Verity's mother only gave a judicious nod before getting in the car and driving away.

Then Verity was truly on her own. When she had started college nine months before, it had been the same—except then, nobody had even tried to be friendly. She glanced around at her peers, who were jabbering happily. She didn't know them at all, she had nothing in common with them, and she would be staying here with them for the next three months—she, the odd stick, the left foot. If it were possible, she would turn and run. She would vanish.

The strangest thing happened. The others began to talk to her. The tall blond-headed guy with the long, beautiful hair asked her where she was from, and when she said San Jose, he asked her where she went to college. He seemed impressed when she said Berkeley.

*   *

Verity made her way back to the cabin and lay down in her bed. The darkness was a relief, as was the smell of dust. She heard occasional shards of conversation as people walked by, but thankfully, nobody came in. Meeting people was very tiring for her, especially those who were handsome, well-off, and—more than anything—easy in their skins. She had gone to a regular high school, but in high school, such people had their own separate world. In some ways, that made it easier; they let you be. She didn't think these people were going to do that. The pretty girl, Leslie, wasn't going to ignore her. It filled her with hope and anxiety.

5

YOU ARE JESUS TO THESE KIDS

In mid-afternoon Verity walked slowly down to the dining hall for a kitchen-workers orientation. These trees, how tall were they? Verity stopped on the path to look at them more carefully. She couldn't really see the tops. It hurt her neck, bending back to look straight up.

Inside the dining hall, she found a dozen young people splayed out on chairs, some of them talking, some not. Verity recognized only one from the group she had met when she arrived—a girl with brown flipped hair whose name she had not caught. Verity took a seat at the edge; nobody said hello. There was one Black guy, tall and lanky, with skin the color of midnight. One Asian girl. Everybody else was white, tanned, and at ease.

Right on time, a pair of jovial adults bustled in, introducing themselves as Trudy and Rich, the dining hall supervisors. Trudy was ample and motherly with dimples; Rich had a thick spade of beard and an accent full of North Carolina. They never stopped smiling, but they stuck to business, making the crew walk through the mealtime routine, from setting tables to seating campers to serving campers to clearing tables to cleanup. Each server would have responsibility for seven tables, and each table would choose a gofer to run to the kitchen. "Otherwise, you'll never keep up, and your feets is gonna kill you," Rich said. Verity decided his accent was fake. The work was six days a week, beginning at dinner on Sunday and ending at breakfast on Saturday. You had to be on time, no excuses. If somebody got sick, the rest of the kitchen staff would have to fill in.

"And here's the thing," Trudy said, dropping the dimpled smile as her voice grew soft and serious. "It's not just serving food. You are Jesus to these kids. A lot of them come to Mount of Olives knowing that this is a Christian camp, and that's about all they know.

"We have a two-word purpose statement for Mount of Olives, and I want you to think of it every day. Does anybody know what it is?"

After a five-second gap, a dark-headed crew-cut staffer put up his hand. "I think it's something like 'knowing God,' isn't it?"

Trudy smiled. "That's pretty close, Jason. You've been to Mount of Olives before, haven't you? Our purpose statement is 'meeting Jesus.' That's why we are here. We want our campers to meet Jesus. If they do, it will change their lives.

"You might not get a chance to talk about Jesus with the campers, not as a food server or kitchen helper, but you're part of a team. You can make the words that others speak seem real, or you can make them seem phony. It's all how you act. It's a real honor to be chosen for this job, and you've been selected because Mount of Olives believes you are the right person to represent Jesus to these kids. You might be the closest any of them has ever been to seeing Jesus."

Verity started back to her cabin alone, but before she got far, the girl with the flipped hair caught up and introduced herself as Julie. Verity realized that they were sharing a bunk bed; Julie was on top.

"That was amazing!" Julie said. "Had you ever thought about that before?"

"No," Verity said—a response that came automatically though she wasn't quite sure what Julie was asking. That was the wrong way to begin, she knew. She had to try to engage. She had promised herself to try.

"What amazed you?" Verity asked, hoping that her "no" would be overlooked.

"About being like Jesus for these kids. I really had no idea. It's such a stunner." Julie shook her head as though the idea was floating loose inside.

"You really think they will think that way?" The subject made Verity nervous; she had never been around people who talked about Jesus.

Julie seemed momentarily nonplussed, but then she gathered herself. "Don't you think? They know it's a Christian camp but maybe they don't know any real Christians where they come from. They're going to see us every day, three meals a day."

"But Jesus? You think they will think we are Jesus?"

Julie shook her head. "Not literally. It's a metaphor. If we are nice, then Jesus is nice. If we are mean or lose our temper, then Jesus is mean too, and they reject him. That sort of thing."

Verity thought, *It's not a metaphor*, but she said nothing. She couldn't act like the smart one. Verity would tie herself in knots to keep from acting smart.

* *

That evening all the camp staff ate dinner together. When Verity opened the door to the dining hall, the roar assaulted her. It was just thirty-five people, not the hundreds they would feed tomorrow, but they all talked at once, almost shouting to be heard. The concrete floor and low ceiling concentrated the sound, unbearably, painfully for Verity. She stopped just inside the door and felt her heart pounding in her chest.

Most of the tables were full and some had chairs tilted against the side, saved for somebody. Where was she going to sit? Julie spotted her, called her name, waved her over. She had saved a seat. She was so pretty, so normal looking. When Verity sat down, she discovered she had landed with most of the group she had met in the dining hall that afternoon. They all seemed to know her name. Leslie was sitting on Verity's left, smiling. The tall blond boy across the table was shouting a question at her; she smiled apologetically but couldn't hear him over the din. He stood up—he had that wonderful blond hair—and walked around the table to her, putting his mouth on her ear. She flinched, surprised; it felt too intimate.

"What did you do this afternoon?" he said in her ear and then pulled back and smiled, as though it were a joke. He went back to his side of the table and cupped his ear, waiting for her answer.

"I didn't do anything," she said.

He smiled more broadly and leaned forward to hear.

"I didn't do anything," she shouted. "I rested."

Raising his eyebrows, he put both hands on the side of his face and tilted his head, feigning sleep. Verity nodded vigorously, and he gave her an energetic thumbs-up. He then turned to talk to his neighbor, whom she recognized as the skinny boy who had first greeted her when she arrived, who looked like the movie alien. The two of them seemed to be friends.

Verity tried to volunteer to be gofer, ferrying food to the table, but everybody vied to do it and she didn't come close to getting anyone's attention. Running food would have kept her from having to attempt conversation.

As it turned out, she needn't have worried. Julie was a talker, a source of non-stop verbiage who opened her mouth and released a river of information. Her conversation stayed rooted in facts, mostly about herself and things she had done, people she knew, places she had seen. She talked a lot about Mount of Olives. Like Leslie, she had been there as a camper and always dreamed of becoming a counselor. "Of course, I didn't get to do that this year; I'm just a server like you, but that's okay. Maybe I'll get to do it next year."

Julie offered no opinions except that everything and everybody was wonderful, which you couldn't dispute. Halfway through the meal, Verity couldn't listen to Julie any longer; her mind went off on its own and wouldn't come back. Julie kept talking.

The food was basic: dry hamburgers; limp, oven-baked French fries; a salad of torn lettuce and cherry tomatoes. Verity, who had never been a good eater, got stuck after two bites of hamburger and began to feel nauseated. She moved her plate out of the way and put her head down. Julie kept talking. Nothing would stop her; she would continue talking when the sky turned black and the roof came down. Verity's vision turned white, shining like the sun behind clouds. *Oh, no,* she thought. Her hands were trembling; she tried with all her power to stop them and could not. Her vision blinked black, then white again, then black.

She collapsed on top of Leslie, dropping onto her like a tarp. Leslie held her, clasping her chattering body.

6

THE BROTHERS

Howard and Sam walked back to their cabins together, talking soberly about Verity's seizure. Neither one had observed the moment she fell, but multiple shouts had quickly turned their heads. They saw Verity entangled with Leslie, the doll-like girl with magnetic eyes, as though the two had been caught in a Twister game gone wrong. Verity lay twitching and unconscious until the ambulance came.

"I thought she was dying," Howard said, his voice still high with excitement. He was the tall blond with shoulder-length hair. He was speaking quite loudly now and didn't even realize it.

"I knew she would be okay," Sam replied quietly. He was a little less than average height, with short, dark hair and handsome brown eyes. "I had a friend in high school with seizures. I think that was grand mal, though. Big bad."

The two knew already they were going to be friends, maybe best friends, though they had met just that day. Christian books had quickly connected them—they each brought a small collection, which they noticed while moving in. Besides, they both went to Stanford, which was important to them though they treated it nonchalantly.

"You think she'll be all right?" Howard asked.

"Oh, sure. She'll sleep, and then she'll be fine. I don't know whether they'll let her stay, though. Imagine if she did that in front of the campers. It would freak them out."

Howard was planning to major in history, Sam geology; they had never met at school and their interests led in different directions. Howard sang in the chorus and liked to drive his VW bus to San Francisco for concerts at the Winterland. Sam was drawn to the rocky Pacific shore. He didn't have a car, but whenever he could hitch a ride he went exploring. That was one reason he had chosen to work the summer at Mount of Olives instead of his dad's business in Kansas City.

"You want to walk up to the cross?" Sam asked. Counselor training began in an hour, but he thought they had time and he wanted to make an impression.

He led Howard on a steep pathway that started behind their cabins and wound up through the forest—an open, sunny hillside of widely spaced conifers that allowed sheets of golden light to bathe the forest floor. Sam moved tirelessly uphill with the smoothness of a cat, while Howard soon was panting and beaded in sweat. Several times Sam paused to let him catch up, but as soon as Howard came even, Sam was off again. Neither one made a comment. At length, they emerged into a patch of thinning brush with a wide view of the surrounding mountains. On those rounded tops, thick with trees, not a building or a road showed.

"Just a little farther," Sam said. "The cross is over here." He acted as though he didn't notice that Howard had his hands on his knees, breathing noisily.

A rough wooden cross had been erected on the brow of the hill. It stood no more than eight feet high, with a couple of benches beneath it. Sam dropped onto one and sat gazing at the cross. Howard joined him, still sucking air.

"How'd you know this was here?" Howard asked when he could speak.

"I've been here before," Sam said, leaving to Howard the question of when. He had come to Mount of Olives for a spring weekend and discovered the cross on one of his hikes.

Standing and walking toward two small trees with dull, leathery leaves, he asked, "Hey, do you know what these are?" He waited, seemingly interested in the reply. Howard shook his head. "Olive trees. We are on the Mount of Olives, get it? Literally."

"They don't look like they are doing that well," Howard said of the scrawny trees, which were more like bushes.

Sam smiled. "I believe they're warm-weather trees. Up here it's foggy and cold."

"Did the name of the camp come first, or the trees?"

Sam shrugged. "I'm guessing they decided to plant the olive trees because of the name. It just goes to show, you can't fight your true nature, no matter what you call yourself. This place really isn't the Mount of Olives. It should be Mount of Redwoods."

"Or Mount of Douglas firs," Howard said. "They like it better up here than the redwoods."

"Really?" Sam tipped his head to one side. The comment didn't fit with how he placed Howard: as a city boy.

"Redwoods like to have their feet in the water, near a stream. These are firs."

"So, you know a lot about trees?"

"Some," Howard said. "That was one of my merit badges. I'm an Eagle Scout."

"Oh," Sam said, duly impressed. "Anyway, there's a lesson in it. You can give something a name, but that doesn't make it real. Just like you can call yourself a Christian, but unless you have a personal relationship with God, it's not going to do you any good." He had thought of this comparison when he came here in the spring.

"That's good stuff," Howard said. "I might use that with my cabin."

"Be my guest," Sam replied.

"You know what?" Howard said as they descended again, their footsteps thudding the steep trail and raising a thin cloud of dust. "I want this to be a fantastic summer. It shouldn't be just another camp. I want us to live in a way that we never have. All of us. And I have the feeling it's going to happen. I think God is going to do something amazing this summer."

Sam didn't respond, but he cautiously squirreled the comment away. He was growing in his admiration of Howard, who wasn't bothered that Sam had to wait for him when he got out of breath. When Sam provided a lesson plan for misplaced olive trees, Howard freely appreciated it. And he had seen Howard go out of his way to welcome Verity, who seemed like a difficult case—self-conscious and hard to talk to.

* *

They just made it on time for the counselor training, which took place in the small club room, crowded with worn upholstered sofas and inspirational posters tacked to the walls. Howard managed to nab a seat next to Leslie and immediately began telling her about his hike to the cross. She looked at him with her hypnotic eyes, not saying a word but smiling beautifully.

The lead counselor, Nate, began the meeting. He looked scarcely older than the rest of them but stood apart with his seriousness. After barely welcoming them, he began emphasizing the responsibility they were given. "The parents of these kids trust Mount of Olives, and that comes down to trusting us. We're the ones with their children every day and all day. And the first thing that means is safety." He went over some rules. No candles. No smoking. No food in the cabins. These were absolute and you could get sent home for violating them.

"We had a girl," Nate went on, "who stuck her finger in the crack behind the door, where the hinges are—I have no idea why—and when somebody came running into the cabin, the door slammed shut and cut her finger off." The counselors gave an involuntary cry. "We spent like an hour hunting for the missing part of her finger."

"Did you find it?" The question came from the back of the room, spoken as though in agony.

"We found it. In the dirt outside the cabin. Somebody had kicked it off the porch, I guess. We put it in a bag of ice, they sewed it back on at the ER, and she was fine. But please understand that this gets serious in a hurry. I don't want to make the phone call to some mother to tell her that her little darling doesn't have a finger anymore.

"So, safety. We want everybody to stay safe, have fun, make friends, and have a great time. But more than anything, we want them to meet Jesus.

"You are the key to that. You should be looking for a chance to get to know your campers, to listen to their worries and their problems and show them that Jesus is the answer. The morning devotions give you a great opportunity to start that conversation. And it should be a conversation. A good devotion isn't one where you talk all the time. When your campers talk, their hearts open."

A hand went up from a small, round-headed girl with short bangs. "We only have them for a week. That's not very long. How do we get to know them?"

Nate did not even crack a smile. He took a deep breath and blew it out. "Let me tell you something about camp," he said. "You have entered a time machine. A week at Mount of Olives is like six months anywhere else. By the end of the week, these kids will have made the best friends they ever dreamed of. When they go home on Saturday, half of them will be crying because they are leaving their friend-for-eternity. And that might be you. I hope and pray it's you because when you get welcomed into somebody's heart, you take Jesus."

Howard closed his eyes and leaned his long frame forward. This was what he had hoped for.

"You're in charge of skits," Nate said. "Very important. It probably seems lightweight, but it's key to making everybody welcome and relaxed. Any of you in drama?" A few hands went up. "Any of you think you're a comedian?" There was a chortle or two, but no hands. "Well, this may be your best chance at stardom. We need great skits. I mean, the cornier the better. I promise you, if you are funny, they will love you. But if you bomb, they can be cold. No mercy." For the first time that day, Nate smiled.

"In the late afternoon, you lead a Bible study for your cabin. Again, this is a great chance to get to know your campers deeply. I don't think I've ever seen a week go by without somebody committing their life to Jesus through the Bible study. If you get to witness that, you'll never forget it. This summer we're studying a passage from Second Corinthians, which is an incredible part of the Bible, and I promise you that by August, you will have gone over it so many times you will know it by heart."

A short, muscular counselor named Brian raised his hand. "When do we get some free time?"

Some of the counselors laughed, but only a slight, sardonic smile came on Nate's lips. "That is a very good question. If you want free time, this is probably not the place for you. You're in charge of between six and eight very squirrely kids, and there's nobody else to take over for you. You are here for those kids. I can't stress that too strongly. You are here for them, not for your social life.

"The kids go home by lunchtime on Saturday, and you have free time until Sunday afternoon when the next group arrives. That's when you get your free time. A lot of people just want to sleep."

When Nate asked for volunteers to lead skits and games, Brian jumped in eagerly. "Come on!" he complained when others were slow to join him. "Haven't you ever been to camp? C'mon! This is the most fun ever!"

7

FIRST WEEK

N ext day, the camp was overrun by skinny limbs and high-pitched voices. Howard was surprised to see how young they were—many barely out of junior high. Six energy-charged boys followed him like newly hatched ducklings. They weren't rebellious or surly, but he could see they were apt to do goofy things. Activities began after dinner and continued non-stop until they stumbled into their bunks past midnight. It was like a basketball game with no lines and no whistle.

Howard lay in his bunk, exhausted but still too wound up to drift off. He listened for the sounds of breathing—the deep, regular signals of sleep from his six campers. Cautiously he got up out of bed and stood, listening. No one spoke or stirred. They were all deeply asleep.

Tiptoeing out the door, Howard found his way in the deep darkness to Sam's cabin. He knocked lightly on the door, waited, then knocked again. The door opened and Sam poked his head out. "Want to talk?" Howard whispered.

They sat on top of a picnic table. Dog tired and knowing they would drag themselves out of bed at 6:30 the next morning, they were bursting with things to say. Soon they were joined by other staff who dribbled out one by one and took seats.

Their only light came from dim yellow bulbs above the door of each cabin, circled by a ghostly galaxy of moths. A fire would have been wonderful, but they feared being discovered. (By the rules, they should be in bed.) It got cold. Sometimes they saw a bank of fog sweeping up the mountain, blotting the stars.

Brian talked the most. He was coarse—a little too loud, a little too full of himself, but entertaining. He thought his campers were hilarious. They could all picture the kids' dorkiness or hear their dumb dialogue when he mimicked them. In complete contrast, Howard began talking about his cabin's first Bible study time. He spoke thoughtfully and sometimcs brilliantly, Sam thought. Between the two of them, they captured the moment: manic fun and serious faith. Sam didn't say a word; he only listened.

The next day they launched the skits. Brian turned into a maniac who somehow got kids laughing no matter what he said or did. They laughed at him or with him, but no matter: they laughed. Howard had worked up a Beach Boys song, "California Girls," and swung his hair in rhythm. It was so popular that they sang it every night that week. The campers jumped, shouted, clapped, and sometimes danced. (There were a few surprisingly talented dancers.)

With Nate's help, they organized mass games on the field every afternoon. Cabins competed against each other in relay races, with Brian adding crazy elements. They played a version of capture the flag as Romans and Christians. The energy was manic, with scores of campers swarming each other, barely under control.

On Thursday afternoon, Sam saw a boy from his cabin—a silent, dweeby kid named Roy—sitting alone at the pool, plunked himself down next to him, and asked how camp was going. To his alarm, Roy began to cry. What came out through his mucus-strangled voice was that Roy had silently, anonymously prayed along with the speaker on Wednesday night when he explained how to ask Jesus into your heart. Nothing had happened, and Roy didn't know whether God had rejected him. Sam was able to assure him that Jesus had answered his prayer and come into his heart, whether he felt anything or not.

Sam told this story at the ten-minute counselor debriefing they had every morning just after breakfast. He could feel the jubilation rise as he spoke. This, precisely this, was why they were here.

Saturday morning, Sam sat next to Roy near the post office while waiting for his parents. Just as Nate had predicted, girls cried at leaving their newfound best friends, and even boys solemnly told each other that they were cool, promising to stay in touch. Parents, when they arrived, shook hands with the counselors and said thank you. It had been an amazing week, they all agreed.

In the suddenly peaceful dining hall, the staff ate lunch, dazed by the completion of their first camp. It amazed them how happy they were. They felt years older. The week had, indeed, taken six months.

* *

Verity had returned from the hospital on Wednesday. Everyone asked her how she was, but she was soon tired of talking about her illness.

Mindy, a tall, slender blonde, leaned across the table to ask, "Do you have to take medicine now?"

"I've taken medicine since I was little," Verity answered, trying not to sound curt.

"And the doctors didn't change the medicine? Not even the dose?"

"No."

"Do you think it could happen again?"

"Do you think we could talk about something else?"

The topic turned to what to do that afternoon. "I need to sleep," Julie proclaimed, saying she was worn out. Somebody wanted to go on a hike; they had heard of a place where you could see a waterfall. The majority sentiment was for doing something, anything, it didn't matter what. Like Julie, they were tired after a week of constant activity and little sleep, but they wanted to be together. They wanted to talk and play and simply look in the eyes of others who could hear the same high bells. Howard took charge and organized them all toward the Santa Cruz boardwalk. Anywhere would do.

Verity stayed at the camp. She wanted to go but knew she was nowhere near ready to relate to so many people. With remarkable kindness, Leslie stayed behind with her, even though Verity said that wasn't necessary.

* *

Howard's Volkswagen bus had once been green, as you could tell from the paint swatches where ancient bumper stickers had peeled off. Rust and oxidation had turned the rest of it the color of split pea soup mixed with coffee grounds. Seven staff piled in, and four more into a white Mercury Comet driven by Julie, who decided that she did not need to rest after all. In minutes, they were transported from the serenity of the trees into freeway traffic. "This feels really weird," Brian said to Howard from the passenger seat. "I haven't been in a car for a week. When has that ever happened?"

Going down the hill, Julie's Comet passed Howard's bus. She cut him off so abruptly that he had to brake hard while she hit the horn in a long, mocking wail. Hands waved out the window and mouths ballooned in inaudible jeers.

The bus chugged ahead, speeding up gradually but inexorably until Howard was able to shoot past Julie, beeping on the bus's high-pitched horn and cutting in front of her. It terrified Mindy; she clutched her seat, preparing for a crash. Howard kept going, dodging through traffic as Julie pursued him. Her car had marginally more power, but the road was crowded enough for Howard to stay ahead until suddenly they came up on slower traffic blocking both lanes. Breaking suddenly, Julie maneuvered alongside Howard. Exhilarated passengers in both vehicles shouted at each other.

Parking just a block from the ocean, they split up to explore. Mindy went with Scott and Randy to walk along the cliffs toward Steamer's Lane, pausing to watch a handful of surfers work the breakers. Howard, Sam, Julie, and Brian strolled the boardwalk and bought sticky colored popcorn. Another group rode the roller coaster and other rides. Eventually they all drifted to the beach, where they threw themselves down.

The day was cool and still, with a low pearly overcast. Only a hundred yards of dirty-brown sand separated them from the boardwalk, but they felt far-off and alone. A mechanical blare of music from the rides made a distant, scratchy noise. Mindy noted how subdued they had become, from the hallooing ride down the hill to this tranquil scene.

"I'm going to get my guitar," Scott said. "Anybody want to come?" Randy jumped up off the sand and they walked back to the Comet. When they returned, Scott played with surprising skill. He sang Beatles songs, camp songs, and silly Christian sing-alongs that they had learned that week. A handful of them clustered near him, singing along. Brian stripped off his clothes—he wore a bathing suit underneath—and ran into the surf. Several of the group had earlier tested the freezing water with their bare feet. Now they watched with fascination as Brian's short, compact frame bustled through the soft sand toward the water, splashed violently in the shallows, and then launched like an artillery shell into the dull, glinting surf. He came up spouting and shaking off water like a dog, a corona of droplets visible in the air around his head. They all smiled involuntarily. Brian made a broad gesture inviting them into the gunmetal swells. "You couldn't pay me enough," Randy said.

Something about Brian's bravado loosened them, though. They talked louder, laughed more, comparing high schools, talking about their colleges—memories that seemed to come from very long ago. Scott again picked up his guitar. The sun was going down by the time Brian came out of the water, his chest purple-pink from the cold. When he realized that nobody had brought a towel, he ran up and down the sand to dry off. He was buzzing with energy, telling them each time he passed that they were cowards and were missing the experience of a lifetime.

Howard had been patrolling the beach, picking up driftwood. When the sun expanded into a blob of red jelly on the horizon, a book of matches appeared from his pocket, and he set to starting a fire.

"An Eagle Scout special!" Brian shouted as he jogged past.

It was, too. The sun went down, and the flickering blaze lit their faces as they gathered around it. Six pelicans rowed their way across the horizon while three seagulls hopped closer to the fire, watching intently for food. More people sang with Scott. He evidently knew the words to every Judy Collins and John Denver song ever recorded. When Howard and Sam began talking about the Jesus Movement, Mindy and Julie scootched closer to listen.

"Howard," Julie said with admiring incredulity, "have you *joined* the Jesus Movement?"

He said it wasn't something you joined. "It's a Spirit thing," he said. "It happens, and you have to ride the wave."

"But how do you *know* so much?"

"I got to know it in high school," he said. He explained that in his sophomore year he had accidentally stumbled onto a beach baptism. Initially it repelled him, so un-church-like, so irreverently casual. He denounced it in his head and then gradually shifted ground until he found himself arguing against his own premises. "I had to rethink everything I'd learned," he said. "What was so great about holiness and dignity that nobody on the beach could understand? I wanted to be part of something alive, something Californian."

Mindy had read about the Jesus Movement in *Life*. What she remembered were pictures of kids with long, golden hair tied back with red bandanas and fingers pointed toward the sky. When Howard learned that Mindy went to Berkeley, he referenced a group known as the Christian World Liberation Front. Mindy had never heard of it; was it part of

Campus Crusade? No, Howard said, this was radical. "It started up in the Free Speech Movement. You know about that, don't you?"

She wasn't sure; she thought she remembered hearing about it.

Randy asked Howard what they should tell their campers. "I don't think Mount of Olives is going to like us talking about a Christian Communist Revolutionary Front."

"It's not Communist," Howard said. "It's Christian World Liberation Front, which if you think of it is exactly what Jesus would be about. Jesus brings liberation to the whole world."

"Okay," Randy said, "but what should we say to our cabins?"

Howard appeared to be thinking. In the quiet that had overtaken the whole group, they heard the sounding of waves smashing onto the shore.

"Do we have to say anything?" Sam asked in a low, tuneful voice. "You know St. Francis said to preach the gospel at all times, using words if necessary."

That sounded so wise that nobody knew what to say.

"The key is prayer," Howard said. "We need to pray. Ask the Holy Spirit to bring power, and he will. If we let him.

"I picked up a hitchhiker last year," Howard continued, suddenly gaining energy. "I was praying, praying, praying that somehow God would open the door for me to talk to him about God. But I was too fearful. We talked about everything—the weather, the war in Vietnam—but not God. I dropped him off, and just as he was getting out of the car, literally with his feet already on the pavement, I finally said, 'Are you interested in spiritual things?' He stopped with his head already out the door and got back in the car. He looked at me and said, 'Buddy, if you know how to find God, tell me.'"

"And then did he disappear?" Scott asked.

That confused everybody.

"I've had two people tell me about a hitchhiker who says something amazing and then disappears," Scott explained. "One guy said the hitchhiker warned that there's only one year left before Christ returns. They think it might be an angel."

"I don't think an angel would be confused like this guy," Howard said. "He was very mixed up."

"Confused about what?" Mindy asked. She was very curious.

"He talked about the Buddha's eightfold path and lots of ideas from the Hare Krishna. My point is that people are searching."

The night had crept over them, leaving their fire as an eyedropper of light against the blackness of sand and sky. Across the beach, the boardwalk's gaudy brilliance appeared as though on display from another planet. Mindy observed that she was cold, which made all of them aware that a chilly breeze had kicked up. They edged closer to the fire, and thus closer to each other. Howard stood up, stripped off his coat, and offered it to Mindy. She protested but ended up taking it. Not having planned on staying so late on the beach, she wore only a sleeveless summer dress.

"I think we should pray for that girl Verity," Julie said.

Sam was surprised. He had taken Julie for a thoughtless, pretty girl.

"She's okay, isn't she?" he asked. He pictured Verity's thin, awkward body and stuttering speech. "They wouldn't have let her come back if they didn't think she was all right."

"Should we pray for healing?" The voice came from behind the circle; they turned to see that it was Randy. Of everybody in the group, he seemed most intensely conventional, and it came as a surprise to Mindy that he would bring up faith healing.

"Definitely," Howard said. "If she's an epileptic, she could have another seizure any time."

"She acted so uncomfortable with us," Mindy said. "She wouldn't look at anybody."

"She needs friends," Sam said in a low voice.

"She has them now," Howard said.

"What do you mean?" Mindy asked. "I'm not getting you."

"Right here," Howard said emphatically. "We are her friends. God brought her here. There are no accidents with God."

"The Bible says that when you welcome strangers you might be meeting an angel," said Sam.

"I don't think she's an angel," Mindy said, wondering why she felt so uncomfortable with the direction the conversation had taken.

8

BY THE POOL

Verity was staggered when Mindy asked her to meet at the pool Monday afternoon. Why would she do that?

Afternoon swim time was the social pinnacle of the camp day, a period of unstructured activity during which girls could watch boys and vice versa, and the mountain sun stroked them all and warmed their skin. Verity and Mindy found a bench against the fence, out of the way of the trotting, dodging, shouting kids. Verity wore a huge, floppy straw hat that almost covered her face and neck, plus a dark coverall. She assiduously applied lotion to her feet, virtually her only body part left exposed to the sun's rays. Mindy, by contrast, had on a green one-piece that exaggerated her fair skin and hair and long legs. She sat with those legs pulled up underneath her, leaning into the conversation, while Verity leaned away, looking into space.

"Aren't you supposed to be with your cabin?" Verity asked.

Mindy flicked it away with a swat of her hand. "Most of them are here," she said. "I can see them."

The whole camp scene was strange to Verity, both frightening and seductive. Ten times a day somebody asked how she was feeling. She wanted very much to take their concern at face value, but she didn't trust it. Why should they care? Like anybody else, she had her fantasies. She dreamed of a boy finding her alluring, or a circle of girls opening and inviting her in. She recognized those as dreams, however. At Berkeley you could be diagnosed with a terminal disease and all anybody would want to know was when you would vacate your room.

Verity stared at Mindy as though she were trying to see inside her brain. "I'm just surprised you want to talk with me," she said.

"Verity!" Mindy said with mock scolding. "You're interesting! Very interesting!"

"I never was to anybody before."

Mindy meant what she said, however. Rarely, if ever, had she encountered someone so lacking in evasion. Verity asked questions that Mindy had never entertained, and she asked them from an upside-down perspective. It was hard to say whether she was pursuing deep issues or was simply utterly naive.

"What do people mean when they talk about a personal relationship with God?" Verity asked.

Mindy at first took the question as skepticism, but she soon realized that Verity really didn't know what the phrase meant. Where to start? "It's like saying that you really believe, you're not just going through the motions."

Verity hadn't even known what kind of camp this was. "But you knew it was a Christian camp," Mindy said.

"I knew but I didn't realize how serious that was," she said and gave a little mistimed chortle. "I thought it was like Bluebirds or Brownies or something like that."

Mindy pondered how that could be. How could you apply to work at a camp without knowing what it was about?

Where most people would have shrugged and moved on, Mindy moved closer, like a museumgoer stepping nearer to a painting to see the brush strokes. "Didn't your mother say something?"

"My mother didn't want me to come here. She was completely against it. She grew up Catholic, and she hates all this religion."

"But you are a Christian, aren't you?" Mindy asked. "I thought you had to be to work here."

"I am," Verity said simply. "They asked about that on the application."

"Is your father a Christian?"

Verity shook her head, and a sly grin crept over her face. "I've never met him. At least, not that I can remember." Both of Verity's parents had been born in Poland and emigrated as children.

"What happened to him?"

Verity blushed. "I don't know. He left when I was a baby, and my mother doesn't talk about him."

"Not ever?"

"Not ever."

Mindy wrapped her arms around her knees and smiled in embarrassment. "I'm sorry, Verity. I hope I'm not upsetting you."

"It's okay."

"So, how did you become a Christian?" Mindy asked.

Verity sighed. She seldom told this story. "When I was in junior high, I heard some music coming from this Baptist church in my neighborhood, and I thought it was interesting because it was Sunday afternoon, not the morning, and the music didn't sound American. The door was open, so I went inside, and it was a Chinese church. They made me so welcome, and I didn't have many places where I felt that. Like no place. So, I started going to the church, and later on I was baptized."

Mindy put out a hand and Verity involuntarily jerked back. They were both embarrassed by her sudden reaction.

"I'm sorry," Mindy said. "I didn't mean to be rude. It just touches me to hear that you became a Christian without anybody in your family helping you."

"I don't know if it took, though."

"What do you mean?"

"I mean, I've asked for a lot of things, but I don't know if God is listening."

"I was always told that God answers, but sometimes he says no," Mindy said gently.

"I know; they said the same thing in my church."

"Can you give me an example of something you've prayed for?" Mindy asked.

"I don't know if I want to," Verity said, shamefaced.

Mindy did not want to pry. However, something in Verity's demeanor communicated that she welcomed Mindy's probing. They sat in a very public space with kids running past them, and yet it felt to Mindy as though they were alone. The pool was on a shelf overlooking the softball field; on the other side were towering redwoods. The campers' cries were high-pitched, like seabirds.

"It would help me to understand," Mindy said. "I won't tell anyone."

Verity stared at her, then slowly opened her mouth. "Mostly it had to do with friends," she said. "I asked God to give me friends, but nothing happened. I really don't know anybody at school."

"Where do you go?"

"To Berkeley."

A smile bloomed all over Mindy's face, starting slowly at her eyes and spreading down into her mouth. "Are you kidding? I go to Berkeley too!" she said. "Where do you live?"

Verity didn't smile but let her dark, sad eyes travel over Mindy. "Stern," she said. "That was last year. I don't know where I'll be this fall."

"What's your major?"

"Math," Verity said.

Mindy stared. "Oh my. You must be one of the smart ones."

She was surprised to see Verity frown. Mindy had thought all women felt flattered when somebody called them smart.

"Well," Mindy said, "I think God just said yes." She looked very pleased with herself, and Verity could not understand why.

"God said yes to what?"

"You asked for friends," Mindy replied. "I'm going to be your friend."

Verity was not sure how to respond.

"And everybody at this camp will be your friend!" Mindy added. "I know they will."

9

HOWARD'S GIRL

By the second week of camp, Julie made up her mind that she wanted Howard for a boyfriend. "We are a perfect fit for each other," she told the others in her cabin, who were stunned that she said it out loud.

Verity kept her face impassive and her mouth shut. The other girls kept quiet, too, but Verity could see their skepticism. Julie was the wrong kind of pretty for Howard—too accommodating, too sweet. She was not dumb; she had her own ideas. But she was not Howard's type.

While the counselors led their Bible studies, girls working in the kitchen gathered in Julie and Verity's cabin to talk. They teased Julie for her crush on Howard, and sometimes she mocked herself. "Don't you see he's bound to fall for me?" she asked with a broad smile. "He has no choice. I'm so beautiful!" She flounced her hair and threw her head to one side. She didn't lack confidence.

One morning Julie caught him coming back from the cross. "Where have you been?" she asked teasingly. He tried to deflect her, but she didn't let him off until he told her about his morning routine. Each day at six a.m. he walked up the hill to the cross. Technically, he was supposed to be in the cabin with his kids, but none of them woke up before the camp bell at six-thirty, so he slipped out the door into the solitude of the hill. Blanketed by the foggy air, he knelt at one of the benches to pray.

He didn't like Julie knowing his secrets and was irritated when he realized that she told everyone what he did.

"I was thinking I could join you," Brian said. "What time do you get up?"

"I don't want company," Howard said, hurting Brian's feelings.

Howard didn't mind Julie's adoration. If she wanted to sit next to him, he had no reason to resist. One day Julie squeezed in next to him at the craft table, an extra-long picnic table set under the redwoods, strewn with paper and paste and paints. He was intent on gluing beads onto a piece of construction paper in an elaborate pattern of circles.

"Ooh, that is so lovely!" she cooed. "It's beautiful! What is it?"

"It's a collage," he said.

"No, you silly," she said, punching him on the shoulder. "What does it mean? What does it stand for?"

"It doesn't stand for anything. It's not representational art."

"Representational art," she said. "You are so intellectual. Why are you a history major? That sounds so boring."

"It's not boring at all," he said. "History is stories." He glanced at her, which was something; she could count on the fingers of one hand the times he had looked at her. "You must have had some bad teachers in high school."

"Well, I'm sure I did," she said. "But what does that have to do with art?"

He threw an exasperated glance at her. "Who's talking about art?"

"I am. Look at you. You make these amazing things and then you ask me who's talking about art."

A softening crossed over his face like a cloud scudding on the wind. She could see that she had touched him. Why? What had she said?

"The art I care about is film," he said. "Ever watch French movies?"

She colored. "No."

"Like Francois Truffaut. It's not dirty. Film is where storytelling meets visual art. Sergei Eisenstein."

She cocked her head. She had no idea what he was talking about.

"Movies?" she said. "Like Hollywood?"

Frantically, she watched his face close. "I'm just asking you," she said. "Tell me. I'm listening."

He relented. "Not Hollywood like most people think. Not James Bond. Not Lawrence of Arabia."

"What, then?" Julie's voice had fallen softer. She was trying to keep him; like a bird, he could be gone in a heartbeat.

He sighed. "It hasn't been done, what I want to do."

"That's your dream," she whispered.

* *

It wasn't planned. Howard was going for a walk and Julie tagged along. He let her. They ended up down at the creek, which ran in a slow trickle. Overhead was a green canopy. Except for the sound of water, everything was still. Howard picked up a round stone and chucked it as far as he could. He was describing *Jules and Jim,* which he had seen for the first time that year. Julie wasn't following. She thought a threesome sounded immoral. It irritated Howard when she asked him about it. He had his mind on the film, not on Julie. She came up behind him and threw her arms around his chest. Losing his balance on the rocks, he lurched forward, and they almost fell. Who caught whom, it was impossible to say, but they ended up holding each other tightly, face-to-face. For just an instant they were caught at a tipping point, and then Julie kissed him tenderly on the lips.

Mindy knew that something had happened when she saw them come into dinner. She watched Julie lingering with Howard, though she was late for her serving assignment. Howard inclined his head slightly toward her, listening.

Mindy smiled to herself. *Unbelievable.* She had not thought Julie could do it.

After the meal, Verity came hustling by her table, elbows flying. She was physically awkward but through maximum effort moved fast. Mindy gestured to Verity to come near and mentioned what she had seen. They had talked about Howard and Julie once or twice, mentioning that they were a mismatch; they had nothing in common. Now a rosebud smile appeared on Verity's lips—a look of pure amusement. "How did that happen?" she asked.

That night, when the campers were in bed, Mindy went by Verity's cabin. She was curious to see Julie, who surely would be unable to contain her triumph. Julie was gone, however. Mindy didn't go in; she stood on the porch. Verity came outside to stand with her.

"Where is she?" she asked.

"Who?"

"Aren't you looking for Julie?"

"I bet she's with Howard," Mindy said.

"Sure," Verity said. She gave an embarrassed giggle. "Are you jealous?"

"What? No!"

"You don't like him?"

"Not that way." In fact, she didn't particularly care for him in any way. He wasn't humble. He had dreams but they all featured him. Perhaps, she thought, people from Stanford act that way, but Sam came from

Stanford, and you couldn't get him to talk about himself. After a pause, Mindy asked, "Do you?"

Verity giggled. "Well, he is very good-looking." She giggled again.

The next day, Mindy, on her way to lunch, noticed Sam and Leslie gliding mysteriously alongside each other. Apparently, they, too, had become a couple. Sam was so serious, almost monk-like, that she had assumed he was unavailable. How had Leslie done it? Unlike Julie, she was serene, lovely in every way.

Once she connected with Sam, she quietly changed her look, ditching the jeans and men's shirts for flowing, ankle-length dresses. "She looks like one of Meg's sisters," Howard joked at their morning counselors' meeting just as Leslie came in the door. The women surreptitiously glanced at each other. Had he really read *Little Women*? That was a girls' book.

Coming so soon after Howard and Julie, Sam and Leslie's example tipped the whole camp toward romance. Crushes multiplied overnight, mostly silent and miserable, sometimes openly longing. Neither Verity nor Mindy was part of this rush of would-be relationships. Mindy might have attracted a boyfriend since she was tall and slender and blond. Boys never got far with her, however. She was nice to everybody but didn't seem to register any particular interest.

Verity was interested, but she didn't project girlfriend qualities. Wherever she sat down, people made friendly attempts at conversation. It ended there, however; boys didn't approach.

* *

When the little clique went back to Santa Cruz on their second Saturday, Verity was invited as a matter of course. She had become more than a project; she was one of them. They joked about her celebrity status and took some pride in it.

They needed four cars, since a bunch of other staff joined them. Brian got two guys to go into the water with him. The waves were bigger than last week—big enough to bodysurf. The others watched the surfers' heads bobbing out of the swell like apples. Seagulls screamed and wheeled while Howard once again gathered driftwood for a fire. Stretched next to Mindy, Verity traded observations. She thought, *I'm beginning to relax. I'm beginning to feel at home.* Then she smiled to herself: when she was home, she never felt at home.

Bags of potato chips got passed around, along with some bananas and apples. A package of hot dogs appeared. Two of the boys bent coat hangers straight, and impaling the hot dogs, tried to roast them over the fire. They were unsuccessful: the coat hangers weren't stiff enough, so the sausages drooped onto the sand. When they doubled the coat hangers, they weren't long enough, and the boys burned their fingers. One after another, the dogs fell into the flames.

"I didn't want to eat those hot dogs anyway," Randy said. Everybody laughed. Brian tried to pull one out of the fire, but it burned his fingers and the sausage fell apart into the sand.

Scott was joined on his guitar by another boy with a mandolin. Prone on a beach towel, listening, Verity thought they made a pretty sound. Scott went on to play some complicated licks from songs she didn't recognize. Sometimes three or four separate conversations went on simultaneously, then merged into one. Howard's voice often rose above the others. They talked about a book that was circulating: *Woman: The Queen of Creation*. All of them had heard its thesis that women had a distinctive role, which feminism undermined. To some of the staff—Howard was in this camp—the book was ludicrous, but some of the girls stood up for it. They liked the idea of being treated like a queen.

"We don't want to be dated," Lilly, a pale redhead, said. "We want to be courted."

"You want us to grovel," Howard said.

"Yes, that's not a bad idea," Lilly said.

Listening to them go back and forth, Verity wished they could discuss the topic more seriously.

Eventually, the conversation moved to the campers. "I'll swear to this," Howard said. "Not one kid is going to leave my cabin without my showing him the love of Jesus. Which means I have to *know* the kid. I have to enter his world and spend time with him even if it's doing cannonballs off the diving board. Sometimes it might look like I'm goofing off, but none of it is."

Sam leaned forward to say something in his ear. Howard smiled, then leaned back and laughed. "Sam says here on the beach we're not wasting time either. Which is true. God has the chance to shape us right here. Why don't we talk about that? What is God doing in your life right now? What is he saying to you?"

It was such a dramatic turn that it startled them into silence. Howard looked around the fire circle, trying to catch the gleaming eyes. "This can't be right," he said. "Isn't God part of your life?"

Still there was no response. Nobody wanted to go first, exposing themselves. Surf pounded the shore and faint, reedy music reached them from the boardwalk. Then, to everyone's surprise, Verity spoke.

"Well, I don't know if it's God," she said. Her tone was almost musical, as though she were about to tell a funny story.

"Everybody has been so nice to me," she went on. "It feels like a miracle." She hesitated. "I guess you've been worried about the seizure I had. I know it's scary to watch. I've never actually seen one. I just have them. Not very often. I mean, I might not have another one all summer."

"Have you had them all your life?" asked somebody in the dark beyond the firelight.

Verity looked up and her eyes widened, as though she were surprised that somebody was interested. "I had my first attack when I was in junior high. They're usually not as bad as what you saw. Sometimes I just freeze for a few minutes. You might not even realize something is wrong."

"Are they dangerous?" Leslie asked. She was sitting across from Verity, her legs tucked demurely under her denim skirt.

"They could be." Ordinarily, Verity hated drawing attention to herself, but now, under the warmth of the group, she felt herself nervously enjoying the scrutiny. "Like if I choked on something. Or if I hit my head, falling. I get some warning it's coming, but I usually can't do anything before it starts."

"You mean you don't have time to sit down or brace yourself?" Scott asked. He was sitting behind Leslie, his knees under his chin. "I saw you fall. It was like somebody had pulled the plug. You really could hurt yourself."

Verity nodded. "I never have. Maybe that's God protecting me."

"Definitely." Howard spoke firmly. "God is in everything. He protected you, Verity."

She lowered her head almost into her lap, speaking so quietly only those seated next to her could hear. "I don't know. I wish he would make it go away."

"What did you say, Verity?"

She lifted her head again and said it for Howard.

"You've asked him to heal you?" Howard asked.

She hesitated, looked at him, then nodded. Something in his tone frightened and thrilled her.

"Verity, do you have faith that God can do it?"

She was staring intensely at him across the fire, with a look that could be angry or could be tearful. "That he could heal me?" she asked. "I don't know. I've asked a lot."

A smile broke over her face. "I even went to a healing service in this huge auditorium in San Jose. People started jumping and falling down. There was a lot of shouting. I couldn't get into it. I tried, but I couldn't relax."

"Did somebody pray for you?" Brian asked. He was listening with intense interest, like a dog on point.

She shook her head, still with the silly smile plastered to her face. "I couldn't. You had to go forward. Well, that's not exactly true. I was up in the balcony, and some of the people who were sitting near me came over and prayed for me. They wanted me to go down to see the minister, who was praying for people in wheelchairs and stuff like that, but it was so loud, I just couldn't do it."

Howard stood up. With his tall frame and the firelight playing on his long hair, he made a dramatic sight. "Verity," he said, "do you have faith in God?" He said it distinctly, as though he were in a play.

Verity's smile disappeared. She looked at Howard, then looked away. "I don't know," she said.

"Do you have enough faith to pray with me?"

"Now?" she asked. Her heart was racing.

"Right now. We can all pray together. If you're willing."

She put her head down again. "Okay," she said in a barely audible voice. Then, more clearly, she asked, "What do I need to do?"

"Nothing," he said. "Just stay where you are."

"What are you going to do?" she asked with a mix of fear and curiosity.

"I'm just going to pray. We'll all pray. I'll lead, and anybody can join me." He walked around the fire to where Verity was seated, then kneeled next to her. "Do you mind if I put my hand on you?"

"What?" She was trembling.

"I'll put my hand on your arm. And some of the others might want to touch your shoulder or your head. Is that okay?"

She didn't answer but put her head down. Howard reached out and softly placed his fingers on the upper part of her arm. "Come on," he said, without looking around. "Let's come near."

Verity, who had shut her eyes, felt the weight of hands on her shoulders and arms. When Howard prayed, her heart beat so hard she could not attend to anything else. But she felt something, like a cold streak of light arcing through her ribs. Her breath caught in a little sob, and Howard suddenly stopped praying.

"Did you feel something?" he asked.

She nodded but could not speak.

"I felt it at the same moment," Howard said, and then continued his prayer. She didn't hear it because she was intent on the light she hoped would play through her again. Before she knew anything, Howard had stopped praying and was standing.

"I believe God healed you," Howard said, and some of the others murmured, though most were silent, just observing.

10

INDEPENDENCE

The next morning, Verity woke up with a happy heart. Her epilepsy and its possible cure she hardly thought of. Instead, she marveled at her place in the group who had prayed for her. Never had she felt so exposed; never had she so wanted to be.

After lunch, Sam asked if he could talk to her. She had picked him out as somebody to admire, but there had never been much conversation between the two of them. She hadn't been sure he knew who she was.

He had short hair and small eyes, hooded as though a crease had been ironed into the skin of his eyelids. Sitting across from him at a table, she watched him closely, nervously.

"When we prayed for you," he said, "did you feel pressured into it?"

"No," she said. "Not really. I mean, I was fine with it."

"You went along."

Verity felt something ominous in that assertion, but she nodded in agreement.

"And you had faith that God could heal you?"

"I don't know," she said, wishing she knew where these questions would lead.

Sam seemed to lose the thread and let his attention go wandering off into the dark trees, where a jay was screaming. Verity sometimes followed those trees all the way into the sky; they were so tall you got lost trying to locate the top. Now, however, she didn't want to watch the sky. She studied Sam's face closely. Some of the girls thought he was handsome, but she didn't see it. He wasn't somebody she would notice for his looks.

He finally came back to her and spoke. "I was reading in James this morning, and it said that a person will be healed by a prayer offered in faith. I wondered whether you had faith."

That agitated her. "I wasn't the one praying."

"I know; it was Howard. But James doesn't say whose faith—he just says a prayer offered in faith. It could be yours."

Hesitating, she asked, "How do you tell?"

"Good question," he said at once. This was the moment he had anxiously anticipated all morning. "Do you take medicine for your seizures?"

She nodded.

"One sign of your faith would be if you stopped taking it. If you have faith in God healing you, you don't need meds."

It came like a rush to her head, both frightening and seductive. "I'd have to ask my doctor first."

"Why? If you're healed, you're healed. Aren't you?"

* *

She made Sam promise he wouldn't throw the pills away but would keep the little orange vial in case she needed it. He looked at her gravely, expressing doubt that this was a demonstration of genuine faith. But when she gave him the bottle, he took it.

By dinner, word had spread. Very suddenly, all the camp staff looked at Verity as though she had done something strange and beautiful. No longer a mere celebrity, as she had been after her seizure, she became a saint. Counselors she had not even met came up like old friends, with tears in their eyes. Then word spread among the campers. Out of the corner of her vision, Verity caught skinny girls making eyes at her, as though they had spotted a movie star.

For a few days, Verity swept through every gathering on a bow wave of attention and love. It embarrassed her, but it caught at her throat a dozen times a day: to be so loved. And for what? She hadn't done anything.

Of course, she was the one taking a risk. No one could say how important her medicine was to her health. It was prophylactic; you weren't supposed to notice anything if it worked as it should. She had been taking it religiously for years without feeling any direct effect.

In a week the novelty had passed. Verity's new fans didn't want to actually know her, it seemed; they were just excited by something to talk about.

That was not so with her little group, however. She was included now in whatever they did, whatever activity, whatever conversation. She had gained a reputation for courage, which was an entirely new experience.

Brian approached her outside the dining hall to ask if she would like to join the Fun Club. "That's what we call ourselves. We do the skits and games and we lead the singing. It's a lot of fun."

He didn't have to explain that; she knew what it was. Brian was not her favorite person—he was too bumptious, too loud—but he was good at leading games and singing. He had a loud voice and his energy spilled over to the rest of them. Everybody knew who Brian was by the second day of camp.

That was not Verity. In a million years, she would not have considered joining the Fun Club.

"I don't see how I can," she said. "I'm in the kitchen."

"Not in the evening meeting," he said.

"I don't think I'd be very good at it."

That night, when she stood at the front of the hall to help lead the singing, she felt terrified. Everybody was looking right at her, she thought. But gradually she realized she was almost invisible. Nobody was worrying about her, and she found it strangely thrilling to be before an audience. *This is my new home,* she thought, *with these friends, in this strange and defenseless position.*

* *

At the beach one very warm Saturday, Verity sat on the sand with Mindy and Leslie. They had been stretched out for hours, talking and slathering each other with clear golden baby lotion. Others from their group filtered in and out, but mainly the three of them kept to themselves. Two weeks had passed since the healing prayers; that seemed ages ago. The afternoon stretched endlessly. Verity was aware of the deepest contentment, a timeless satisfaction.

"Isn't this great?" she said, which was unlike her. She didn't effuse.

"It's a little hot," Mindy replied.

"I don't mean the weather. I mean, it's great that we can say anything we want without worrying that it will be misunderstood."

Leslie rolled over and propped herself on her elbow. She was wearing a daring electric-blue bikini—quite a change from her floor-length skirts and embroidered blouses. The swimsuit rattled Verity. Her mother always insisted on clothing that did not reveal. A person should not stick out; the high daisy got chopped. Added to that was an undercurrent that she had absorbed from Mount of Olives: modesty in all things. Only recently had the camp allowed two-piece bathing suits.

Verity admired Leslie so much; she was so kind, so peaceful, so gentle.

"Verity," Leslie asked kindly, "have you been misunderstood a lot?"

She didn't immediately get the question. "No, not particularly."

"But you said you worried about being misunderstood."

Verity made the connection, recognizing in a rush that for her to be misunderstood was as ordinary as rain in January. Embarrassed, she couldn't meet Leslie's eyes.

Mindy sat up and put out a hand to touch her. Verity's eyes blurred with tears, and she pressed Mindy's hand against her chest. "Don't worry, I'm not upset. I've never been this happy."

After a suitable silence, Mindy picked up the thread. "It does feel like heaven, doesn't it?" she said. "To be in this beautiful place, with so many wonderful people."

"Everybody our same age," Leslie added. "All Christians."

"You are so nice!" Verity said. She was conscious of letting all her defenses down. "I can't believe that everybody prayed for my epilepsy. That you actually cared."

"That was Howard," Leslie said. "He led the way."

"But Sam too!" Verity insisted. She wanted to give him credit because he was paired with Leslie. "He wanted to help me. He showed me the meaning of true faith."

Mindy, who had been indolent all afternoon, suddenly spoke energetically. "This camp is just overflowing with people who are sold out for God. You sit down with somebody you don't even know, and you won't be talking about trivial things; you'll be learning and growing by leaps and bounds. It's so inspiring."

Leslie nodded rapidly. "No matter where we all go after this summer, we have to stay together."

They ought to make a list of everybody's address and telephone number, Verity said.

Scott, who had been lying motionless nearby, sat up. Scott was quiet and neat, easily missed when he slid in and out of gatherings. His dark hair was kept short; his clothes never drew attention to themselves; he rarely spoke and when he did, it was brief and to the point. The three young women liked his guitar playing, and since he hung around with their group, they were used to him, though they felt that they barely knew him.

He spoke in a carefully guarded but fiercely concentrated way. "You should take your medicine," he said, looking straight at Verity with a stare that could bore holes.

"What?"

"It's not a sign of faith to quit taking medicine. That's Christian Science, not Christianity. You should have faith in your doctors."

Embarrassed, Verity waited for Mindy or Leslie to speak up. To her surprise, neither did. Scott seemed poised to get an answer. His dark eyes looked into hers with a terrible intensity. Was he trembling?

"Sam said if I really believed in God's healing, I'd show it by giving up the medicine."

"That makes *great* sense," Scott said caustically. "And if you really believe in God's protection, you'll jump off a cliff. Don't you know that Jesus told us not to test God?"

She didn't know it. She didn't know anything. She waited again for Mindy or Leslie, but they said nothing. "Scott?" she said after a considerable silence. "I don't know what to say. Can you talk to Sam?"

Now he finally looked away, down into the sand. Verity noticed that his shoulders were red; he had been in the sun too long. She also noticed that he had suddenly gone limp. It must have taken all he had to say what he did. "I'm not worried about Sam," he muttered, swallowing his words.

"Pardon?"

"I said I'm not worried about Sam. I'm worried about you. I'm sure the doctor prescribed those pills for a reason."

"But what if I've been healed?"

"God can heal you with or without the pills. How do you know he's not using medicine to heal you?"

Fortunately, Leslie finally spoke up. "Scott, you've thought about this a lot, haven't you?" she asked. "Did something happen to you to make you feel so strongly?"

Right before their eyes, he seemed to shrink. "I just don't want her to get hurt," he said. "Medicine is important."

"Can I get you some sunscreen?" Mindy asked. "You look like you're burning up."

He put a finger on his upper arm and watched as the pale dot turned red. "Oh," he said. "I always forget."

11

SKITS

By the fourth week of camp, the counselors had found their stride. They stopped worrying about making mistakes and instead raced to outdo each other. The Fun Club had kids screaming with laughter at their skits; the singing was so energetic that it hurt your ears. Howard got up an Elvis impersonation, slicking his hair into a ducktail and buying an Elvis outfit from a costume shop in Santa Cruz. He sang "You Ain't Nothin But a Hound Dog" while playfully swiveling his hips. The kids shrieked and crowded the front. He sang, "Love Me Tender" with a big, sloppy smile, but Mindy could see from the looks in the girls' eyes that it wasn't entirely a joke to them.

The Fun Club repeated the same silly skits week after week, but Brian was constantly egging them on to make them more extreme. There was, for instance, the toothpaste skit, which they always saved for the last night. It involved a line of counselors sharing the bathroom; one brushed his teeth, spit out the water into a cup, then handed the toothbrush and cup to the next counselor, who brushed and gargled from the same cup and handed them both to the next person, and so on down the line. At first only the guys would do it, but then a loud and raucous girl counselor named Linny volunteered. She became the final tooth brusher, the one who always drove the kids to insanity when she spit her mouthful of water on the floor and shouted at the top of her voice, "That tastes foul!"

To make the skit more insane, Brian had the third tooth brusher squirt toothpaste on his bare chest before scraping it off with his toothbrush and proceeding.

Beach Ball Ballet involved Brian and a very tall counselor named Jack dressed in tutus and holding a beach ball between various body parts while *Swan Lake* played. It depended on hamming it up in compromising positions, an effort that played perfectly to Brian's enthusiasm.

Verity was completely taken aback when Brian asked her to take a part in a new skit.

To that point she had only helped lead the singing, moving beyond self-consciousness and gradually, cautiously, edging into self-parody. Right from the start she quite naturally got the songs' hand motions confused and lagged on the beat. Now she did it semi-deliberately and let everyone laugh at her addled self. There was a song about Pharaoh that involved a little fake-Egyptian dance, which Verity couldn't do. She frowned and focused and still missed the beat, pretending not to notice that kids were pointing at her and laughing.

That was the limit of what she wanted to do, but Brian refused to let her say no. They had a new skit, he said, and she would be perfect for it. She didn't have to say a word; she just had to chew up some things and spit them out.

He wouldn't say more. The skit depended on surprise, he said, and it would work better if she were surprised, too. Verity hesitantly agreed to do it, and all that day she lived with a turbulent mix of pride and anxiety.

When the time came, two counselors carried a makeshift table onto the stage and then held up a sheet to block the audience's view while Brian hustled Verity under the table. They had cut a hole in a sheet of plywood; she crouched under it and put her head through the hole. As soon as she came through, the sheet was thrown over her.

She couldn't see but she could hear Brian talking like a county fair shill offering the latest and best food processor. He claimed it would dice and slice and grind and liquify any food to make a healthy meal for your family. You had heard, he said, of the Veg-o-matic. This new, advanced triumph of science was the Head-o-matic. He whipped off the sheet to reveal Verity's head poking out of the table, which drew a sustained peal of hesitant laughter, starting and stopping and starting again, as though trying to make up its mind.

"Say you want to make a nice ham salad," Brian was saying. "You want that ham diced nice and small. What do you do? You take your ham and put it in the Head-o-matic!" *Sotto voce* he told Verity to open her mouth wide and stuffed ham slices in. "Chew," he told her. "Chew it up fine, and then spit it out." It was harder to do than she would have thought. Bits and pieces fell out of her mouth; Brian kept stuffing in more ham until she almost gagged. She could hear the laughter growing and see the kids' faces lighting up with delight. With one last heave, she spat out the remaining chewed-up ham.

Then olives.

Then Jell-O cubes.

Then peanuts.

It got messier with each item, and Verity, hearing the waves of hilarity, grew more exuberant in chewing and growling and spitting. Never had she dreamed of doing comedy. Her jaw was getting tired, and she was still nervous, but she was almost enjoying herself.

"So you want to dice some potatoes?" Brian asked. "Let's just take a nice hunk of potato and stick it in the Head-o-matic!" He suddenly thrust a large chunk of raw potato into Verity's mouth. It wedged between her teeth and all the way to the back of her throat, so large she could not bite down on it. Letting out a loud, gargling sound, she wagged her head back and forth.

"But let's save time beating up our eggs!" Brian said. He began picking up raw egg yolks from a bowl and, with his bare hands, throwing them into Verity's mouth. She felt them trickling to the back of her throat, but with her mouth wedged open, she could not swallow. Almost immediately, she felt panic rising; she was going to drown. Rolling her head, she tried to get leverage on the potato to spit it out, but it was lodged tight. Her gag reflex kicked in; she could not breathe. Panicking, she struggled, her body writhing, until finally she managed to dislodge the potato and eject it. It launched across the table and onto the floor. The sound of hilarity was tremendous, but Verity could not appreciate it. She was sucking in air. Only after a minute of helpless heaving could she extricate herself from the hole in the table, stand up behind it, and take a bow to thundering applause and stomping feet.

In many ways, it was the best moment of her life.

* *

Leslie had the idea of doing a makeover on Verity. With the right haircut, clothes, and makeup, Verity could look much better than she did. She was not ugly, but she needed help.

"You'll feel so much better about yourself," Leslie explained when Verity did not immediately take to the idea.

"Why?"

"You'll see! You'll get so many compliments. Trust me."

Leslie got Mindy and Julie to help persuade her. Julie was extremely enthusiastic, Mindy less so, though she thought it would be a fun experience—a chance to bond together as females. Julie drove off in her Comet to buy products.

Saturday afternoon, the four of them crammed into the bathroom, almost sitting on each other, giggling. They began with a haircut. That was the hardest part of the makeover, since Verity had followed her mother's lead in regarding her hair as a treasure. She had never cut it; it flowed down to her waist like a thick, black waterfall.

They tipped a dining room chair back against the sink and poured water over Verity's head from a plastic pitcher. Mounds of suds soon ran down her shoulders and back. Water drizzled onto the floor and puddled underfoot until they were all splashing. Rinse, rinse, until her hair squeaked, and then Mindy dried her with a thick, coarse towel. Julie did the cutting—she claimed to have experience—and soon it was too late to stop. Verity felt an agony of uncertainty but kept her peace, letting the others' enthusiasm roll over her hesitation. Long, shiny strands fell on the floor while Mindy stared at her with a great, benevolent smile. They wouldn't let Verity look in the mirror until Julie was satisfied.

She didn't recognize herself. Julie had gone for a pixie look, very short, and it made her look like a thirteen-year-old boy. Verity decided not to hate it. Her friends seemed delighted. She looked at herself in the mirror, patted one side and then the other.

"What do you think?" Julie asked hopefully. "Do you like it?"

"Not really," she said.

"I think it looks great," Mindy said. "It opens up your face. And your eyes."

"Anyway, we're not done," Leslie said.

"I wonder what you'd look like as a blonde," Julie said, studying her, and that made them all laugh.

While Leslie applied makeup, they talked about the things they never talked about in mixed company. Julie had sized up every boy in camp. With detailed analysis, she tried out each one on Mindy and Verity, certain that they were on the hunt. "Oh my goodness, those freckles!" "Did you hear his voice? It sounds like a train whistle." They got tickled at the descriptions and laughed until tears came streaking down their cheeks.

When Leslie declared her work complete and Verity looked in the mirror again, it frightened her. The makeup had taken over her face, crusting her eyes with a thick dark line, pinking her lips, shading her eyelids with blue. The others acted very pleased. "You look so elegant!" Julie kept saying. "Nobody will know who you are."

12

MEDS

On Monday, while they were serving lunch, Trudy, the dining hall supervisor, told Verity that her mother had called. "As soon as your work is done, you can call her back on the office phone," Trudy said.

The office was a small back room, stuffed with desks and littered with papers. Verity felt like a trespasser as she crept in. Giveaway calendars hung on the wall; note cards were thumbtacked to corkboards. A small window, the only window, had a crack angling from the upper right corner to the lower left.

Verity dreaded the conversation. She had received three short notes from her mother, which she had yet to answer. Verity knew that failing to respond was irrational, that the surest way to alarm her mother was to exclude her. Yet when she thought of writing back, she couldn't. Her mother would ruin it somehow if she gave her a chance.

She was surprised, therefore, that her mother didn't bother to complain about her unanswered notes. She asked if Verity was okay, whether she had everything she needed. "Is the work hard?" she asked. "You've never really worked before."

"You never wanted me to work," Verity said. Her mother had insisted that she take summer classes at the junior college.

Remarkably, her mother left it at that. "Do you have enough medicine?" she asked. "I realized I didn't get you any extra."

This pierced Verity like a sliver of glass. "I'm fine," she said.

"You're sure you're okay?"

"Yeah," Verity said. Then she slipped. "I'm not taking it now, anyway." Later, when she thought it over, she couldn't understand why she said that.

The more she explained, the more upset her mother became, to the point where she threatened to come and bring her home. She had no use for faith healers, she said, and if she had known the camp was full of that kind of nonsense, she would have refused to let Verity work there.

Verity did not raise her voice to match her mother's. She did not cry. Teetering on the verge of losing the happiest time she had ever known, her brain whizzing with fears, she managed to say as little as possible because that was the only way she had ever managed to placate her mother.

In the end, she had to promise that she would take her medications. It wasn't such a hard promise to make; she had felt ambivalent all along. What was hard was the thought of telling her friends. She knew they would be profoundly disappointed in her.

When Verity emerged from the office into the lazy warmth of afternoon free time, she blinked in the light like someone who has taken a profound shock. Mindy had followed her from the dining hall and waited outside the camp office, sitting on a stump, soaking in the sun. She saw immediately that something was wrong.

"Verity! What happened?"

Verity gave a shrug. Her string bean arms and hollow shoulders made the gesture more expressive than she realized.

"Are you all right?" Mindy asked.

"I'm fine," Verity replied. "My mom got upset with me, that's all."

"You're sure you're okay? What was she upset about?"

Her eyes full of misanthropy, Verity looked at Mindy closely. "If I tell you, you have to promise not to tell anyone."

"Of course," she said. "I promise."

"I don't want anyone else to know."

"They won't," Mindy said. She was dying to be told.

Verity closed her eyes, unable to bear her friend's response. "My mom found out that I wasn't taking my medications. She thinks it's stupid. She hates the idea of faith healing." Verity stopped short and shook her head. "She made me promise I would take my pills, or she would call the director."

A smile dawned on Mindy's lips. "Oh, Verity," she said. She had feared something awful.

"I have to do it," Verity said. "I gave my word."

"Oh, Verity, of course!"

"But I don't want you to tell anybody. You promised."

"I won't. But Verity, I don't think they'd be upset."

"Yes, they will. They'll say I lack faith."

Mindy looked at Verity with quizzical wonder. "Well, you don't have to tell them. We can keep it to ourselves."

They went to change and met again at the pool. Mindy swam laps, dodging fourteen-year-olds splashing through the water or jumping into her path. Verity sat by the fence in her floppy hat and coverall, eaten up with misery. She did not believe Mindy's assurance. Keeping secrets from the others felt like lying. She couldn't bear to be with her friends on such false terms. They had trusted her, they believed in her, and they had even made her part of the Fun Club.

At four-thirty the camp bell rang, and everybody headed back to their cabins for Bible study. Verity went to her bunk and lay down, turning her face to the wall. She heard others come in and recognized Julie's voice, but could not turn to greet her. Julie would be the worst. Except her boyfriend, Howard. Verity could not imagine telling Howard.

When the time came to serve dinner, she thought her face told everything but soon realized that could not be true since nobody asked her what was wrong.

After the post-meal cleanup, the kitchen staff crowded together at a long table to eat. It was a cheerful, gabby time, and still no one seemed to notice Verity's silence, probably because she was generally very quiet anyway.

As soon as she could get away, Verity took a long walk by the creek. Usually, she headed for the evening program; but they wouldn't miss her. The night fog was beginning to come in from the ocean in wisps and feathers. Pale blues and pinks textured the sky. She wanted to avoid people, and she told herself that she needed to think. Unfortunately, fear kept her from that. When she tried to say a prayer, her mind went careening off in panic. In the distance, she heard singing from the assembly, an almost tuneless chanting, and then amplified voices she couldn't make out. Occasionally she heard a burst of noise like static, which she eventually realized was laughter.

Just as it began to get dark, she went back to her cabin and picked up a book to read. She had finished *Dune*, her fourth reading, but she had one of Robert Heinlein's novels. It couldn't hold her attention. The other girls came and left again.

Verity was trying to decide whether to join the nightly gathering at the picnic tables. They would miss her if she did not go. They would ask her where she had been. So perhaps she had to go; it only made it worse not to.

And she wanted to be there. Listening to the sounds of camp closing down for the night, she heard bursts of laughter, the distant hum of conversation. Soon, only occasional shouts punctuated the silence. Julie came in to get something and asked if she was coming. She said she wasn't sure.

But she had to go; she knew that.

Verity waited until she knew the conversations had begun, then dragged herself out to the picnic tables, hoping that nobody would notice her. Trying in the dark to find a spot to sit, she bumped into somebody, who turned out to be Leslie. They made a slight commotion as they identified each other. Leslie slid over to make room. Howard was talking, though Verity had not caught the subject. In looping her leg over the picnic table bench, she kicked somebody else, who said "Ow!" very loudly.

Howard stopped what he was saying. "Who *is* that?" he asked.

"It's Verity," Leslie said.

"Verity!" Howard said, joy in his voice. "How are you?"

It was meant to be an innocuous question, and Verity could have easily said, "Fine," except that she had spent the whole afternoon in dread. This was precisely what she shrank from: lying to her friends.

"I've had a terrible day," she said, her voice breaking. "I had to promise my mother that I would take my medications."

The silence, as she heard it, was loaded with condemnation. She had no faith; she had given up on God's healing.

Howard's voice, when it finally came, had a light, ordinary timbre. "Why?" he asked. "Why did that happen?"

"She got very upset with me. She was ready to come and get me, because she hates having me here with a bunch of holy rollers, and I couldn't. I can't go home. I can't miss this summer. She made me promise, and I did." Verity began to sob loudly, her throat catching.

Before she knew what was happening, Leslie was putting a hand on her back, comforting her. Soon other staff were trying to comfort her. They all said it was fine, not to worry. "Verity. It's okay! You have to listen to your mother."

"But I have no faith!" Verity sobbed. "I can't leave here! I just can't!"

"You have plenty of faith," Howard said. "We love you, Verity."

Then she began really blubbering, from joy. They were not condemning her. She would spend the whole summer here.

"We don't care about the meds," Howard said. He had slid across to join Leslie, rubbing her back. "We care about you."

* *

The next afternoon, Mindy and Verity lounged on the steps of Verity's cabin, their arms wrapped around their knees. Sunshine streaked through the gaps in the trees. Mindy was supposed to be with her campers, and Verity wondered how she justified sitting with her. Probably it had something to do with last night. She herself was still catching up with that.

The gracious reaction of her friends, their forgiveness of her faithlessness amazed Verity, but she wasn't sure she believed in it. Every molecule of her being had gone into her decision to abandon the security of her meds and throw herself into the miracle-working hands of God. And then, to call it off? To just say, "Oh, my mom doesn't want me to do it?" It was a betrayal. "We love you!" they said. How could they?

"So what do you honestly think of your new look?" Mindy asked.

That was so far from her mind. "I'll have to get used to it."

"It's really nice," Mindy said. "Different. I don't know about the makeup."

Verity smiled. "I'll never wear makeup like that. But please don't tell anyone. I wouldn't like it to get back to Leslie."

Mindy put out a hand to touch Verity's. "Thanks for letting us use you as our guinea pig. We had fun."

"Oh, I had fun, too."

"What about your hair?" Mindy asked. "Do you hate that too?"

"No, it's okay. It's just hair." She hesitated just a twitch and then added, "My mother will hate it."

"Oh! What are you going to do?"

Verity grimaced. "There's nothing I can do. She can't make it grow back." She gave a chortle. "Though she might try."

Mindy sat up straight and stretched. Her curiosity was engaged, and she lifted her head like a cat who hears rustling in the high grass. "Can you explain your mom to me?" she said. "She seemed really nice when I met her, but I get a different idea from you."

Verity winced. Thinking about her mother was hard—a pain in the head. "I wouldn't call her nice, but she has good intentions."

"About what?"

"About my life. She wants what's best for me and she never lets up."

"What does she want you to do?"

That stopped Verity for a moment. What did her mother want her to do? Everything, every minute. "She's so demanding. I don't have a life; she tells me what my life is." She paused, startled by her own vehemence. "Most of the time it's about studying. She wants me to get good grades and get ahead. That's the secret of life, she thinks."

Mindy, who had grown up in an easygoing family, could hardly relate to Verity's emotion. What surprised her most was the mismatch between Verity's feelings and the unspectacular nature of her complaints. Verity spoke with a repressed hysteria, as though about to explode, but she described the most ordinary of lives. A single mother trying to maintain control. No abuse. No deprivation. Mindy couldn't see what upset Verity so profoundly.

"Can you talk to your mother?" Mindy asked. "Let her know how you feel?"

Verity controlled her reaction, but it required obvious effort. She managed to calm her face and then said quietly, "My mother would hate that. She doesn't have room for feelings."

"At least she would know."

"She doesn't want to know."

"What does she think about your spending the summer here? She seemed happy enough when she dropped you off."

Verity stopped to think. It still amazed her that her mother had agreed to let her go.

"It was my decision. I applied without her knowing, and when I got accepted, I just told her."

"But she said yes. She even drove you. She talked to us very nicely."

"That was just an act. She knows how to put on a show. All the way here she would hardly say a word."

Mindy smiled and wrapped her arms more tightly around her knees. "At least," she said, "you can be thankful she pushed you into coming here. Just by being so difficult. Even if she wasn't intending good, she did good. That's the way God works."

Verity seemed to tense up, a porcupine lifting its quills. She didn't say anything, but Mindy added, "You know, like Romans 8:28, God works all things together for good. If your mother weren't so hard to live with, you wouldn't have come."

Verity had never thought of it that way, and when she took in the implications, they dumbfounded her. "Where did you say that was?"

"Romans 8:28. You don't know that one? It's kinda famous."

From Mindy's point of view, the conversation ended there. Verity pulled into herself, deep into her own thoughts. She had to get a Bible and look up that verse.

The idea was terribly important, she knew at once: that God was working not only to override facts, like through miracles, but to undermine facts by working through them, to bring good out of carelessness *through* carelessness, out of hostility *through* hostility. Nothing was wasted in this economy; God worked in everything. That idea of God was deeper and more complex than anything she had imagined. No, not even an idea—a power as subtle and inescapable as quantum mechanics. She wanted to be alone to think.

When she got a Bible and read the verse, she found even deeper matters to ponder. It spoke of God's groaning in pain. In fact, there was groaning all through it: the whole creation groaning.

She was in her cabin, alone on her bed because she wanted no interruptions. It was huge, what she grasped, encompassing everything, surrounding her in power. It frightened and thrilled her. She knew she had stumbled on something that would never let her go. No, not something, she corrected herself. Someone.

13

THE KISS

Since nothing she could do would estrange her from these friends, Verity opened up. In her hesitant, halting way, she freely pursued all sorts of questions—questions that would never occur to anyone else. She wanted to know why people closed their eyes to pray. What was a soul, and what was the difference between soul and spirit? She had asked questions from the beginning, but now she did it with abandon. It tickled people. Little smiles followed her, but they weren't mean. She was like a child visiting a museum, and they were happy to explain every picture, every coat of armor, every dinosaur.

In this, Howard and Verity came together as an intellectual fit: she had endless questions, and he had endless answers. If God created the universe out of nothing, how? She wondered about slaves in the Bible. Why did they hold elections every four years instead of five? Howard loved to talk and explain. Verity wanted to understand.

Julie usually wandered off, leaving them to themselves. She never thought of Verity as a rival. Even after her makeover, Verity wasn't pretty. She had a flat face and narrow eyes. Her hair was good, but she didn't know how to dress. Julie had a well-developed figure and an attractive, smiling face. She moved athletically. Boys always liked her. She knew how to talk to them with her eyes, signaling that she was eager for their company. Verity knew nothing about that kind of communication.

Howard, however, knew lots of girls who signaled. That was background noise to him. A woman who only wanted to understand—she was intriguing. He marveled at Verity's hunger for knowledge.

Nobody would say they made a handsome couple. Verity was plain, introverted, and cryptic. Yet he kept thinking of her. When he found time to talk to her—which came seldom since he had no spare time—he ended up inexplicably pleased. Sometimes, when he was intent on some task, he would feel that he had forgotten something and only slowly grasped that he wanted Verity's reaction. The thought surprised him.

During Tuesday afternoon free time, she was sitting by herself outside her cabin. The air was perfect: warm and liquid and still. "Want to go for a walk?" he asked.

She looked up as though he had told a joke. As everybody knew by then, she didn't exercise. She never walked if she could help it.

Seeing that he was serious, she said, "Sure."

Their path required them to edge along a narrow trail indented into the creek bank. Howard had gone ahead, talking as he walked, assuming that Verity was just behind him. When he didn't hear her, he looked back and saw that she trailed him by ten yards. His first reaction was irritation: she had missed everything he was saying. Then he saw by her face that Verity was frightened. She walked as though on a high wire, fearful of falling.

It made him feel tender. He told her it wasn't difficult; just don't look down.

If she fell, she would slide twenty feet down the bank into the shallow water. That wouldn't be so terrible. He wasn't concerned, but Verity was creeping down the trail, one foot splayed in front of the other, trying to keep herself almost on the ground. He started to laugh because she looked so pitifully ridiculous, but he stopped himself in time. "Wait," he said, and went back for her.

Putting out a hand, he tried to talk her into standing straight and reaching out to him. He couldn't really help—he couldn't stop her if she began to fall—but confidence was what she needed.

The first step was the hardest—he could see her knees trembling—and then she gained courage for the second step. The third step was easier yet, and then she was out of trouble.

She didn't know it yet. Her face was still locked in fierce concentration, pushing one foot ahead, then bringing the other forward to join it. A feeling swept through him: like love. She wasn't beautiful but she was darling: so focused, so courageous. He put out a hand again to guide her, but she shook her head sharply and continued her edging, halting progress. He studied every inch of her. When they finally reached the water's edge, where a small triangle of gravel gave them room to stand together, Howard reached down, scooped her into his arms, and kissed her.

He felt her surprise. She tried to pull away, but he held her. Gradually she relaxed and began kissing back, quite eagerly. Her lips were soft, pliable, rubbery. Howard had kissed lots of girls, but this was novel and experimental, the lips of a girl who had never been kissed.

She pulled away before he was ready. Looking at him in deep seriousness, she asked, "What are you doing?" Her eyes seemed dark as midnight, black holes sucking him in.

"Kissing you."

"Why?"

She reminded him of a little girl, asking why for things that cannot be explained. Rather than try to answer her question, he kissed her again.

* *

Verity knew she had not done anything wrong, but she felt so guilty. Howard had been the one to kiss. She had only responded. Happily, yes, but how could she be blamed for that? She had never given Howard a seductive glance. In fact, she had no idea how to do such a thing.

Nevertheless, she was sure that Julie would vilify her with the white-hot anger of a woman scorned. Julie would not blame Howard. Only Verity would merit condemnation. This was a devastating thought. Having just found a place where she was loved, Verity didn't see how she could endure judgment.

When they started climbing out of the little canyon, she asked, "Will you tell Julie?"

For the longest time Howard gave no response. Finally, he said, "No. She'll figure it out."

"Don't you need to talk to her?"

"There's nothing to say," he countered. He was walking ahead of her, and she wished she could stop him, turn him around, and see his face. "She'll get over it," he added.

She assumed that Howard's response was right but knew she could never imitate it. By the time they reached camp, Verity looked like a poisoning victim. Her steps were heavy, her head down, her shoulders slumped with a heavy weight. Howard walked beside her and tried to slip his hand into hers, but she couldn't do that, not in public.

Howard stopped in front of the snack shack, in full view of a line of kids waiting to buy ice cream sandwiches and gummy bears. Putting his hands on Verity's shoulders, he looked at her and smiled. "I have to go be with my cabin," he said. "I'll see you tonight."

He put a finger on her chin and lifted it. "Smile! I thought you liked me. Why aren't you happy?"

"I'm worried about Julie," she said.

"Don't worry about her! She'll get over it. You're my girlfriend now."

The word seemed to float lightly in the air. Until that moment she had thought the issue was a moment of random kissing. It was more, much more.

"I've never been anybody's girlfriend. I don't know how to act."

Howard's face broke into a wolfish grin. "You don't have to act. It's not something you do, it's who you are. Just be yourself."

He put his finger on her chin again. "Cheer up," he said. "We can talk tonight. I need to go."

Ordinarily Verity was sedentary, happy to sit in one place all day, but now she wandered over to the pool, then to her cabin, where she sat on her bunk for a few minutes, then back to the creek, trying to summon memories of the kiss. She was so anxious that she couldn't sit still. What an extraordinary day it was.

Passing by the pool she saw Julie from a distance, bright in the sunlight, and turned away. Her secret would destroy Julie, and the power of that knowledge made her sick. Julie wasn't her favorite person, but she didn't want to see her crushed. Her own suffering made her sensitive to others'.

When the bell rang and all the campers headed back to their cabins, Verity wandered toward the dining room. Ordinarily she would go back to her cabin to change, but she wasn't prepared to face Julie, who would also be there. She took a seat on the bench outside the dining room, thinking that she could wait quietly. To her surprise, however, Julie rounded the corner. She had on snug jeans and a sleeveless lemon chiffon top that accentuated her figure.

"What were you doing with Howard this afternoon?" she asked, smiling broadly.

For an instant Verity thought she was asking about the kiss. She started to blush before realizing that Julie couldn't possibly know what had happened.

"We went for a walk," she said. "Down by the creek."

"What were you talking about?"

"I can't remember." She wasn't lying. All she could remember was the kiss. Had they talked about anything?

Julie still wore that smile. "I went looking for him and he was nowhere to be found. He likes talking to you."

Speaking carefully, Verity said, "I like talking to him. He's very interesting."

"Don't get too interested!" Julie said it as a joke, but of course she meant it. The problem was what to say in response.

Verity wanted to tell Julie the truth, but Howard had said it was better to say nothing. Let it sleep; it might go away. She knew that was impossible, but for now she wanted simply to snuggle down in the present, in which Howard had kissed her and nobody knew.

While serving dinner, Verity saw Julie talking to Howard. They were standing close together by a window. From their faces she saw that it was a serious conversation. The room was noisy, and their words were inaudible.

"You liar!" Julie appeared out of nowhere, her face close and distorted by rage. "You can't remember! You can't remember! What a liar you are!"

The roar of the room drowned out Julie's voice for all but those nearby, but anybody could see that Julie was outraged, yelling and red-faced with the effort. Verity would have run, but she was afraid to turn her back. Fixing her eyes on a spot just under Julie's chin, she faced the assault like a swimmer bracing for a wave.

Julie grabbed her upper arm and pulled hard toward the door. "What are you doing?" Verity gasped. "I have to do my tables."

"You have to talk to me," Julie said. Slamming the door open, she hauled Verity out the door and spun her around. By now, most of the dining room was watching.

Julie had her face inches away from Verity's, close enough to bite. "You are *not* Howard's girlfriend," she said, spitting out the words like nails. "I am Howard's girlfriend. You can stay away from him."

Verity had already given up the fight. "I will, Julie, I will. I didn't do anything."

That little speech further enraged Julie. "What did you do with him? If you weren't talking, what? You have to tell me."

"Nothing!"

"It wasn't nothing. You know that."

No, it wasn't nothing. Verity was too factual, too trusting to lie. Frozen, she shut her eyes, as though she could escape into darkness.

"Tell me! What did you do? You have to tell me."

The barrage was so forceful she couldn't help giving in. "He kissed me."

For an instant there was silence, and with it the possibility that Julie had somehow been quieted, perhaps charmed. Then the storm broke. "You kissed? You kissed?" Julie went for her eyes, and Verity barely fended her off. Julie screamed, her words distorted and incomprehensible. Verity's arms defended her face, but Julie's nails tore into her skin. She shrank into herself, trying to become so small she would disappear. Afraid to turn her back or drop her guard, she stood and bore the assault until others pulled Julie off.

Other servers finished Verity's work while she went to her cabin and lay down. She felt so limp that her body disappeared to her, becoming like water. She was as lacking in agency as a twig twirling in the creek, carried downstream. Her wonderful summer was over.

Howard's voice floated into her consciousness; he was talking to someone outside. Then he was beside her, running his hand over her forehead, smoothing back her hair. "Don't worry," he said. "I'm settling Julie. She can't act like that."

"No," Verity said in alarm. "Don't, Howard. It's all right. She is your girl-friend. I had no right." She could not bear for Julie to be crazy.

"Don't talk like that," Howard said. "Leave Julie to me." He said he had to go, and he leaned over to kiss her on the lips.

Later, she got up to wash her face. In the distance she could hear the camp singing in the Big Meeting, but it did not penetrate her heart as before. She tried to think of Howard stooping beside her bed, but her mind slipped off that. She felt so sorry for Julie. Howard was all she lived for. Howard was like Julie's religion. It was not that Verity was ready to relinquish him; she had been, for a few hours, as happy and as content as she had ever been. She had never dreamed of somebody like Howard; she couldn't believe that he called her his girlfriend. Julie's plight seemed almost a separate category.

After the evening program, Verity heard campers chattering as they returned to their cabins. It was not long before Julie came in, accompanied by Trudy, the dining hall supervisor. You could tell they had a plan by the way they entered, not talking, with Trudy glancing at Julie. She planted herself by Verity's bed, and without looking at her, asked if they could talk outside. "Just for a moment," she said.

They stood in the darkness. Perhaps it was easier if nobody could see.

"I'm sorry," Julie said.

"For what?" Where that challenge came from, Verity did not know. Somewhere buried in her heart must be anger; she had not been aware of it until this moment.

It took Julie the better part of a minute and a nudge from Trudy before she answered. "For yelling at you."

"Not just yelling," Trudy said.

"And for..."

"Attacking you," Trudy prompted.

"I'm sorry for attacking you."

"Why did you do it?" Verity asked, though she knew the answer perfectly well.

* *

Verity expected that she would surrender Howard back to Julie. He had come to her like a lost penny—a lucky chance for her, but nothing that she planned to spend. Seeing Julie, though, stirred up something self-righteous and assertive in her, something she had not known she was capable of, except with her mother. She liked being Howard's girlfriend. She hadn't done anything wrong.

Then she saw Julie's face, not in reality but in her imagination. It was almost like looking at a painting of the crucifixion: Julie wretched and tear-stained, her pretty face distorted with suffering, blotched with red. Verity felt sorry for her. Such an extraordinary feeling, to be on top looking down, to be an agent of concern rather than wishing somebody—anybody—would care for you.

Howard, meanwhile, suffered very little. He was entirely sincere in assuring Verity that Julie would get over it. He had seen it before. Girls put up a huge fuss, and they only make things worse. But it wouldn't last long.

He saw the marks on Verity's forearms, long, red digs still angry from the assault, which brought out his pity. He intended to talk with Verity in just the way that had brought them together: her questing mind meeting his nimble and wise understanding. He wanted her to ask questions, and later perhaps they could find some privacy and kiss. This, he expected, would put Julie's attack behind them.

He found instead that Verity was profoundly wrapped up in Julie, not with anger or fear over her assault, but with pity for Julie's suffering. When he said she would get over it, it was almost as though Verity skipped right over his words and carried on with her worry.

"Do you think I should go talk to her?" Verity asked him.

"No!" he said. "Let her work it out herself." Julie would not like a visit from Verity, he knew.

Verity could hardly avoid Julie, however. They shared a bunk bed. That night neither one went out to the staff rendezvous; they both got ready for bed. Verity was startled by Julie's face, usually so smooth and put together, as she stood in front of the bathroom mirror rubbing cream into her forehead. Her eyes were sad in a way that captured her whole face. Verity wanted to turn away, but she couldn't; she had never seen such sorrow.

"I don't know what to say," Verity said.

"You don't have to say anything," Julie replied, while still rubbing on cream. "I know you'd say you were sorry if you really were sorry, but you don't need to say that. It won't do any good. I've lost him and I'll never be happy again. You'll never understand how miserable I am."

Verity searched for a response. She had plenty of experience with misery and thought that surely Julie would someday be happy again. But she didn't say this; she couldn't form the words.

"I don't know what I did wrong," Julie said. "I was so devoted to him. I thought about him all the time. I did everything he wanted to do, and if he had asked me, I would have done anything. He just got tired of me. I'm not smart enough for him. I'd say I'm not pretty enough, but then why would he choose you as his next girlfriend? That wouldn't make any sense."

Verity was glad she was no longer being blamed, and she wasn't really bothered that Julie didn't think she was pretty. Verity herself didn't think she was pretty. While wanting to say something to draw Julie out of her misery, she knew from experience that when you make up your mind to be wretched, nothing can stop you. Instead of responding, she washed her face and hands and brushed out her hair. Julie watched her, not saying a word but appearing to critique what she was seeing.

"He's not as great as he thinks, you know," Julie finally said, as though picking up the thread of an earlier conversation. "He's very proud, you know. He acts like he knows everything, but there are lots of things he doesn't know."

Listening, Verity thought that perhaps Julie was working her way to thinking, *Good riddance.* She hoped for that, but it was not to be. Verity watched in the mirror as Julie's face cracked open and she began to howl. "I love him so much. Am I asking for too much that he should stay with me for the whole summer? I don't blame you for going after him, but couldn't he have waited until we went back to school?"

"I didn't go after him," Verity said. "I just like to talk to him."

14

STICKS ON THE FIRE

Contrary to Howard's prediction, Julie did not get over it. Misery filled her stomach, and she vomited it out: over the campers at her tables, the girls who shared her cabin, the camp counselors. For long hours at a time, Julie disappeared into Trudy's tiny, cluttered office. And she ate. One of the girls drove with her to Safeway, where she bought a gigantic bag of Oreos that she kept next to her pillow. She called them comfort pills and made no bones about eating day and night. Within two weeks she had noticeably put on weight. "I was slim," she said to anybody in range. "So slim. You remember?"

Verity knew it was a show—she was capable of drama herself—but she also knew that something real lay behind it. She went to find Mindy, who had kept her distance during all the commotion. "I don't know what to do," she said, her voice cracking. "With Julie so miserable. It's just unbearable. Howard says she will get over it, but she's not getting over it."

Mindy looked at her coolly. "Is that really your business?" she asked.

"I feel responsible," Verity said.

"Why are you responsible?"

Doubt flooded Verity's face. "I don't know. I didn't do anything."

"You did something. You didn't have to let him kiss you."

"No," Verity said, her face showing nothing but gloom. "What would you have done?"

Mindy shrugged. She seemed not at all the kind and understanding friend Verity had expected. "It's water under the bridge," she said. "The question for you is, do you see any future with him?"

"I don't know."

"To tell you the truth, it's hard for me to see it. You two are so different."

That made her mad. Verity decided on the spot that everything was fine. She said so to Mindy.

Even so, Mindy's skepticism nagged at her. She had gone to Mindy because she was the epitome of calm, common sense, but she hadn't calmed Verity. If anything, she made it worse.

Howard also changed in the way he related to her. She wanted to ask him questions and hear him spin out wisdom as effortlessly and joyfully as a sea otter floats on its back. Somehow, he didn't do that. Was it impossible now that she was his girlfriend? They went on walks, they stretched out on the sand at the beach on Saturdays, they made out when they found a moment of privacy, but the stimulating talk ebbed. She found it difficult to remember her questions, and when she did think of them, he would joke with her, sometimes in a way that felt condescending. He didn't talk as he used to.

Verity swallowed her pride and asked Mindy whether she had noticed any change in Howard.

"Why, don't you like him?" Mindy asked, which was such a disconnected response that Verity hardly knew what to say.

"I like him," she said. "Of course. Don't you like him?"

"He's not my boyfriend," Mindy said with a laugh.

Verity became more and more unsure of her path. She had gotten more than she dreamed of, yet something was off. She had no idea what she should do.

One night in the seventh week she went out, as usual, to be with the staff as they gathered at the picnic tables. She felt that these get-togethers had changed. The same conversations went on, but they did them by rote; the spontaneity and excitement were gone. Finding her place by Howard's side, she let him wrap both arms around her, holding her in front of him. She liked this position; it felt cozy. Sometimes Howard's hands wandered, and she had to hold them tightly, but even that felt reassuring.

Verity felt Howard's body rock, at first gently and then more violently. It took a moment for her to realize that Julie was behind them, that she had grabbed on to Howard and was trying to pull him away. The struggle was silent until Julie began to shriek: "Take your hands off her!! It's disgusting!" Howard's arms stayed wrapped tightly around Verity until he suddenly released her. She spun to see that he was pushing Julie away, while she grabbed at him.

Verity began shouting at them both: "Stop! Don't!"

Some of the other staff grabbed Julie and held her, while she burst into sobs. Howard was yelling at her: "Leave us alone! I've told you!"

"I don't care!" Julie shouted. "I just want to hurt you."

"Julie, you can't do that." Randy held Julie, trying to talk reasonably to her.

"I will!" Julie insisted. "I'm going to hurt myself. I'll run in front of a car."

She eventually allowed herself to be led away to their cabin. "Can you believe that?" someone said. Howard was uncharacteristically silent.

"Where am I going to sleep tonight?" Verity quietly asked him.

He laughed. "You think she might strangle you in your bed?"

Verity didn't find it funny. "You said she would get over it." She felt deeply estranged from everything, as lonely as she had felt when she first came to camp.

Howard shrugged.

"I'm going to go to bed," she said and left him without ceremony.

The lights were on in her cabin, but the lump on Julie's bed did not move. Verity brushed her teeth and changed into pajamas, then climbed under her covers. The lights were on—the other girls were still out. It felt strange to be directly underneath Julie. Verity tried to hear her breathing.

"Julie?" she asked tentatively. "Julie, are you awake?"

"Yeah," Julie said.

"I'm sorry, Julie," Verity said softly. "I'm sorry it's worked out like this. I don't know what I can do."

"Neither do I," Julie said. "I should just kill myself."

"Don't say that."

"Why shouldn't I say it? I mean it. I'm so low I don't see what the point is."

Verity tried to be logical. "You aren't looking at the big picture. You're nice looking. Boys like you."

"I'm fat."

"Only because you're so upset, you're eating all those cookies. You'll be thin again, and you always look nice."

"That's all that matters," Julie said. "Look nice for the boys."

"I don't mean that. You're going to USC. You're smart. You have a good family, don't you?"

Julie was quiet. Verity could hear her breathing, which she took for a good sign until it turned into whimpering. "I don't have Howard," Julie said.

For a good half hour, they went around and around that way, Verity talking calmly and logically while Julie listened and then spun back to her grief. "He's so beautiful," she said. "He's going to be a star, and you'll be there with him."

Verity could not even begin to imagine that. It was so far over her horizon that it had no meaning. If she tried to put herself into that picture, there was no picture.

"I doubt I will be there with him," Verity said.

Unexpectedly, that tipped Julie back into hysterics. "That is so *cruel*," she said. "How can you *say* that?"

"Why is it cruel?"

"You steal him from me, and you don't even want him."

Verity had no answer. Did she want him? She had not chosen, really: he had picked her, in a choice that now seemed completely baseless.

"I didn't steal him, you know. I wasn't even thinking about him that way."

Julie kept hyperventilating, making little mewing sounds.

"Why does that make you so upset?" Verity asked.

"You weren't even thinking about him. He wanted you, and he didn't want me! I would follow him anywhere, and you don't even care about him. He's nothing to you."

That wasn't quite true, but Verity could understand that from Julie's perspective it might seem so. She felt awful for Julie, which was a novel feeling for somebody used to living in the prison of her own woes.

"Julie," she said. "You can have him back. I'll tell him in the morning. As long as you'll still let me talk to him, and not get all jealous."

Julie said nothing.

"Really, I'll tell him. I'll say I don't want to be his girlfriend, that he should go back to you because you deserve him."

What else could she do? She didn't like it, but she saw no other option.

* *

To her surprise, Howard put up only token resistance. "Are you sure?" he asked her. "Do you need time to think about it?" He accepted her decision so easily it seemed dreamlike. As she went about her cleanup work, it came to her that their relationship had ended before she even made her decision. He had already moved on. She was no longer what Howard had in mind for himself.

While walking toward the dining hall at lunchtime, she saw Howard and Julie together, oblivious to the rest of the world. *I'm glad,* she thought. And yet, it hurt.

She felt lighter, but empty and apt to fly away. When she had been with Howard, she knew what direction to turn every day. Now, her trajectory disappeared in the air like jet contrails.

That night she went to Victory Circle and found a spot in the back, looking down to the firepit. Mindy gestured for her to come to the front, but she stubbornly shook her head.

The campers flooded in, crowding the bleachers, crowing and laughing. After some singing and a short, inspirational talk, the counselors began their weekly routine of throwing a stick on the fire. They had done this every week of camp, so their words were well rehearsed. Verity stared at the fire, a barely visible flickering eye from her vantage at the very top of the risers. The fire was a symbol for God, she realized. The counselors threw their sticks in as though their lives were to be immolated in God's very being.

It is only a symbol, she thought, pulling herself back, but then she remembered the Second Corinthians passage. When anyone turns to the Lord, the veil is taken away.

She remembered the verses Mindy had tossed out. All things work together for good, for those who love him, for those who are called. All things. Tears began to flow, and she doubled over her knees like a person in pain. The love of God. Of course, it was in everything.

God appeared in her mind's eye, sorrowful, watchful, his face bruised, blood on his forehead. He was dying. She was overwhelmed by the vision. This is what she wanted—not boyfriends or friends or approval or anything else in the universe.

15

FAREWELL

Mount of Olives had a tradition that after the last camp of the summer, the staff stayed on for one final night—a barbecue with a whole roasted pig and a talent show. Typically, they stayed up all night and left the next morning, bedraggled and nostalgic.

Trisha told Verity it would be fun. "You see sides of people you didn't know were there."

"Can you be more specific?" Verity said.

"Some people are really funny," she said. "You have no idea."

Saturday morning, the cooks began digging a pit for the roast pig. This attracted the attention of departing campers, who trudged down the hill bearing their sleeping bags and duffle bags and stopped to watch. By noon, the parents had come and taken them away, leaving only staff. All around camp, you encountered singers furtively practicing for their talent show performances.

Sam found Howard and invited him for a final walk to the cross. Already feeling melancholy about the summer's end, he wanted to bookend their time together. They had started at the cross; they should end there.

Howard was much more fit than he had been in June, Sam noticed; he climbed the hill effortlessly. When they reached the cross, both paused in silence, looking up at it.

"How would you sum up the summer?" Howard asked. "What was your most meaningful experience?"

Sam felt suddenly shy. "I had a great time," he said. "I think we all did." The truth was, his most meaningful experience was meeting Howard.

"But..." Howard said suggestively.

"No 'but,' really. It was all great. I can't think of a single regret."

"How do you think we will remember it years from now?"

Sam sighed. "I'm sure I'll have happy memories, but I expect they'll fade. It makes me sad to say it, but I think it's inevitably true. Nothing lasts. We'll move on."

"I can't agree with you," Howard said. "This summer began something that will grow, not fade."

"For you," Sam said, "that could be true. I don't know about the rest of us. We've had a magical time, but I expect to turn back into a pumpkin."

"Sam!" Howard smiled.

"It's not negative. Pumpkins are good. They just don't carry you to the royal ball."

Howard laughed. "That's good," he said. "I've got to remember that. But let me give you another way to look at it. Ever seen a pumpkin vine?"

"Yeah, I have."

"You know how they send out so many shoots one plant can cover the garden? I think this summer is a pumpkin seed. You're going to marvel at how far the shoots grow."

* *

The meal, set out buffet style in the dining hall, proved disappointing. A whole roasted pig sounded exotic, but what they got was overcooked pork hacked up any old way and dumped into two stainless-steel chafing dishes. Next to them sat a mammoth plastic bowl of green salad with bottled dressing on the side, macaroni salad lubricated with mayonnaise, and saggy green beans with bacon slices on top. The dessert was the best part: make-your-own ice cream sundaes with vast amounts of whipped cream and enough maraschino cherries to make you sick.

"It's the same meal we've been eating all summer," Brian complained, stuffing it down while seated at an outdoor picnic table.

"Oh, come on," Leslie said.

The food didn't really matter. Everybody was talking to everybody, mingling happily. They were relieved to be done with a summer's work and excited for a party with no need to get up the next morning and start all over again. They had found, just by luck or grace, the most beautiful summer.

Week after week they had sat cross-legged with their campers in the assembly hall, listening to speakers. Now, it was their show. A chunky girl from Stockton named Michelle circulated, reminding those who had volunteered for the talent show of her clever plan for staging it. Nobody knew exactly when they were scheduled to perform; they only knew who was on just ahead of them, so they could be ready to get onstage immediately when their time came. Michelle pleasantly warned them that somebody else would take their place if they weren't ready to go.

The scheme worked. There were no delays. The first hour was almost all singers—some with guitar, three with piano, and one, sadly, *a capella*. Most sang love songs, full of loss and grief. One small and introverted young man, who came all the way from Seattle, played a crashing Rachmaninoff on the out-of-tune piano, and one blond girl from Castro Valley tried her hand at stand-up comedy. Nobody had explained beforehand that they were supposed to laugh; and when they finally realized it, they were embarrassed for her and couldn't make themselves laugh. She was a good sport, though; she kept trying one Jack Benny joke after another until she had exhausted her entire supply and backed off the stage, bowing, while the audience cheered wildly, relieved that at last they knew what to do.

Three staffers provided a very silly skit they had done for the campers all summer, wedging themselves together under a sheet so that one operated the feet of a tiny man, another provided the hands, and a third posed as the head. Everybody liked the skit, even though for most of them this was the tenth time to see it. Edgar the dummy shaved himself (shaving cream everywhere), drank a cup of chocolate milk (everywhere), and ran a high hurdle race. The only innovation was that Edgar had been renamed Rich after the dining hall supervisor and had been provided with a beard and an atrocious North Carolina accent. This tickled them all to an incomprehensible extent.

Verity had only seen Edgar once before. She got the giggles and absolutely could not control her own laughter. Keeling over onto her side, she lay on the floor holding herself and laughing silently.

"Verity! Verity! Get up," Mindy whispered. "Howard is coming."

Mindy and Verity were sitting together. After Howard was returned to Julie, Mindy had warmed up again.

Howard had on the same huarache sandals, T-shirt, and jeans he had worn every day all summer. With Scott playing guitar for him, he began to sing a song he had written to the tune of "Like a Rolling Stone." He did a creditable Bob Dylan imitation, and at first, he seemed serious.

"How does it feel?

To be on your own?

With no letters from home?

A complete unknown?

With a cabin full of drones?

Kids who don't know a Bible from a ham sandwich?"

That last line, spun out in Dylan's whining drawl, got a chuckle.

He went on in the same vein, skewering camp food, the monotonous repetition of the program, the idiocy of the games, the vapidity of the camp songs. They were starting to like it. It was moderately clever; he got a laugh from each line. "How does it feeeel?"

Then he switched to the tune of "Eleanor Rigby."

"Sam O'Bryan,

Acts like he's thinking deep thoughts in the back of his head,

Lives in a dream."

He worked his way through at least half of the staff. Verity was amazed that he remembered all the words without looking at a cheat sheet. Julie was compared to an overfriendly dog. Mindy got dinged as Marian the librarian. Brian was Preacher Man, sermonizing from a comic book. The words were clever enough, Verity thought, but what made the performance mesmerizing was the enormous energy and charm that Howard put into it. He believed in what he was doing, and he was so very likeable.

He went into caricatures, imitating six or eight of them, capturing the sound of their voices, their way of moving, and exaggerating their preoccupations. Up until now he had spared Verity, but when he turned into an awkward, arm-swinging, tooth-sucking old woman, he didn't have to explain who it was; they all knew and roared as the old woman asked questions one on top of the other. They turned to look at Verity with their faces alive with hilarity. She lifted the hem of her sweater to cover her head.

He did Leslie. He did Scott, even though he was so straight you would have doubted he could be caricatured. Verity was dazzled; they all were, laughing until they couldn't catch their breath.

It was a hard act to follow, but Randy got up to sing, accompanying himself on the piano, and gradually they all settled down. Randy proved to be surprisingly gifted. Nobody had known.

By then it was late. A feeling settled over them that it was time to wrap up the show; they had seen what they came for and were ready for Michelle to get up and thank everybody who had participated. Then

Brian came running into the room from the back, wearing a long, blond wig. He skidded to a stop and solemnly opened a Bible, then began to speak in a dead-on imitation of Howard.

That prompted a giggle, followed thirty seconds later by a little shock when they realized he was preaching from the passage in Second Corinthians that they had studied all summer. He expounded with sputtered references to scholars and Greek words and Old Testament texts that were an absurd embellishment of Howard—learned, showy, self-infatuated. He shook the wig, swinging the platinum hair around his head. He compared Paul's teaching to various Beach Boys songs, most notably, "Help Me, Rhonda." Everybody swiveled toward Howard, who was sitting off to the side with Julie; Howard's face was alive, and he was laughing. That made it all the funnier and all the more fun. Brian ended with an altar call in which he hummed "Just as I Am" and beckoned Howard to come forward. He persisted until Howard got to his feet, and to a roar of approval approached Brian and was thrust to his knees. Brian said a mock prayer over him, and then shouted, "Hallelujah!" He ran to the back and plucked a guitar off the back table, leading them all in three verses of "Just as I Am," which most of them knew by heart. Then it was over.

Verity did not realize how warm the hall had become until she stepped outside and felt the moist air coming up the mountain. It cooled her face and provided the finishing touch to the last day of summer. She felt unbelievably happy. Nothing like it had ever come to her. Never had she fallen on the floor laughing, without shame, without self-consciousness. It was hard for her to believe that she had been made the butt of jokes and yet felt no humiliation—rather a sense of being loved.

She knew some of her friends would stay up all night, but she had never seen the romance in losing sleep. Her mother would come very early tomorrow to get her if she knew her mother. Verity headed up the pathway to her cabin.

Mindy caught up with her. "Wasn't that awful?" Mindy asked.

"Why?" She was caught completely off guard.

"They were mocking Mount of Olives, and the Bible, and everybody here. And you."

"I thought they were just having fun."

"It's not nice to make fun of other people. And they were mocking what makes this camp so special. You shouldn't make fun of the Bible."

"You mean Brian."

"Yes."

Verity kept quiet. She wasn't sufficiently sure of herself to challenge Mindy. Maybe she had a point. To judge by the crowd's laughter, though, nobody else thought so.

"Did Howard's part offend you?"

It was Mindy's turn to be quiet. She said nothing as they pushed up a steep section, climbing the hill. "I guess it did," she said when they got to the top and Verity paused to catch her breath. "I thought it was mean."

They went on silently for thirty seconds. "Weren't you offended when he imitated you?" Mindy asked.

Verity had to smile. "No," she said.

"Really?"

"That's where we're different," Verity said. *Mindy has never been left out,* she thought to herself.

* *

The next morning Verity got up before anybody else in her cabin. They had all stayed out late; she had heard them come in. After washing and quietly finishing her packing, she hauled her bags down to the parking lot. She would be ready to go as soon as her mother appeared.

It was a surprise to find that eight or ten others had the same idea; they sat on the concrete stairs chatting languidly. Bright morning sunlight poured over them. Verity looked at the brilliant, purpling sky and remembered her first day, ten weeks ago. Leslie had pointed out the magnificent, soaring trees to her, but she had been too nervous to see them.

Howard was there already, and soon Julie arrived, too; she went straight to Howard and clung to him like a limpet. Last night she had been stiff and unfriendly toward Verity. Now she seemed merely oblivious. All her attention went toward Howard. He would be at Stanford, she at USC; they might never see each other again. She moaned out loud, as though nobody else were there to hear. Howard's head swiveled around, looking for somebody or something. He gave Verity a little nod; he didn't say anything.

Sam and Leslie came down looking smart and sleek. Sam dropped a heavy duffle bag next to Julie and Howard. Almost immediately, Howard began talking to him about renting a house off campus where they could have talks and Bible studies and plan rallies on White Plaza. He knew musicians from Southern California he could get to come north to play. He brimmed with ideas for spreading the faith.

Scott appeared with his luggage and his guitar; he pulled it from its case and began tuning. "Play something we can sing," Mindy said, and when he began "Hey Jude," the afternoons on the beach came back as they joined in. "Here Comes the Sun" seemed to capture the moment. Then "Humble Thyself in the Sight of the Lord," and "I've Got a River of Life Flowing Out of Me." Julie stood up, tears streaking her cheeks, gesturing for them all to form a circle, arms awkwardly over each other's shoulders. "Oh, the deep, deep love of Jesus, vast, unmeasured, boundless, free." Now many of them were weeping.

Just then Verity's mother drove up. She was the first parent to arrive, and nobody but Verity seemed to notice. They kept singing while her mother, dressed in culottes and sandals and a frilly white blouse, got out of the car and stood by it, looking them over. Verity turned her eyes elsewhere. Leslie, though, waved, smiling. The others noticed and followed Leslie's eyes. It was a sign: time to go. The song fest broke apart. Everybody wanted to embrace Verity one last time and say how much they loved her and hoped they would see her again. She had a hard time focusing on them because she was conscious of her mother.

"Hey, everybody," Howard cried out. Automatically he got their attention. "We should make a plan. When are we going to get together?"

Thanksgiving, somebody said, but somebody else said that wouldn't work; they would be with their families. Christmas vacation was another suggestion, but no location was offered.

Howard put a stop to it, holding up his hand. "I'll put out a newsletter," he said. "Make sure I have your address."

So, they put off making any plans, leaving it to Howard to organize a reunion, and of course it never happened.

1983

16

L.A.

Under the airplane's wing, Los Angeles unrolled like a scroll: a manuscript of low, rectangular buildings and surface streets. The undeviating two-dimensional cityscape looked menacing to Sam—bleached, anonymous. Bone-colored hills were no more friendly, rising like heaps of porridge out of the plain. *California.* He rarely came back, and when he did, he felt torn between a thousand happy memories and his sense that the land was hostile.

His family and friends in Kansas City could have sworn that he loved California, from the way he talked about it. Cynthia was in the habit of humming "The Impossible Dream" when he started in on Stanford. Thinking of this made him smile. And it was true, he did love California. And sometimes it made his skin crawl.

He didn't understand the reaction. As far as he could think, everything about his years at Stanford had been good. He had never been humiliated, never done anything shameful. After graduating he had gone back home to work with his father, not because he wanted to leave but because the California economy offered no entry-level geology jobs. Anyway, he had an intuition that he needed to go underground, which is what returning to Kansas City felt like. He needed to get out of Howard's space and figure out for himself who he was.

He would be forever grateful for Howard, but it was hard to know yourself in Howard's company—all you knew was him. After living like twins in college, their communication had dwindled to an occasional drip. He called Howard sometimes; Howard almost never initiated.

Still, Howard had sounded quite enthusiastic when Sam proposed a visit. He was famous now, just as everybody at camp had expected. A year or so after graduation he wrote a children's book, *The Hedgehog's Tale*, which got published by a tiny New York firm and improbably won the Newbery. It was in all the bookstores—Sam saw it himself in a downtown

Kansas City store named The Literary—and Howard got a five-minute interview on one of the morning shows. That was crazy, to see his close friend on national TV. Nobody had expected a children's book from Howard, but it stood to reason that whatever he chose to do would win awards.

After that it became difficult to stay in touch; you left messages but received no return call. Other camp friends asked Sam about it, knowing how close the two of them had been. Sam never complained. Howard was busy. Howard was his friend for life.

On the freeway toward Santa Monica, Sam smiled, anticipating their meeting. He thought he might hint at his own transformation. Maybe Howard would want to hear about it, though he might not approve. When they were students, the Bible had been everything for them—the all-purpose salve, the knife that could cut to the heart of any issue. Sam hadn't deviated from that, at least to his mind, but he had expanded.

Even in college, he had been interested in probing beyond a purely rational faith. He felt drawn toward a wider and deeper way, though he couldn't tell you much about it. There is a reason they call it mystery, he would say.

* *

The freeway ended in Santa Monica, dumping Sam onto surface streets. He couldn't make sense of Howard's directions and had to pull over to look at his map. During his Stanford years he'd visited LA on multiple occasions—once for a football game, twice for spring break with a roommate who came from Canoga Park. He'd done a summer internship with an oil company in Bakersfield, which gave him a chance to visit LA on the weekends. He always found getting around the city a pleasure. With the grid of freeways and streets, you could find anything. Sure enough, he located the right street and pulled up in front of a condo. Two blocks from the beach, with palm trees and hibiscus in the front yard. Obviously, Howard was doing well.

Julie answered the door and threw herself on him. "Look at you!" she cried, holding his head in her hands. "It is so good to see you!"

She looked better than he remembered: skinny and tan. "Good to see you," he said. Practically squirming with excitement, she led him inside.

He was taking in the tasteful Danish furniture and abstract paintings when Howard came out of the back. He lunged toward Sam and hugged him hard around the chest. "You're here!" he almost shouted. "Can you believe it?"

They sat on the outside patio, grinning at each other like lunatics. Sam hadn't seen Julie since their wedding. Howard he'd met in passing a couple of other times—once at their five-year college reunion, once randomly bumping into him at O'Hare. Julie brought glasses and they sipped Chardonnay while Howard lifted the bottle and read from the label. "It's a little place in Sonoma," he said. "Better than Napa. And cheaper." He cackled as though he had said something funny. "Man, it's good to see you."

"It's good to see *you*," Sam said. When they first met at camp, he had fallen for Howard like a schoolboy with a crush on a pretty girl. Nothing in his feelings had really changed. He felt the way he imagined a person might feel who had been saved from drowning.

Howard wore big, owlish glasses and had short hair. "Come sit, honey," he called to Julie, who was bustling over something in the kitchen. "Come talk to Sam."

"I will," she said.

For a moment Howard looked blank, as though he had forgotten who Sam was. "So tell me," he said after rebooting. "What are you up to? How's that church of yours?"

"The church is great," Sam said. "Really great. Some very deep stuff is going on." He loved his church. It was small, but for him, numbers were unimportant. A sense of holy anticipation came on him every time he joined a meeting, uncertain what might occur or what he might learn.

"So, tell me."

Sam weighed how much to say. "It's very casual. We were able to buy a building from a Lutheran church that wanted to move. Have you ever heard of John Casey? We're very tuned in to him."

Howard shook his head. "Is he a writer? A teacher?"

"He writes books, but you really have to experience him. I wouldn't exactly call him a teacher. Maybe a prophet."

"What does he prophesy about?"

"The Holy Spirit. The Last Days." Sam smiled, thinking that he had just put out bait. He would see whether Howard would bite. Casey would be at the gathering Sam was attending in Orange County this weekend.

Howard looked around the garden. "So what brings you to California? Does this Casey live here?"

"No, he's a Canadian. I'm here for a pastors' conference."

"Oh? Where?"

"Down in Orange County. At a place called Tree of Life."

"I've heard of it. So what's the conference about?"

"It's called 'The Power of Praxis.'"

"Well good grief, that tells me nothing."

"Sam is speaking at it," Julie said. She brought a plate of crackers and cheese. "I saw an ad in the *Christian Chronicle*."

"I'm just leading a seminar," Sam said. He was studying Julie. Positively skinny. Her hair was longer and running down her back in a dark braid.

"About what?"

"About what our church is doing in the inner city."

Howard raised his eyebrows. "You have an inner city in KC?"

"Yeah, we do. We send teams there every week."

"To do what?"

"We feed people, and we pray for them."

"But that is so wonderful!" Julie said. "Howard, tell Sam about the project you're working on."

"Which one?"

"The one about the high school football coach."

Howard took a sip of his wine. "I'm writing a script for MGM about a football coach who finds out that one of his kids is dying of cancer. Nobody else knows, not even the kid, and the coach is carrying this burden through their season." He turned to Julie. "Why did you want me to tell him about that one?"

"Because it's so good!"

"My agent swears it will be big," Howard said. "He thinks I'm onto something that will make us a lot of money. But you know—Hollywood. Everybody has fabulous plans."

"Tell him about the one with the lion."

Howard looked slightly bemused by his wife's enthusiasm. He paused for another sip, then said, "That's more a long-term project. I'm just starting to pitch it. I need to find the right approach because it's kind of wild. The story of a man who comes back from Africa with a pet cheetah, and he's traveling the country trying to make a living by showing it at schools and Rotary meetings, stuff like that, when he meets this woman who kinda likes him and has an idea for making a movie about a cheetah." Howard chortled, pleased with his own thoughts. "It goes on from there. Kinda wild, like I said. It's a great story. I think that one could really hit big."

"Don't forget the hedgehog," Julie said.

Howard smiled indulgently at her. "You know my book," he said to Sam.

"Of course. It's famous."

"They want to make a movie out of it. Animated."

"Is the book long enough to make a movie?"

"That's the tricky part. They want me to make it longer."

"Howard has so many projects," Julie said.

"Which one is your number-one priority?" Sam asked.

"Whichever one they cough up the big bucks for!" Howard said, laughing uproariously. "Well," he said, standing up. "Shall we go get some lunch?"

* *

The restaurant was a shack, literally on the beach, with tables set on the sand. Howard ordered another bottle of wine, while Sam stared at the oversized menu offering expensive seafood dishes. He had been glad to sit down when they reached the restaurant. Drinking wine in the warm sunshine wasn't his habit; it left him a little dizzy. When he asked Julie what she'd recommend for lunch, she looked slightly panicky but suggested the shrimp po'boy. Sam wasn't sure who was paying so he was glad the sandwich was on the lower side of the price list. Howard got tuna tartare and Julie said she would have a salad. "I'm on a diet," she explained.

"If you lose any more weight you'll blow away," Sam said, and he almost meant it. The more he looked at her, the more struck he was by how thin she had become.

"Don't be silly," she said. "I'm as fat as a pig."

"You're forgetting," Sam said. "I knew you at Mount of Olives."

Her face crumpled up in a smile. "Oh!" she said. "I weighed more than I ever have since. Was I disgusting?"

Sam shook his head and smiled.

"So who are you in touch with?" Julie asked. "We've lost track of so many of those old friends."

"I hear from a few of them," Sam said. "Let's see. Brian—you remember Brian? He's in my church, so I see him all the time. In fact, he's an elder."

Howard had seemed to drift away while they discussed Julie's weight, but at the mention of Brian his attention snapped back. "How did Brian end up in Kansas City?" he asked. "He's a Californian."

"His wife is from the area. But I think they moved to Kansas City to be part of the church."

"I remember he had a lot of theories about the Bible," Howard said. "Is he still spouting off?"

Sam smiled. "I remember when he got in an argument with you," he said. "What was that about?"

Howard shook his head. "I have no idea. I just remember that he was full of himself."

"And so were you," Sam said. "We were all so full of ourselves."

"It was such a wonderful summer," Julie said. "I wish I knew where all those people are."

"Howard, didn't you promise to organize a reunion?" Sam said. "Whatever happened to that?"

"Yeah," he said. "People always say they won't forget each other, and then they do." He shrugged.

"What about Verity?" Julie asked. "Do you know where she is?"

"Verity," Sam said. "Wow. I think she's still in the Bay Area. She graduated from Berkeley, I know, and I think she's a computer programmer. Other than that, I don't know much. Mindy stays in touch with her, I think. I still get a Christmas card from Mindy. She's living in Redwood City, working as a teacher."

"Did she ever get married?" Julie asked.

"No, I don't think so. Neither did Verity."

"I'd love to see them all. Wouldn't you, Howard?"

"Sure. We should organize something." Howard had drifted away again. He seemed only half engaged, which frustrated Sam.

He was jealous of Howard, he admitted to himself, and fearful that he would look down on his church. A lot of people disparaged charismatic churches; that came with the territory. Sam himself wouldn't want to characterize his church as charismatic, but he knew that was how people pigeonholed it. For him, what mattered was God, not what brand you claimed to follow. He accepted that you weren't going to make everybody happy, but Howard's approval still meant something. Sam would love to bring Howard along to the conference.

Howard was eating his tuna, paying the closest attention to it. Sam asked Julie what she was doing.

"I'm a teacher," she said. "Fourth grade. I adore it."

"What's the school like?"

"It's small. Have you heard of classical education?"

Sam had heard of it, but only barely. "You read Aristotle to your fourth-graders?" he said, expecting a laugh.

Julie didn't even smile. "In fourth grade we do Plato. Aristotle comes in fifth grade, along with Aquinas. Of course, that's only part of the curriculum. We read literature, learn mathematics. There's music. And Latin."

"Latin?"

"It's easier to learn when you're young."

"But why Latin?"

Howard suddenly checked back into the conversation. "The rigor and logic of it is great for forming the mind. For most of European history you couldn't be an educated person if you didn't know Latin."

"I'd think you'd want to know Russian. Or Chinese," Sam said.

"Latin is a great foundation for learning other languages," Julie said as Howard went back to his tuna. "You have kids, don't you? What kind of education are they getting?"

"We just have one," he said. "Cynthia plans to homeschool."

Julie couldn't help herself; her face screwed into an expression of dismay. Her impression was that homeschooled children filled out worksheets. She was too polite to say that to Sam, though. "I've seen a homeschool curriculum for classical education," she offered tentatively. "I couldn't swear that it's any good, but I don't see why it couldn't be."

"All right, that's good to know," Sam murmured. He couldn't bring himself to look at her.

Howard rescued them by standing and announcing that he was going to the bathroom. "I'll be right back," he said cheerily.

Julie watched him leave, studying his back with an intensity that Sam found alarming. When Howard had disappeared, she shifted her chair toward Sam and leaned in. Her eyes had narrowed to slits and her words came out in hard bites. "Sam, could I ask you to pick up the check? Howard will try to grab it, but he doesn't know that they've cut off our credit."

"Sure," Sam said. "I can do that." He didn't see that he had any other choice.

She scooted her chair even closer. "It would embarrass him to death, you know. He's so proud."

Sam didn't know what to say, so he took his preferred approach and remained silent. Tears started in Julie's eyes. That caused a quiet surge of panic in him. He didn't know what was going on.

"He can't finish anything!" she said in an urgent whisper. "He has all these brilliant ideas, but he's getting a reputation. I don't know what to do."

Still unable to find anything to say, Sam watched Julie closely, trying to look sympathetic. As a pastor, he had been called to help many people, so it felt weirdly familiar—but weird nonetheless, because they were talking about Howard. A moment ago, he had been jealous.

"But you have a job. And what about Howard's book?"

She shook her head, her face crimped into an expression of pain. "It's not enough. My school hardly pays me anything, and the book money..." She closed her eyes. "We live well. We have to. It's Hollywood; you have to look successful. And everything is so expensive!"

She stopped suddenly, realizing that Howard had appeared behind her. "What are you doing?" he asked in a low drawl. "Airing our dirty laundry?"

"She was telling me about her job," Sam said guiltily. On principle he didn't tell half-truths, but it came out of his mouth before he could think.

"You're telling Sam we're broke? That's what he needs to hear? An old friend comes by after years, and you have to tell him your sob story? He didn't come to see you—he came to see me."

Sam watched Julie's face collapse like a bubble in a mud geyser. "I had to tell him!" she wailed. "I'm saving you from embarrassment! They stopped our credit!"

That information seemed to jolt Howard for a moment, but he arranged his face and went on. "And Sam needs to know that. Did you want to print up our bank statement for him? Maybe a credit report?"

"She just told me you had a cash flow problem," Sam said. "That's all." Another half-truth, for which he felt ashamed. "Come on, Howard; sit down. It's no big deal. Everybody has money problems. Believe me, I know—I'm a pastor."

"I can't believe you came all the way here to get a load of this," Howard said.

"It's nothing."

For a moment Sam thought Howard might sit down. "Howard, please," Julie cried, still sniveling.

The sound of her voice seemed to reactivate his indignation. "I think this lunch is over," he said. "I'll leave you two lovebirds to sort out the cash flow problem." With that, he walked off into the sand, onto the beach, leaving them.

"How long has it been like this?" Sam asked after a suitable silence. It was a question he had learned to use when counseling alcoholics and adulterers; it led a bit but left the content open.

"He's like a grass fire," Julie said. "He burns hot and then it's like nothing ever happened."

"But the money?"

"He got some money from the book when it first came out. Since then, we've lived on my income."

"But that's not enough."

"No. He's borrowed from his parents. And maybe other people. He doesn't tell me."

Sam remembered Julie as an unreasonably cheerful person, hopping with optimism. Now she looked drugged by misery. Her face was heavy; her skin sagged like old rubber. She looked ugly. Sam wanted to hit the side of his head to straighten out his perceptions.

"Do you have a pastor you can talk to?"

"We go to church, but it's this huge place and we don't know anybody."

"Does Howard have any friends who could talk to him?"

She was silent, thinking. "I'm not sure. I think maybe he's used them up. He meets with people, but I don't know most of them. Hollywood people, he says."

"His parents?"

She sighed deeply. "His parents are wonderful. His father is like a saint. He's so wise. I thought Howard was just like his dad when we got married. He tries to help. They both do. I think they give him money, but he won't let them give him advice. Nobody can tell Howard what to do."

17

JOURNEYS

Howard stalked the beach trying to eat up time until Sam was gone. The sun was uncomfortably hot, and he felt utterly humiliated. Why had he acted like that? He was sure that Sam would be telling everybody they knew. When his friends heard, what would they think? They would see right through him. They would see that he had nothing. At the thought of it, Howard wanted to fall down and writhe in the sand.

In this state of mind, he couldn't write. He had talent, he knew he had talent, but why couldn't he use it?

It had been different starting out. He had set up his home office just as he liked it. *Hedgehog* had spun itself out of his head like a spider throwing a web, and right away he knew it was good. He had been bursting with ideas—so many stories blowing up his head, he couldn't wait to start writing them down. *Hedgehog*'s success got in the way of that: people to talk to, book signings to attend. The publisher had never had a real bestseller before, and they wanted to squeeze him dry. Which he had happily agreed to! But it kept him from writing. He thought it was just a temporary delay, and it was. You think fame will go on forever, but it's a bitch goddess that demands to be fed. He didn't feed it. He *couldn't* feed it. When he finally had time to write, he got so distracted. It was easier to talk to people, to do lunch, to plot strategy—who to work with, which people were at the top. He would sit down to write and in fifteen minutes he couldn't sit still; he had to get up and walk around. Why not call somebody to make an appointment to meet, or to tell them what he was working on—anything but work.

He had perfected the art of pretending to be a writer. He knew where to go for lunch, what to order, how to dress.

You had to produce something. You had to deliver the goods—a script, a story. Sometimes he managed to get something down on paper, filling him with overwhelming relief. The next day it was never any good. He couldn't let anybody see that. He had to junk it.

He blamed it on Julie sometimes. That wasn't right, he knew, but it was emblematic of the mess they had made of their lives. Thinking about her left him hopelessly tangled. She tried to encourage him, and he hated it. He hated the feeling that she had her eyes on him. She believed in him so much, but she didn't know anything about the business. When she told him how wonderful he was, it felt like nagging. Of course, that wasn't right; she was just doing her best to buck him up. Plus, she wanted the money he could make. She had no talents to make it herself, but she thought about money a lot. Why was the money so important to her? It wasn't like she had gone without. He didn't care about money; why did she?

He walked far down the beach until his legs became heavy and a deep bodily weariness came over him. Surely, he thought, Sam had by now given up and gone away. His conference was in Orange County; he would probably go down there tonight. The thought made Howard unbearably sad. Sam could have stayed overnight with them; they had room. It hadn't been necessary to go out to lunch. They could have eaten at home. Then they could have talked all day. This whole thing could have been avoided.

Howard sat down in the sand, which he ordinarily would never do in nice clothes. The sand would be in his pockets and his cuffs. He felt so utterly stricken. His best friend. He knew he should pray, but he couldn't. Words wouldn't come any more. Wordless prayers, just thinking of God, were too vague: his worries came piling into the empty space in his mind.

His father thought he knew exactly what was going on. His chummy way of approaching Howard made him out to be the wise old man who would simply listen and nod. When Howard thought about it, a blind rage came into his chest. For his father, it always came down to the Lord. Which was completely true, Howard knew, but it didn't help. His father urged Howard to attend church regularly. He tried to give Howard a book on prayer, and he even offered to collaborate with him on a book about angels that a publisher wanted. Howard couldn't talk to his father anymore.

* *

From his hotel room that night, Sam called Cynthia. Her voice was a welcome signal from a familiar world—warm, faintly hoarse, ironic in tone. She said the baby was asleep and she was worn out, ready to go to bed herself.

"What a day," she said. "I think Russell is getting sick. He was so crabby, and he might have a slight fever. I hope he sleeps. And the phone was ringing all day with people from the church wanting to tell me about Jeff. There's something brewing, like there might be a meeting called when you get back. Do you know anything about it?"

He didn't. Jeff was the youth pastor—a very gifted, brash individual whom he'd recruited for the job, accepting the conventional belief that a strong youth program was needed to build the church. Jeff had firm opinions that didn't necessarily agree with Sam's, but that was fine. He worked hard. Sam didn't expect his church staff to rhyme on everything.

"Oh, boy," he said with a sigh. It meant that he would be listening to a parade of people when he got back. Once a week, pastors got to get up and preach. The rest of the week, people preached to them.

He had not become a pastor to run a complaints desk. Not to preach, either, really. He had come home from college to work for his father, who owned a Caterpillar franchise that was rapidly dwarfing the rest of his construction company. His father intended for Sam to take over the business, which appealed to him.

Two years in, he met Cynthia. She was the company's tax attorney and wanted his father to cut out some of his financial shenanigans. He wasn't doing anything that would send him to prison, but money moved in and out without leaving much of a paper trail. Sam's father ignored Cynthia at first. He may have thought he could bulldoze her. Sam was in the meeting when she laid down the law. She said her piece very pleasantly, and the whole bland room of managers and vice presidents grew suddenly quiet and alert. "Mr. O'Bryan, I have the impression you are ignoring these regulations."

His father gave his rogue smile. "Miss, I've been running this company for thirty years. I'm not doing anything different from what I've done all along."

She smiled back. "I'm sure that's true, Mr. O'Bryan. And I expect you plan to continue. However, I am obliged to inform you that if you do, I will cease representing your firm. That would be my ethical obligation."

As the firm's legal representative, Cynthia was obligated to maintain confidentiality, but she knew perfectly well—as did his father—that word would spread quickly if she quit. She got her way—the only time Sam ever saw his father reined in.

His father gladly let Sam take over legal representation; he didn't want to deal with "that woman" anymore. Thereafter, Sam had a good business reason for inviting Cynthia to lunch. She was a few years older than he and ran marathons. Like many marathoners, she had a lean, eagle appearance. Cynthia was nothing like Leslie, who had broken up with Sam shortly after their summer at Mount of Olives. She was not sleek. She wasn't soft in manner, either. Sam treated her with the utmost respect, having seen how she could undercut those who underestimated her. When he asked her out to dinner—a date—he was extremely nervous. "I'd love to," she said with a warmth in her face that he had never seen. Quite soon, they were going out every week.

Cynthia seemed happy to leave things there, however. At least, she made no move to push forward—and Sam wasn't sure what he wanted.

He had never known anyone like her—so calm, so factual, so sure of herself. She made him explain everything. A building couldn't just be ugly; she wanted to know what made it so. His political opinions, his theology—it was more examination than he wanted.

The truth came to him suddenly one night as he was driving home from her house. He had the car windows down and was enjoying the moist, fertile air of a spring night. The problematic person wasn't her; it was him. It wasn't that she took all the mystery out of life, as he was fond of joking. It was that she wouldn't let him be mysterious. She wanted him to explain what was going on in his mind, which he often didn't himself know.

He liked to keep things vague. Poking around too deeply was distasteful to him. This had been his way from childhood—a means of avoiding conflict with his father. His high school girlfriend had suffered terrible and unnecessary hurt because of it: he didn't want to tell her the truth, that he had lost interest in her. Even during his brilliant summer at Mount of Olives, he stayed in the shadows.

In principle, Cynthia recognized that there were gray areas where a lack of information might keep you from a conclusion. She was a lawyer, after all, and the law is full of uncertainty. However, lawyers do their research in order to reach conclusions. Her default reaction was that vagueness was a symptom of laziness. If you didn't know, you should be trying to find out.

He had perfected the art of slipping out of the moment to stand sideways, watching. He liked to go silent and let others account for it as charm. It could be an advantage to be mysterious, but Cynthia wouldn't let him.

At one point, he wasn't sure he could sustain life in the glare of Cynthia's clarity. Yet he wasn't sure he could go back to his old ways, either. Sometimes when Cynthia impaled him with her matter-of-fact questions, it felt like she was gutting a fish. But sometimes he felt that he was being sprung free.

Part of that was career reassessment. It seemed increasingly unlikely that a mystic should run a business selling work machines. That was a negative assessment, a recognition that he didn't fit in his own plans. That was nothing, however, compared to the positive reassessment. He slowly gained an ambition. A silence sat beside him. He was drawn to know that silence.

He knew all about God; he could talk about God intelligently. This felt like something quite different. He discussed it with his pastor, who gave him a few books to read. He devoured them. Slowly he understood that he was not the first nor the last to probe the silence. Before he quite understood what was happening, he was leading a small group of men from his church who were willing to talk about it together. Then he enrolled in a class at a Catholic seminary, and then in a whole course of study with the Methodists at their seminary south of town. He was not thinking of career training, but as the journey unfolded, he found himself preparing to be a pastor.

A year into that process he asked Cynthia to marry him. He knew she would make him be honest.

Now, in his hotel room, he told Cynthia about his visit with Howard and Julie. He had walked Julie back to the condo, hoping and dreading to see Howard again, but the place was empty. Sam pulled away as soon as he could.

"Don't worry about us," Julie said bravely as she walked him to his car. "We adore each other, you know." She said it while holding the car door open; he couldn't drive away until she let go. Even distressed as he was, he could see she meant what she said.

He told Cynthia that now, but she didn't offer a sympathetic ear. "Maybe she does still love him," Cynthia said, "but Howard better get himself together soon, or she won't."

Sam asked her why she thought so.

"Money, Sam," Cynthia said. "If you can't trust him with money, you can't trust him anywhere."

* *

Sam did not sleep well. Thoughts of Howard kept returning in an almost continuous loop. At one point he got out of bed in disgust; he wanted to sleep, he needed to sleep, but Howard would not let him go.

The morning crept in without birdsong or visible sunrise, only a sense that a dimmer switch had been turned. California had seemed friendly in Santa Monica, but now, looking out his window onto a parking lot, it seemed hostile again. Whenever he left home, he was confined to these beige hotel rooms. Feeling overwhelmingly weary, he considered junking the conference and heading back to Kansas City.

Casey would be there today; it would help somehow. Sam thought of him as someone who had penetrated the silence, someone who truly knew God.

After a leisurely breakfast in the hotel restaurant, he drove his rental to Anaheim. The conference met in a glass-and-plaster industrial ware-house, low-slung and unadorned, without a cross or any religious symbol. Feathery tropical trees floated over the parking lot, and the buildings sported numbers the size of wine barrels. Sam found his way into the auditorium—a vast, carpeted space with stackable chairs and a long stage fronted by a row of ficus plants. Nothing was happening yet except sound checks.

The room was as faceless as his hotel room, but inexplicably Sam relaxed. He took a chair, and as the room filled, he watched handfuls of people mosey in, save seats, and greet friends. They wore shorts and short-sleeved shirts and sport sandals. They were mostly white, mostly young.

He hadn't been completely truthful with Howard and Julie about keeping in touch with Verity. She had called him after he mentioned John Casey in a family Christmas letter. With her usual curiosity, she wanted to know all about him. Even as he sat in the auditorium, hearing a growing hum of human noise, he could imagine Verity's deep, scratchy voice as she hemmed and hawed her way through questions. She had been in therapy—weird therapy where you sat in a room and screamed until you were hoarse. Her therapist told her she had been abused as a child, and she believed him, though no evidence or memory of any abuse surfaced. God only knew how much she spent on that stuff. Sam didn't ask what made her pursue it, but he thought he knew. Everybody has a hole they try to fill. Like him, Verity was seeking God, and church life wasn't really delivering. Unlike him and everybody else, she made no pretense of being okay.

18

VERITY AND MINDY

Verity met Mindy for tea at Allied Arts, a sedate Menlo Park institution that seemed to belong to an earlier age. They had been there before. Both enjoyed the oddity of being young among the well-off matrons, dressed up and drinking tea in the flower gardens. They sat at little cast-iron tables and sipped from china cups.

For years they had practically lost touch, first in college where Mindy forgot all about her pledge to befriend Verity, and then in the working world when neither one realized they both lived on the Peninsula. Mindy bumped into Verity at an Asian market in Redwood City, and they got talking while standing on the narrow sidewalk, surrounded by bins of melons.

They both recognized the pleasure they gave each other. Mindy remembered just how odd Verity was, and Verity felt Mindy's open and non-judgmental curiosity. She could ask or say anything to Mindy, which was hardly true in the wider world.

"What do you think about Pentecostalism?" was Verity's question when they had ordered. Contrary to her norms, she had worn a dress, an ugly shift made from coarse cotton cloth stamped with a floral design.

Mindy had come straight from work, wearing the same jeans and a blouse she wore every day teaching preschool. "Pentecostalism!" she said. "Why Pentecostalism?"

Verity ducked her head as though avoiding a right hook. "Don't you think it's interesting?"

"Maybe. I've never really thought about it."

"Well, do you believe in miracles?"

Mindy smiled. "Of course I do. They're in the Bible."

Verity seemed surprised by this. "You really believe in them? Like, people getting healed of cancer? Have you seen one?"

Mindy said she had not and seemed bemused. "What kind of miracle would you like?" Mindy asked.

Verity laughed in the absurdly shy, ticklish way she had. "A man would be nice," she said.

"You don't need a miracle for that."

"No? Do you have one available?"

Mindy suspected that the mention of a man was a dodge, drawing her off Verity's real designs. "So where have you met Pentecostals?" she asked.

Mindy noted the way Verity answered or didn't answer. "I started going to a church in San Jose," she said.

"San Jose? How did you end up there?"

"A guy I know at work invited me."

"A guy?" Mindy remembered from their camp days that Verity liked men. She had enjoyed teasing Verity about it.

"Yeah," Verity said. "He's married."

"Okay," Mindy said. "So what takes you to that church? It's a little far, isn't it?" Depending on what part of San Jose, it might be a twenty-minute drive.

"I like that they take the Bible so literally. Jesus sent his disciples out to heal the sick and cast out demons; they go out to heal the sick and cast out demons. And it happens."

"What do you mean, it happens?"

"I mean, people get healed. They cast out demons. It seems like it happens all the time."

Mindy was taken aback. "Exorcisms?" She only knew about them through movies. "You've seen this?"

"I haven't actually seen that, but they talk about it. I've seen healings."

"Really? What kind of healings?"

Verity seemed embarrassed by the question; she tightened her mouth into a small smile and appeared ready to blush. "Last week they prayed for somebody with a bad back who'd been in a car accident. I mean, I couldn't see anything change, but she said she felt better. I guess you could question that. They say they've seen people cured of cancer. Like, the doctor told a guy he had a tumor, and two weeks later, after they prayed for him, the doctors said there was nothing there."

"It could have been a mistake."

"Well, maybe," Verity said. She paused and pursed her lips. "It's pretty interesting."

At this moment their waitress came with tea, and they kept quiet while she set the china plates and cups on the table. High tea at Allied Arts was a ritual with a calming effect for Mindy. The idea of praying for healings and exorcisms rattled her.

"I don't know, Verity," she said. "Be careful. You remember when we tried to heal you of epilepsy at camp?"

Verity smiled. "That wasn't so bad. What do you think could happen?"

"I don't know. I guess that's the trouble. I don't know. It just seems questionable to me."

"Are you sorry that you prayed for me when we were at camp?"

"I was never that comfortable with it. Looking back, it feels like we were just a bunch of kids playing with magic."

"But like you said, it's in the Bible."

* *

After coming home from tea with Verity, Mindy stretched out on a chaise lounge in the backyard, her head propped up on her elbow, a book in her hand, happily relaxed in the hours before dinner. She was not that interested in the book, but reading was her preferred way of withdrawing into herself. Her housemates watched TV or went out, but she more typically found a chair in the backyard and read. She steadily ate up paperbacks that she bought in library book sales or borrowed from friends. She was like a knitter who makes scarves but doesn't mind whether anybody wears them.

Today she kept losing her place, thinking of Verity, and wondering what drew her to that church. She imagined it as loud and self-promoting. Why would Verity want such a thing?

Verity was searching for something, she thought, and she might end up going somewhere, since she was in motion and Mindy was not. Verity threw herself into the open sea, while Mindy stayed in sheltered waters.

"It will all make sense when the right man comes into your life," her mother had told her when she hinted at her lack of direction. Lots of people assumed that was the missing piece Mindy was waiting for, but she doubted it.

Mindy put down her book and stood up. She had read and reread the same paragraph multiple times. Going into the house, she wandered into the kitchen and looked at what her housemate Helen was cooking, chatted with her a bit, and then went out the front door, intending to walk. She could not have told you what Helen was cooking.

She felt she should take charge of herself. To do what, she did not know.

* *

Verity woke up groggily, having stayed up very late reading science fiction in bed. Her tiny efficiency apartment had only one window in front and a small, frosted window in the bathroom, making a cave-like environment. She was happy there. Its close darkness made it a snug place to read, as she loved to do.

Today being Sunday, she was anticipating going to The House of God. The church didn't seem right for her: extroverted where she was private, spontaneous where she was guarded. That might be why she liked to go. It was different and therefore intriguing; it promised to get her out of herself.

She arrived at 9:55 for a service that was meant to start at 10:00. The door of the church was open, but nobody was inside. She sat down in the back. The room was a modest rectangle, with a pulpit and an electric organ to one side of the stage. A wooden cross was the only decoration. At five minutes after the hour, a drummer took up position at the drum kit on stage, whacking the drums nervously a few times before a guitarist joined him and plugged in.

As people filtered into the room, several members sidled up to Verity to shake her hand and say welcome, but their friendliness didn't go beyond that. They seemed to have things to do and moved off without making much effort at conversation. From Verity's point of view, that was just the right amount of friendliness. Eventually, a small, middle-aged man appeared at the front of the room. He was bald on top, dressed in a light-blue suit and tie. When he began to sing in a light baritone and threw his arms out wide, he seemed inordinately pleased with himself. Seeing him made Verity feel cheerful. She did not sing.

Throughout the service, various leaders tried hard to get the congregation involved. When they called on everybody to stand, Verity did stand, but she didn't clap or cheer or otherwise make a sound. Anybody who knew her could have seen that she was happy, though.

After the service, they were invited to the fellowship hall for a cup of coffee and a bite to eat. The hall was in the basement, with pipes running overhead and linoleum tile on the floor. It smelled of ammonia. The bite to eat was donuts, cut in half. Verity took hers and sat down at a table. She had no expectation that anybody would come over to talk to her, since they had not the previous week, the first in which she had stayed for the fellowship hour.

Now, however, a man sat down opposite her. He introduced himself as Cass and said that he had seen her before. Verity tried to guess how old Cass was. He had light-colored hair and a receding hairline, which made him look middle-aged, but his build was slight, and his face seemed youthful. She found herself interested in him.

"How long have you been in this church?" she asked.

He thought for a while before answering. "I don't know how to say, exactly. I used to come sometimes, for a year or two, and then I went to Glory Road for a few months, and then I came back here."

"What made you come back?"

"I think the power is here," he said. "We're already seeing miracles. Pretty soon I bet we see somebody raised from the dead." He said it as calmly as though he were predicting a hot day.

"Have you always been a Pentecostal?" Verity asked.

"Oh, no; I only got the baptism about six months ago."

"Here or at Glory Road?"

"It was at Glory Road. But I felt the call to come back here."

"Are you from San Jose?"

"Yeah," he answered.

"Where did you go to school?"

"Mercury Boulevard," he said.

"I don't know that one," Verity said. "Is it a high school?"

"Yeah," he said. "I thought about going to the JC, but then I couldn't see the point. I have a good job."

"Where do you work?"

"At Big O Tires," he said. "I'm a technician. I'll be assistant manager if I stay there for a year."

Verity thought about asking what a technician did but decided she didn't really care. She kept quiet and studied Cass. He wasn't handsome—he had a bland face, and he was calm like a summer day—but she decided that she liked what she saw.

"What do you do?" he asked. "Do you have a job?"

"Yes," Verity said. "I work as a programmer."

His face knotted in uncertainty. "Programming? Like for TV? Or what?"

"With computers," she said. "I write software."

He was silent for a moment. "I have to learn to use a computer if I'm going to be assistant manager," he said solemnly.

"It's not hard," she said. "It's all very logical." And she thought to herself, *I like him. I like him very much.* "I'd be glad to teach you," Verity said. "If you'd like."

19

THE FIRE IN THE CHURCH

Cynthia met Sam at the airport, holding Russell. Sam kissed Cynthia and then ran a hand over Russell's back.

Cynthia said he had an elders' meeting at 7:30. He sagged inwardly but guarded his reaction. He was the servant of the church.

"Do you know what it's about?"

"Not exactly. I tried to find out, but everybody was cagey. Some kind of question that we need to talk about, but they wouldn't say exactly what." He was surprised. Nobody knew how to pry open a secret like Cynthia. "I'm actually a little worried," she said. "I smell something."

"But you don't know what."

"No. Not yet."

He waved it off. "Don't worry," he told her.

When they reached home—they lived twenty minutes from the airport—he was able to wash his face and hands, change his clothes, and play with Russell before dinner was served. His weariness gone, he thought how wonderful his life was.

Dinner was homemade pizza, big squares of cheese and tomato sauce, with a salad made of slices of iceberg lettuce. Cynthia's black hair was damp with perspiration; she kept pushing it back off her face, and the gesture reminded Sam of how beautiful she was.

"I missed you," he said. "When I think of what Howard and Julie are going through, I'm terribly thankful for you."

She smiled at him while pouring more juice for Russell. "How was your conference?" she asked.

"It was great. I don't even know how to explain it. You know how *shalom* means peace of mind, body, and spirit? That's how it was."

"Did you bring back anything you can translate into life in the Midwest?"

He grinned. "I brought back myself. My *shalom*. I hope I can pass that on, but it's not a concept, it's an experience."

Cynthia raised an eyebrow. "We Midwesterners prefer a manual."

Sam got up from the table. "I better go," he said. He leaned over to kiss her, taking his time.

When he reached the church, he was still feeling the warmth of his family. As the men arrived in the Fireside Room, those feelings carried over. Seven men, each one of whom he knew deeply, each one of whom shared his fundamental longings. Two of them were Black and one Korean, which made the unity even more remarkable. Sam loved these men. They were like family.

He said a prayer to begin their time. Then, leaning back in his chair, Sam asked why they were meeting.

Nobody answered. He knew that something was wrong then, and his first reaction was to think that a scandal had occurred. He couldn't imagine what.

"Liam," he said, looking at a young, gingerish redhead. "What's up? You might as well tell me." He asked Liam, who was funny and bright and always quick, because he had a way with words. Surprisingly, Liam acted embarrassed. "Come on, Liam."

"Jeff has been asking questions," he said, avoiding Sam's eyes. "We need to talk to you about it."

A signal flared in Sam's brain. Why didn't Jeff come talk to him? He kept the impatience out of his face, though he thought: I need to explain to him. He needs to know. I owe it to him.

"Questions about what?"

Liam had overcome his initial hesitation. "About the Bible. You believe it's the word of God, don't you?"

"I do."

"And the word of God has to be perfect, doesn't it?"

Sam saw where this was heading. Jeff thought in straight lines. He was instinctively conservative.

"Absolutely."

"So Jeff has been asking why we don't have a church statement that the Bible is infallible and inerrant. He wants to know why we don't ever talk about it."

"Oh," Sam said. "You know, Jeff went to a seminary where they emphasize those words. I've never liked to use them because as soon as you do, it's like drawing a line in the sand. The other guy starts to think,

'What about this? What about that?' He wants to know how Noah's flood covered the whole earth, and why there are two versions of how Judas died. As soon as you answer one question you get another. You end up in a negative argument. My philosophy is, we don't lead with statements, we lead with our lives. We show that we trust God's word by the way we use it. I love the Bible. I love to read it, and I try to follow it reverently. Haven't I taught every one of you to do the same?"

Wilmer spoke, as usual muttering and unsure of himself. He was a butcher at the Piggly Wiggly and one of the kindest men Sam knew, but with words he seemed to be wrestling a steer to the ground. "Don't we need to take a stand?"

"I take a stand every day. So do you."

Wilmer flicked his eyes upward, and for a moment Sam thought he was convinced. Twisting himself in his chair, Wilmer rocked back and forth for a moment. "I mean, put it in writing. Like a contract."

That made sense to some of the men. As they spoke, Sam could see that Jeff had given them arguments. That the Bible was under assault and they needed to defend it. That there was a slippery slope.

At first, Sam wasn't terribly concerned. They weren't philosophers and they might not get the subtlety of his point of view, but they surely knew he would not lead them astray. He kept reassuring them, returning to his argument against setting up a barricade for people to push against.

Yet two of the men got argumentative and quite emotional; the rest of them hung in the middle, pushed back and forth by the argument and not sure what to think. Finally, Brian, Sam's old friend from camp, spoke. He was more knowledgeable than the others, and when he had something to say everybody paid attention.

"I think this is important," he said, "important enough for us to get everybody involved. I'd like to call a meeting of the whole church."

"Brian," Sam said. "Don't you think it will just stir up factions and take us out of the direction we are heading?"

"That's the thing," Brian answered. "This is about our direction. The congregation should decide which way we are going to go."

* *

Sam agreed to the meeting. It was the easiest thing. They would hold it on Sunday, in the late afternoon. Everybody turned cordial once they had that settled. They asked about Sam's conference and shook hands as they parted. On his way home, though, Sam felt as though he had forgotten something important and couldn't think what.

Cynthia was not happy when he told her what had occurred. A meeting of the church could go wrong in a number of ways, as she pointed out. All it took was one emotional appeal for the whole assembly to go careening down the road—any road. As they talked, Sam's sense of turmoil grew. In his mind he saw each of the elders' faces. He had sat with and prayed with most of them through kids gone astray, marital crises, business failures, and job losses. They knew him inside out, but at their meeting they had acted wary and distant. Did they not trust him?

This thought followed him through the rest of the week, diverting his attention from the sermon he had to prepare. He considered calling Jeff, but something kept him from it. He thought he knew what Jeff would say, and in his depths he felt contempt for it. He caught himself talking to himself, as though in a furious argument. Being aware of his own pooled anger made him uneasy and unsure of himself.

While flying home from the conference, he had set his mind on drawing his church into the depth and the love he had experienced. It wouldn't require any fancy rhetoric, just the plain truth, spoken with sincere humility. He so wanted to be the channel for that among people he loved, people who had followed him in seeking God's company. Now, the seed of mistrust was planted. Sam knew he couldn't talk them into the exaltation he had felt; he could only lead them. Some people would be ready, others not. But he couldn't lead anybody if they didn't trust him.

The church met in a boxy, utilitarian structure from the fifties, bought from a defunct Lutheran congregation. They had done little to update it beyond taking out the pews. Sam was growing fond of it the way you grow fond of your grandmother's cooking. The building had memories in it, beginning with their audacity in buying it when they had no money, and built up through dozens of services when their love for each other and for God had circled and spread like the pool at the foot of a waterfall.

Sam encountered Jeff just before the morning service began. He was standing in a hallway with two of his high school students, and he acted unaware of Sam's presence. It suddenly came to Sam, when he saw him, that he ought to double-check that Jeff knew about the afternoon meeting. When Sam asked, Jeff's face broke into a huge smile, almost a laugh. "Oh, I know, I know," he said, and immediately turned back to the students, leaving Sam hanging.

In the few minutes before he began leading the service, Sam was unable to forget that. He knew he had failed to connect with Jeff in the way he should—a younger man, talented, eager to lead, surely in need of a mentor. Two years ago, when they hired Jeff, he had assumed that rapport would come with time. It never had.

Now, standing before the church, looking over his congregation, he couldn't lose Jeff's mocking smile. He couldn't forget how the elders had questioned him at their meeting, as though they didn't know who he was. *Trust is everything*, he thought, *whether with God or with your spouse or your business partner*. Nothing good comes without trust. Always, before this moment, he had trusted his people without a thought.

He bowed his head in a quick, silent prayer and was able to put that worry aside. As Sam led and preached and prayed in the morning service, his words and his manner came out peaceful and hopeful. He watched himself do it, and then he wondered halfway through if it was completely phony. Whether anybody could tell that something was wrong, he couldn't say, but he thought not. His anxiety made a difference to him, though; at one point he felt himself overcome by an impulse to walk out of the service, leaving the congregation to find their own way. Of course, he did no such thing; he wasn't going to act on an impulse.

"Did I seem weird today?" he asked Cynthia over lunch.

She looked at him with an expression at once penetrating and faintly alarmed. "No more than usual," she said. "Why?"

"I felt weird," he said. "Like I wasn't connecting. Like I was talking, but nobody could hear me."

"Are you worried about the meeting this afternoon?"

"No, not at all," Sam said. "Well, maybe a little."

* *

The meeting was at 4:00, which meant that those who came had been playing or gardening or watching football. They came in work clothes or shorts and T-shirts, and some of them brought their kids with them. It occurred to Sam, too late, that they should have arranged for snacks—it felt like that kind of a gathering. He mingled, shaking hands. A few minutes after the hour he called the meeting to order.

About fifty people had come, not counting children, who were sent out to play on the lawn. Their high-pitched voices made a lovely sound, ringing and calling. To begin, Sam read a passage from Psalm 119, an ode to the guidance of God's word. With the reading, he felt the gathering settle into attention in a satisfying way. Then he turned over the meeting to the chair of the elders, a man named Dennis.

They met in the fellowship hall, which doubled as a basketball court but had a temporary platform at one end, about a foot high. Sam opened the meeting standing in front of the stage, at floor level, but Dennis, a paunchy, pale, middle-aged man with a red face, asked him to take questions from the stage. Sam followed directions, but it put him at a distance. He felt suddenly shy peering over the gathering, even though these were his friends. The first question, to his surprise, came from Jeff. "Why don't you believe the Bible is inerrant?"

He stared at Jeff, who had close-cropped dark hair and looked even younger than he was. It was a lose-lose question, like "Have you stopped beating your wife?"

Sam explained that "inerrant" was a "dare-you-to-prove-me-wrong" statement that only created arguments with people trying to find mistakes in the Bible. He preferred positives, like "trustworthy" or "authoritative." Even more, he preferred to avoid philosophical statements in favor of living out the truth—action over argument, as he liked to put it.

He thought he made a good explanation, but hands went up immediately. "Yes, Connie!" She was a young mother whom he had baptized two years ago.

"Was the world created in six days?" she wanted to know. "Do you believe in the Bible over science?" He muddled his way through that, but the next question was about whether God changed his mind, as the Bible said he did. And then came a question about how Judas died, whether by hanging himself or by throwing himself off a cliff. Sam was amazed. He had no idea his people even knew about these textual issues, let alone cared. In ten minutes, they managed to run through the standard village skeptic's repertoire of "stump the preacher."

Sam had the standard pastor's replies at his disposal, but he didn't really care for them, mainly because he didn't really care about the questions. They didn't seem important to him; they didn't rise to the level of seriousness. What did they have to do with God?

He tried to explain. "I understand these questions can seem very disturbing, but as your pastor I've tried to lead you closer to God. I don't find these discussions very helpful in that. In fact, they can get in the way."

That only got him into trouble. Nobody liked being told that their questions weren't helpful. "Don't you believe that the Bible is under attack?" "Don't you believe in defending God's word?" Sam happened to glance at the back of the room and see Jeff with a smile on his face.

Dennis, the board chair, stood up and motioned for Jeff to come forward. "I think we'd like to hear from our other pastor, who has a different perspective. Jeff, could you come up?"

Jeff looked slowly around the room—proprietarily, Sam thought—and said how proud he was of them all. Then his expression grew serious. "I think you all know me enough to know that I believe in the Bible. The *inerrant* Bible, utterly free from error because it comes from God himself. That Bible, God's Bible, is under attack today." He didn't say who was leading the attack, but it sounded like the forces of skepticism were very near. He had a conventional approach, which Sam knew wouldn't convince anybody outside the fold. But Jeff expressed himself well, and he was singing the national anthem to patriots.

When he paused for questions, he didn't get any. What he got was agreement, reinforcement, could he please expand on what he meant about the attack on the Bible? But Jeff wasn't content to simply take his popularity and walk away; he pivoted into a plea. "This church is at a crossroads," he said. "We have to make a decision. Will we continue with sweet, soft, easy talk about coming closer to God? Or will we make this church a fortress, training an army? If we are under attack, we have to fight. I've been here two years and I'm still waiting to hear a battle trumpet."

He didn't say that he was ready to be named general for the war effort, but he didn't have to. It was too obvious. Sam's energy vanished. Wouldn't some of his elders stand up with him? One did: Ronnie, a laconic Black man, got to his feet and testified to how Sam had helped save his marriage. "I knew I could count on him. He was there with me and my wife every step of the way. Whatever we did, he was there.

"So I know that Sam can fight. I've seen him fight. The thing is, he is fighting *for* us. He isn't fighting against anybody."

Sam thought Ronnie's eloquence might turn the conversation around. Instead, the others blew past him as though they hadn't heard. Andrea, a woman whom Sam had married, asked Jeff where he would like to see the church go. Answering like a candidate seeking office, Jeff explained how they ought to be reaching their neighbors, inviting them to church, knowing they would hear from God's word when they came. He also grew expansive about the youth, who he believed ought to be part of everything the church did, who ought to be learning leadership skills instead of playing games.

It seemed to Sam that Jeff had the floor for hours. Yet Sam wasn't completely prepared when Andrea said that she had asked Jeff his sense of direction, and now she would like to hear from Sam. He should have been ready for that. Standing at the microphone, taking his time to look over the faces, he tried to calibrate the moment. Nobody looked hostile. It was their neutrality that disturbed him. They looked at him as though he were a commodity to be evaluated. That broke his heart.

"Look, you know me," he said after a long survey. "I've never been one to make big statements about our plans. Some of you remember how we got this building. We prayed. We asked God to lead us, to show us the way. We had no idea where he would lead us, but here we are. I think you know what I'm about. I'd say, more of the same. More of God. More of listening. More humility. More love. I'm not big on going to war."

For a second he thought he had them. Their faces suggested they were not dead to him; they seemed to stop and consider what he said.

"Is that about it?" Dennis asked as he came forward. "Anything else you want to add?" That broke the spell. People began gathering their things to go. Dennis had started to introduce a closing prayer when Brian spoke up. "I think it would be useful to get a sense of what we're thinking," he said. "Could we take a straw vote?"

The question was followed by an awkward silence. People paused their exit, but their body language showed that they wanted to go home, they didn't want to decide. It was premature; they were still pondering what had been said, and they wanted time.

"Could we get Sam and Jeff to summarize their thoughts before we do that?" That came from the back of the room, and nobody answered it, but you could feel the resistance. Everybody wanted to go home and get dinner.

"It's just a straw vote," Brian said. "Just to get a sense of where we are. We don't need to talk; let's just have a quick show of hands."

"I don't think we want to do that," Ronnie said slowly. "That's just a little too casual for me." There were murmurs of agreement. People backed away from exposing the pastor like a steer on auction at the county fair. Instead, they took the time to cut up slips of paper in the church office, distribute them, and ask each person to indicate a choice—S for Sam or J for Jeff. Though impatient with the time it took, nobody left until they collected the paper slips and Dennis said a prayer. Most people made for the exit. A handful came up to chat and shake Sam's hand, but nobody had the heart to talk about what had happened.

* *

Cynthia had stayed home with Russell, but when she heard about the meeting, she knew she should have been there. "Those dogs," she said. "And nobody said a word!"

"Ronnie did," he said. "Nobody seemed to listen."

"Dirty dogs," she said.

In the night, Sam woke up out of a dead sleep. At first, he thought some noise had awakened him, and he listened for prowlers. Then the Bible story of Samuel came into his mind—a little boy whom God called to in the night. Samuel didn't know it was God; he went to the old priest to see what he wanted.

"What do you want?" Sam asked out loud, and Cynthia stirred beside him. Nobody answered, but Sam recognized a sacred moment. He began to pray silently, explaining to God his fears, asking what he should do. Then, having found peace, he went back to sleep.

When he woke up in the morning, he felt surprisingly peaceful as he showered and ate a bowl of Cheerios. He had slept late; nobody else was in the house. Picking up the phone, he called Jeff.

"I'd like to see you at the church office," he told him without bothering about small talk.

"All right," Jeff said. "I'm free this afternoon."

"No, I'd like to see you now. In fifteen minutes."

Jeff arrived looking slightly sheepish. Sam shook his hand, then offered him a seat. "I don't want you working here any longer. You'll get a month's severance, but I want you to clear out all your things now. Please don't contact any of the kids. That would be extremely unprofessional, as I shouldn't have to tell you. I expect you will want to talk to some of their parents, and I can't do anything about that, but if you contact any of the kids directly, you'll lose your severance pay."

Jeff did not move, but Sam could see the alarm working under his face. "You won't win this war," he said.

"It's not a war to me, and I'm not trying to win. I just don't want somebody who lacks character to be leading our youth." He paused and smiled. "God woke me up last night, and I remembered the story of Samuel. So, I asked God to tell me what to do. I prayed for a long time and didn't hear anything, but eventually I remembered that story again. Not so much about Samuel as about Eli, the priest, who had sons who were ambitious and wanted to make a profit from the ministry. Eli couldn't control them. You remember? You know the story, don't you? I'm not going to say you are like them, but you showed your character yesterday. I'm responsible for you as long as you're in leadership here, and I don't want you with our kids any longer. I'm afraid of what might rub off." He stood up. "So, I'll wait while you clean out your stuff. I'll need your keys when you are done."

* *

After seeing Jeff out the door, Sam felt exhausted. He drove home and told Cynthia what he had done. She was astounded, not because she disagreed, but simply because it was not something she had ever expected him to do.

"I wouldn't have done it," he said simply. "God told me I should."

She shook her head.

Dennis was not so accepting. "You can't do that!" he said when he called later in the day.

"According to my job description, I can."

"It's petty. Just because he brought up a different point of view."

"It was more than a different point of view. It was a coup attempt."

"And it's not over," Dennis said. "The votes were in his favor."

"By how much?" Sam was curious.

"Just by a few. It was close. But still, what are the elders going to say?"

"I don't know. I just know I was following God. He won't tolerate that kind of character in his church."

"Oh, come on, Sam. There are worse characters all over the place."

"Yeah, maybe because God told people to remove them, and they didn't listen."

He felt very clear and cool about it, but when he told Cynthia about the conversation, she seemed genuinely shaken. That was not like her. "What's the matter?" he asked.

She pursed her lips. "I don't want to go back to work," she said. "I like things the way they are."

"Don't worry," he said. "I can always work for my dad again."

Later that evening, reality sank in. He could not be sure how the elders would react, but when he thought of the expressions on their faces in the meeting, their neutral, looking-at-product stares, it brought a sense of dread.

1988

20

REUNION

"Have you got room for Cass, too?" Verity asked when Mindy offered a ride to the reunion. Mindy hesitated. Nobody had said to bring your friends, and Verity and Cass still weren't married. Mindy didn't feel free to say so directly, however. That kind of comment could hurt Verity deeply.

"Does Randy know that Cass is coming?" Mindy asked.

"Sort of," Verity said, and issued a laugh. "I told him I had a friend who might want to come, and he didn't say anything."

Mindy had met Cass several times, but when they rendezvoused on Friday afternoon, she was struck all over again: how did he and Verity fit together? His frequently offered opinions were spoken with the sort of offhand self-assurance that Mindy remembered from boys in high school—as though he was certain that whatever he said must be true, since it had come out of his mouth.

She had plenty of time to hear these observations on their ride up to Tahoe, a four-hour trip. Cass shared that the entire mountain range had been under a hundred feet of ice just before the 49ers arrived to look for gold; that the winters in the Sierra were the coldest in the world; that pine trees grew so fast that there could never be a shortage of wood. Verity just giggled—she was obviously delighted with him—and when Mindy queried his information, he simply repeated it.

Mindy decided to focus on Verity, who was in the front seat beside her. "It's funny how excited I feel about this reunion," Mindy said, "considering it's been fifteen years."

"It was our golden summer," Verity said. She giggled again. "We're bound to be disappointed."

"Probably," Mindy said.

They arrived at Randy's house by the late afternoon and thought they had the wrong address. Mindy had pictured a ski cabin squeezed onto a small lot, with wall-to-wall carpeting, old skis hung on the wall, and a hallway of small bedrooms. Instead, they found an old stone house with a wide flagstone patio leading onto sloping green lawns fronting the lake. Inside was comfortable furniture and an abundance of space. Randy and his wife, Candy, met them at the door. Candy, whom neither Mindy nor Verity had met before, was an ample, friendly woman with a heart-shaped face. She escorted them to their shared upstairs bedroom where a wide picture window looked over the lake and the mountains behind. "Isn't this a view?" she said. "You two get settled while I show Cass where he's staying."

When they were alone, Mindy and Verity looked at each other and began laughing. "Oh, my goodness," Mindy said.

They had left work early so as not to miss a minute. Assuming they were first to arrive, they went back downstairs to explore the grounds but instead found Howard and Julie sitting in the den with a plate of fancy hors d'oeuvres and a bottle of wine. "Grab some glasses," Howard said. "This stuff is great."

"Did you bring it?" Verity asked when she had settled onto a chair. She was not a drinker, but she would nurse a glass.

"Are you kidding?" Julie said. "It's all Randy. There are two cases in there." She indicated the kitchen.

"I had no idea he came from money," Mindy said.

"He didn't. I met his mother once. His father taught high school French. This is all new money."

"Isn't this amazing?" Mindy asked. "I don't even know what Randy does."

Julie did, of course. She said Randy worked in commercial real estate, and he'd made ponds of cash working with the big computer companies. "He did a lot for IBM," she said.

Randy came in with Cass. "Do any of you sail?" Cass asked. "There's a honking sailboat out there Randy said we could use."

None of them professed to know how to sail, not even Randy. "It came with the house," he said. "Kinda funny. I should probably sell it."

"How long have you owned this place?" Mindy asked. "It's fabulous."

"I bought it a couple of years ago. We like to ski, so it made sense. I didn't even think about what a great place it would make for a reunion."

"It's perfect," Julie said.

Virtually everybody was coming, Randy said, but he was vague about arrival times. "We'll eat late," he said, "so everybody has a chance to get here and settle in. I've got lots of snacks to tide us over."

"Do you need help with dinner?" Julie asked.

"Oh, no," Randy said. "It's all catered."

That was a wonder. Mindy had expected them all to pitch in: lasagna, hamburgers. No friend of hers had ever hired a caterer, except for a wedding. She began worrying about how it would be paid for. Almost as though he read her mind, Randy let it be known that he had had a great year and he wanted everything to be on him.

After they finished the bottle of wine, they went outside to walk along the water. Mindy found herself strolling with Julie, who had never been one of her favorite people. Julie could be a great source of information, however. She probably knew everything about everybody.

Mindy asked how her year was going. "Exhausting," Julie said. "I have thirty-eight kids in my class."

"I thought your school was small."

"That was the classical school. I'm in a regular public school now."

"That's a change. How do you like it?"

"It's horrible. I miss my old school, but I had to make more money. We're just getting by on my salary, you know."

Mindy didn't know. It confused her. "I thought Howard was writing for the movies."

"Yeah, he is if he ever would finish anything. He talks a million projects—I've learned to hate that word—but nothing ever comes of it. I don't know what he's doing. I've given up hope."

"Oh," Mindy said softly. Julie's tone of voice was matter-of-fact, with a spoonful of acidity. The Julie Mindy remembered would never talk that way.

They had stopped on the edge of the lake, looking out on a rippled surface. The dark mountains far across the water stood still and sharp, etched with snow. "Are you bitter?"

"I'm tired is what I am. I do all the cooking and cleaning, I make all the money, and he goes to lunch. I took away his credit cards, but he gets money from somewhere. His parents, I think, but he won't tell me. Don't you think I have a right to know?"

"Of course," Mindy said quietly. She felt an inner shiver, reflecting that there were advantages to being single. "Isn't this exciting?" she asked, changing the subject. "I can't believe we are all together, after so many years talking about it. Wasn't Howard going to organize something like this way back when?"

"Yes, but Howard's not good at following through. When Randy wrote, I told Howard we are going. I will not miss this."

"Same for me. Who are you looking forward to seeing?"

"Everybody, absolutely everybody. Sam is flying out. In fact, I think he should be driving up right now."

"But no Cynthia? I wanted to meet her." Mindy had long felt curiosity about the woman Sam had married.

Meanwhile, sitting in two Adirondack chairs on the lawn, Cass peppered Randy with questions about the real estate business. He had thought about getting into it, he said, and he wondered where the best place was to start. Randy inquired about Cass's experience and background and eventually suggested that he might think about studying for his real estate license to sell homes.

"Nuts to that," Cass said. "I want to do the big deals. You make more money for less work."

"That's true," Randy said and turned to Howard, who had come up alongside. "Howard, what are you working on?"

"Lots of different projects," Howard answered. "Movie scripts, mostly. I have productions in various stages."

"Any that will come out soon?"

"Depends on what you mean by 'soon.'"

"Well, this year?"

Howard pooched his lips into a grimace and shook his head. "No, afraid not. Everything takes so long in Hollywood."

* *

Sam and Scott were the last to arrive, just before dinner. They had met at the Sacramento airport and driven up together. By their manner, they gave the impression they were deep in conversation and wanted to continue. The catering company had barbecued two whole salmon, with corn and coleslaw and potato salad on the side. Tables with red checked tablecloths were set on the lawn, and they all filled thick paper plates from a buffet. Sam and Scott took seats across from each other, showing little interest in talking to anybody else. Mindy, watching carefully, noticed that Howard drank a lot of wine. He got more jovial as the evening progressed, regaling Cass with tales of the movie business and slapping Randy on the back whenever he passed within reach. She was surprised that he made no effort to talk to Sam. At one time they had been inseparable.

When Scott went to get more food, Mindy walked over to join Sam at his table. She asked about his wife and family.

"It's been difficult for them," he answered in a somber voice. "Russ has started kindergarten, and Cynthia feels isolated. Most of her friends went to the church."

That was the first hint she had of his struggles. She knew he had become a pastor. She didn't know that he was no longer.

He told her how he had fired the youth pastor, and then the board asked him to resign.

"Oh my goodness," Mindy said. "So what are you doing now?"

"Working for my dad's company."

"Do you plan to get another church?"

He shrugged, his face communicating torpor and dismay. "I think the church was more of a one-time thing. I never wanted to be a pastor. I mean, I didn't choose to make that my career. The church was more like the people that I met on my way to where I wanted to go."

"Where you wanted to go?"

He nodded glumly. "After I met Cynthia, I realized that I had talked about God, and I knew a lot about him, but meanwhile he was right there, and I didn't know how to relate to him. I couldn't really talk to him, to tell you the truth. Imagine that. It took over my life, you might say."

"And that was because of Cynthia?"

He shrugged again. "She asked a lot of questions. That's what she does. She's good at making me think."

Mindy had not intended to wander so far into Sam's story. Life for some people could get so complex, while hers was so simple. Now that she had kicked the scab off the wound, however, curiosity drove her on. "How do you like working for your dad? You worked for him before, didn't you?"

Sam was not looking at her; his gaze followed the high cedars on the property's edge. "It's different," he said.

"Really different from leading a church," Mindy said. "Do you miss it?"

"I do," he said slowly, then gave his head a small shake as though to wake himself. "I'm thinking I might start my own business."

"What kind of business?"

"Something in construction," he said. "Maybe a tile company."

Mindy knew something about the trades from watching her dad build apartments. She could hardly imagine Sam as a tile guy. "That would be better than working for your father?" she asked.

Sam had a chunk of salmon speared on his fork; it had been there for some time, and he seemed to have forgotten about it. Now, at her question, he slumped down, as though she had punched him in the solar plexus. "Mindy, all I want is to be able to think. That's hard to do when you're in an office with other people. If I'm working for myself, I don't have to talk to anybody."

"Think about what?" she said softly.

"What I did wrong," he said.

"What you did wrong."

"It was a dream, the church. I had no plan. It fell into place. God led us in everything, was how I would have put it. All I wanted was to pursue God with people who felt the way I did. Up until the very end, I thought that was happening. I don't know whether I fooled myself all along, or whether something snapped."

"What do your friends say?"

He shook his head. "All my friends were in the church."

"And Cynthia?"

"She is a very practical person. She wants to know how we are going to take care of our son and pay the bills."

"So you don't have anyone to talk to."

The question seemed to disturb him. He scowled and then shook his head, as though trying to clear it. "I guess not."

* *

Through most of the meal, Verity silently kept her eyes on Howard, attentive to every move he made. She noticed not only that he drank too much, but also that he didn't really talk to anyone. Seated next to him, Julie was chatting nonstop, but Howard didn't say much, even though he put on an act of friendliness. Verity had a proprietorial feeling about Howard. He had been her first boyfriend. They had kissed. It felt to her as though they never would be completely separate.

She got up from her seat and went to sit across from him. "Verity!" he said, leaning across the table to kiss her cheek. "Isn't this amazing? After so many years."

"Something is wrong," Verity said. "I can feel it. Do you know why?"

His face was suddenly alarmed and hostile. "Something is wrong? I'd say that's the wrong way to start with somebody you haven't seen in fifteen years."

"I was at your wedding."

He laughed. "Yeah. Okay."

"Cass and I could pray for you. We do that at our church. We pray for lots of people."

Her intensity carried Howard back to their days at camp. Everybody had been intense then.

"No, thanks," he said. "I have my own church."

"Do they know what is going on with you?"

"No, and neither do you."

She smiled and gave a small, apologetic laugh. "I don't always need to know. Cass and I prayed for one of our church members and she found out the next week she had lung cancer. All we knew was that God told us to pray for her."

"So, you couldn't heal her."

Taken aback, she asked him how he knew that.

"Because you said she found out she had cancer the next week. If your prayers had healed her, that wouldn't have been an issue."

"No, that's true; she died. But when we prayed, we didn't even know she was sick. We just knew that something was wrong."

He was grinning now, as though enjoying the conundrum. "Then why would I want you to pray for me?"

Verity's face fell. She was not used to this. The people who attended her church were eager to be prayed for.

"Do you know what's wrong?" she asked.

Howard burst out laughing. "Verity!" he said. "Listen to yourself. First you announce that something is wrong with me, and then you want me to tell you what it is."

"Well, why shouldn't you?" She was quite stubborn. It made perfect sense to her.

"Because there's nothing wrong!" He laughed again. "I'm fine! And if I had a problem, I still wouldn't want you to pray for me."

* *

Scott started playing classical pieces quietly on his guitar. One by one, conversations paused as they turned to listen. The setting sun sprayed pink alpenglow on the peaks across the lake. When Scott moved to the old camp songs, many of them found they had forgotten the words, which caused a little hilarity. Others remembered the words perfectly, together with the hand motions. To Julie it felt as though they had fallen into their slots in this fellowship, formed when they were teenagers.

The sun disappeared, a chilly breeze came up, and they went inside. The front room was the perfect size for their gathering: a vast stone fireplace at one end, a high open lattice of rough-cut beams overhead, and plenty of room for everybody to have a comfortable seat. Coming into the warmth and light woke everybody up and boosted their energy. Several conversations layered over Scott's guitar playing; he sang loudly but nobody seemed to listen. They were talking, they were eating cobbler, a bottle of Scotch appeared and some of them sipped at a glass.

Julie, who never missed anything, had noticed Verity talking intensely with Howard. She went to sit next to her on the sofa. "Isn't this fun?" she said. She had a large bowl of cobbler and offered Verity a bite. Verity declined, sitting very still.

"This isn't what I thought," Verity said.

Julie opened her eyes very wide. "What were you expecting?" she asked.

"This is just nostalgia."

"And?"

"I thought we would be serious. That we would talk about deep things. That's what we did when we were kids at camp; why can't we do that now? We didn't even pray before our meal."

Julie was surprised by Verity's directness. "What were you talking to Howard about? That looked serious."

"He wouldn't even talk to me. He said nothing was wrong. I can tell that's not true."

Julie leaned over and gave Verity a hug. Verity was not a hugger, but she accepted it calmly while remaining rigid. "You're absolutely right," Julie said. "But he's not going to tell you what's wrong. He won't even talk to me."

"He won't talk to you?" It was Verity's turn to be surprised. "You're his wife."

"I know that, Verity." Julie wiped her eyes with the back of a hand. "It's very hard, believe me."

"I offered to pray for him. Cass and I do that at my church. We are on the prayer team."

"What did he say?"

"He said there was nothing wrong."

Julie wiped her eyes again. "Well, thank you for trying," she said.

21

GOING DEEPER

In the morning, Mindy got quietly out of bed. She never used makeup, so it took very little time to dress and slip out the door. Verity was still asleep, and Mindy knew vaguely that she had been up reading much of the night. She might well sleep until noon. That was Verity.

Downstairs stood covered trays of eggs and bacon, pitchers of orange juice and fresh coffee. Mindy examined it all carefully, lifting the covers and breathing the aromas before deciding to wait. She felt like an addict with these friends. The more questions she asked, the more her curiosity grew. She wanted to know about their families, their churches, their memories of Mount of Olives, their work, a million things. But it overwhelmed her. Before beginning another round of talking, she craved time alone.

Outside, the lawn was damp, the air bright and chilly, the lake a mirror. On the path she encountered Brian, dripping water and shivering from the cold. "You going in?" he asked with a grin. "It's *freezing!*"

"Not today!" she said, laughing, and watched him jog toward the house. From a swinging bench, she looked across the water and thought about the day ahead.

Nothing was quite as she had imagined. Howard, their hero and leader at Mount of Olives, was (according to Verity) off the rails in some unaccountable way. Sam the omnicompetent had darkly, mysteriously failed, and he wasn't making the slightest attempt to talk to Howard, with whom he had once been inseparable. Verity, their hopeful project during that summer, was careening ahead in a direction Mindy didn't understand with a man who—she might as well admit it—repelled her. Mindy had expected to recapture youthful idealism at this reunion. Instead, she was seeing it broken. Or wounded, at least.

All of this stoked greater curiosity. She hadn't lost confidence in any of her friends. They just proved more complex than she had expected.

At breakfast, Mindy cornered Brian. She had never taken him seriously, she realized; at camp he had always acted the clown. As she sat down with him, she saw that she was five inches taller than he. She had never noticed.

He seemed to live a very ordinary life in Kansas City: working as a construction engineer, fixing up an old house he had bought two years before. She learned that he was married and had kids.

"And you're an elder in Sam's church," she said. "So I heard."

"It's not Sam's church," he said.

"Not anymore. I heard about that."

"It never was Sam's church. He didn't own it."

She smiled and nodded. "Okay, sure. But he started it, didn't he?"

Brian stopped bristling and took a bite of eggs. "I think that's accurate," he allowed. "I moved to Kansas City to be part of it. I met my wife there."

Now she was getting somewhere. "What made you go there? What drew you?"

He didn't answer right away but took another bite. "I always admired Sam. Right from our days at camp. He was humble, right? He listened to people. The church really was a remarkable fellowship. He did an amazing job of leading. It was almost like he wasn't leading; he was just listening. Yet somehow, we came together, and we got excited. He would say something very simple, and it would turn our minds inside out. Very inspiring, I thought." He went back to eating as though he were done with that subject.

"So what happened?" she asked.

He was bristling at her again, looking offended. "What happened is the elders asked him to resign."

"But what made them do that? It's pretty drastic. Especially if he was such a great pastor."

Brian did not look comfortable. "Well, he fired the youth pastor, who was very well regarded. In fact, we made him the new pastor."

"We?"

"I was an elder," Brian said, obviously defensive. "Look, Sam is my friend, but he was acting like a dictator. We were asking him questions and he refused to listen to us. He didn't want to take it seriously."

"What kind of questions?"

"Questions about the Bible. Whether it's infallible. He refused to use that word. Or inerrant, which is the same thing. He said he preferred to use positive words. Which is fine, but when somebody is asking you if there are mistakes, you have to answer in a straightforward way. And he didn't want to do that."

Mindy thought there must be more to the story, but maybe not. She had heard about these disputes. "What did the youth pastor have to do with it?"

"He was the one asking the questions."

"Really," Mindy said. "Just him?"

"Not just him, of course. But he was spearheading it. None of the rest of us had been to seminary, so he was the one who knew what to ask."

Mindy leaned back, surprise written on her face. "It sounds like he led a coup."

"It wasn't a coup," Brian said and stood up. He didn't want to talk anymore.

He had only gone a few steps when he turned back toward her. "It's all water under the bridge, anyway," he said.

"Really?"

"The church closed down."

*　*

Just before lunch, Leslie arrived. Randy had apparently known her plans because he had her room ready. For everybody else, her arrival was a surprise. Like a cat, she arrived in her own time and in her own way.

Julie felt guilty for forgetting her—she, who knew everything about everybody—but made up for it by grabbing her for lunch. "Come sit with me and help me with portion control," Julie said. "You can't believe how we are eating. The food is fantastic."

Leslie seemed to have stepped out of a time machine, utterly un-changed from college days. She dressed like a grown-up now, but her clothes remained a perfect fit, unwrinkled and tailored. Her eyes were deep and beautiful. Anybody but Julie would have been intimidated.

"You look wonderful," she said. "How is your family?" Leslie was married, Julie had heard, but she didn't even know her husband's name.

"Oh, they're fine," Leslie said. "Getting older, but just fine."

That stymied Julie for a moment. "No, I mean *your* family. You're married, aren't you? I'm sorry, I don't know your husband's name." She smiled broadly, as though to buy forgiveness.

"Oh," Leslie said, "Yes, I was married to Greg, but it didn't work out."

Julie was stunned. "You're divorced?" Lots of their friends in Holly-wood were, of course, but it had never crossed Julie's mind that someone from Mount of Olives would fall into that category.

"Sadly, I am," Leslie said. "We were only married for three years."

Julie recognized that she would have to warn the others. She didn't want Leslie to have to go through the awkwardness of revealing it to everybody, one at a time.

Suddenly she grasped why the group was so tentative. Fifteen years had passed, and they weren't kids any more. She herself had dreaded telling their friends that she and Howard weren't rich or famous. But here was Sam, sitting on the news that his church had fired him; and here was Leslie, divorced; and here were Scott and Mindy and Verity, not even married. It wasn't at all what she had expected. It was sad.

Verity thought they should go into deep conversations, like when they were young. Well, that was Verity. She had a point, though, or at least half a point. They all needed to show some optimism and some appreciation. Thankful hearts were the best hearts, like she told her fourth-graders.

After lunch, Randy and Candy gave options for the afternoon: hiking, horseback riding, canoeing on the lake. "Or you can just loaf around here," Randy said. "Dinner will start about six and it's going to be great. Ribs. If you still remember the pig we ate on our last night at Mount of Olives, I promise you this will be even better."

With a sudden inspiration, Julie stood up as Randy sat down. "I want to add something," she said. "I want us to get beyond chitchat and negativity and really open up to each other tonight. For a start, I want you to think about who has had the most positive influence on your life. Come tonight ready to share that. Tell how God has used that person in your life. Okay?"

Nobody objected and the group slowly dispersed. Howard took out a canoe with Leslie, leaving Julie behind to set up a listening post in one of the Adirondack chairs. She sat lazily reading the newspaper and talking to anyone who came along. By dinnertime, she had learned all about the catering staff—four energetic young people who made her feel quite mature. Randy and Candy, Verity, Scott, and Brian all came by, though none of them lingered.

When the group straggled in, tired and rosy from a day in the sun, nobody was terribly talkative. Some food would restore their energy,

Julie thought, but she wondered whether they would want to talk about deeper personal matters. Well, they would have to see.

They ate at the same tables they had used the night before, and the food and drink really were fabulous. Julie took just one rib but filled her plate with a big green Caesar salad. It remained a quiet group. Julie monitored the mood closely, considering when she should take charge and lead the sharing. She came close to letting it go—to letting Scott play his guitar and forgetting her plan.

But that would not do. Standing up, she rang a glass with her fork. "Would anybody like to go first?" she asked. "Remember the question? Who has influenced you the most? How has the Lord used that person in your life?"

When she was met by silence, she said she would start. "It's so hard to choose just one person," she said with a huge smile lighting her face. She flounced her hair with one hand. "But I come down to Sam. Our friend Sam. A couple of years ago he came and visited us at a time when things were difficult, and he was so understanding. He didn't talk a blue streak, but he said just enough to point me in a different direction—toward God. That's how he was when we first met at Mount of Olives, and he really hasn't changed. Sam is my North Star. He makes me want to be better than I really am. Thank you, Sam."

Somebody gave out a little yip, and there was a scattering of applause. "Who's next?" Julie asked. Brian put up his hand, stood, and grimaced. For a frightful moment, Julie feared that he would try to undo what she had said about Sam. She had chosen to speak of him partly because she thought he needed bucking up.

She need not have worried. Brian's voice broke a little talking about his wife and how patient she was. Glancing over at Verity, Julie thought with a wave of happiness that her experiment was working.

One after the other, they all named someone. It seemed heartfelt and genuine, with the level of seriousness increasing as one example spurred on the next. Julie was surprised that nobody named Howard. At Mount of Olives, they certainly would have—maybe all of them.

Scott was almost the last to speak. "The person who influenced me the most is Mindy," he said, "with her kindness and her constancy." He didn't give any examples, just sat down to silence. Nobody clapped or responded because he finished before they realized he had no more to say.

After him there was only Cass, who would not even be included if it were up to Julie. He remembered his grandmother, who had made a huge spiritual impact on him. As he talked, wandering from one anecdote to another, they gradually realized that he had been very young when she died—four years old, in fact, as he eventually let out.

Randy stood. "There's dessert in the kitchen, and plenty more wine and beer," he said. "Thanks, Julie, for getting us to share." He stood and began walking toward the house.

Suddenly, Howard stood and called for attention. Julie froze at the sound of his voice. He had been drinking all day, and she thought he must feel bad not being at the center of attention. "I know some of you have to go first thing in the morning," he said. "So this is our last time together. I want to raise a glass to Randy and Candy for putting on this amazing weekend. You two are so generous! Thank you, thank you for this beautiful place, for the food, for the wine, for everything. We can't say enough about how wonderful you are!"

They did all raise their glasses and followed the toast with a clamor of happy remarks.

Some lingered at the table, talking. Scott opened his guitar case, but before he could begin to play, Mindy sat down beside him.

"I'm very happy that you think I have been such a positive influence," she told him. "But could you say a little more about when and where?" He lived in Seattle, and she couldn't think when they had even had contact.

He was silent for a moment. "I think of you," he said. "That's all."

"You think of me? What do you think about?"

He gave his head a little shake. "Nothing. Just who you are."

She waited for him to go on, but Scott was a person who felt comfortable with silence. Eventually Mindy said, "Well, thank you; that's a real compliment." Not knowing what else to add, she got up and left.

22

THE COURTSHIP

For a week or more after the Tahoe reunion, Mindy harbored a happy memory of Scott's admiration, but since he lived a thousand miles away, she didn't dwell on it. His surprise telephone call changed all that. He asked her out to dinner, and she didn't have to consult her calendar—she knew she was free and felt unexpectedly giddy about it. Scott interested her. She liked his quietness, his neatness, his modesty.

Once or twice in recent years, friends had hinted at the possibility that she might be a lesbian. A young colleague at her preschool had come out and asked, point blank, "Are you gay?" She understood the curiosity, but she thought their questions betrayed a very narrow point of view. She liked men and had always assumed she would marry one. Men had never defined her, however. She could afford to be choosy, and she was. Why shouldn't she be?

Friday, Scott arrived right on time. Susie, one of her housemates, welcomed him and then came smiling to find Mindy in the bathroom. "He's cute," she said, folding her arms and leaning on the door while Mindy put on lipstick. *Cute*, Mindy thought. It wasn't a word to recommend a thirty-five-year-old man.

In the living room she found Scott sitting on the arm of the sofa, talking to her other two housemates, who were headed for a concert. He looked relaxed and poised. His hair was short and dark, he wore a sports coat and an open-collar shirt, and he swung a foot shod in a penny loafer. Mindy was glad she had dressed up a bit.

"Ready?" he asked when he saw her. He was about her height, she observed—maybe an inch shorter. "Cute" probably came from his stature. Mindy was taller than lots of men she knew, including some she had dated, so it was nothing new to her. She didn't mind, but people noticed.

His rental was a deep blue Pontiac convertible, and he opened the door for her. They went to a very nice restaurant in North Beach, and afterward climbed the steep hills through Chinatown to Nob Hill, where they got a drink in the Tiki Room. Mindy found Scott easy to talk to. He didn't dwell on the reunion or on their long-ago summer at Mount of Olives; he asked about her life and acted genuinely interested in the antics of her four-year-olds. Both of them described their hometowns, their parents and siblings, the books and movies they enjoyed. It was exactly the kind of conversation that suited Mindy, who was always curious to learn what made people tick. Scott seemed happy with it; he slipped into it easily.

When they got back to Mindy's house, she didn't invite him in; from the front door they could hear the TV, and Mindy thought it would be awkward to disrupt her housemates. Scott kissed her on the lips, but it was a brief connection, without ardor. That was fine with Mindy. She did not enjoy fending off amorous lunges.

"Can I call you again?" he asked. "I'm going to be in the area for work pretty often, and I'd like to see you." She said *of course* and meant it.

He called the very next week and took her to a symphony concert. Mindy had grown up with Sinatra, not Beethoven, but she found the music relaxing and elegant. The classic solidity of the San Francisco Opera House appealed to her, and she liked looking at the dressed-up people. Afterward, they drove to a Chinese restaurant, where she was surprised to see Scott using chopsticks. Watching him wield them effortlessly, she thought for the first time that he was authentically handsome. His features were dark and small, and he wouldn't grab attention to himself, but his neatness and care were attractive.

He told her that he loved classical music, having been raised by a mother who played the harp. He also told her, somewhat reluctantly, about his work with Boeing. She asked him why he was so slow to talk about it.

"It's technical," he said. "I don't want to bore people."

"It's not boring to me."

"You're different from most people," he said, clearly meaning it as a compliment.

Even so, she found it hard to get much out of him. His work *was* technical, and probably mathematically impenetrable to her, but he told interesting stories about the customers he met around the world. That was another point in his favor: he had traveled, whereas she had been almost nowhere.

They held hands while walking back to his car from the restaurant, and when he dropped her home, he kissed her again. "I'm going to be here next week," he said, holding one of her hands loosely. "Would you go out with me again?"

She called Verity. "Scott?" she said with surprise and wicked delight. "He kissed you?" She giggled. "That's hard to believe."

"Twice," Mindy said. "But it was just a goodnight kiss. Nothing too potent."

"Still. He's so quiet."

"He isn't as quiet as I thought. When you get him by himself, he can carry on a conversation."

"He did say you were the person who had influenced him the most," Verity added, as though pondering all the evidence. "At the reunion."

"I still don't know why he said that."

Verity gave another laugh. "So, what are you going to do? Are you really interested in him?"

Mindy suddenly saw that she would need an answer to that question. She and Scott were both old enough to get serious in a hurry. "I don't know," she said. "I like him, but I don't feel like I know him very well." She shrugged. "I guess I'll just have to wait to see where it leads."

She found it gratifying to be the focus of a man's attention. She had discouraged so many young men for so many years that they had stopped calling. A date with Scott was something to look forward to. He seemed to have a lot of work in the Bay Area, though he would say very little about who he worked with and even less about the purpose behind it. Once, he let drop that it was military, which she took for an indication that some secrecy was involved. She didn't press the issue.

He took her out more weeks than not. When his work took him elsewhere, he gave fair warning so she wasn't left hanging. Twice he sent beautiful flowers. And yet he made no physical advances. He held hands, he ran an arm around her waist, he kissed goodnight, but he was entirely a gentleman. Mostly, Mindy was happy with that. All previous experiences suggested that men had strong sexual urges and were naturally aggressive. Apparently, with Scott, that wasn't so. If he weren't so persistent in asking her out, she would have thought that he had only lukewarm interest.

She became quite comfortable with him, and yet a patina of politeness ruled their relationship. Part of her wanted to carry on this way forever. Part of her knew that that was impossible. Something earthy had to break in.

Arranging to meet Verity at Allied Arts, she unleashed her wonderings. Verity leaned forward across the wrought-iron table, forgetting to drink her tea. "Just one kiss?" she said and giggled. "Cass has his hands everywhere. He's got a one-track mind."

"It's different," Mindy said. "It's really different."

"Do you like him?"

"I do, but I'm not sure how seriously."

"Because I've always had the feeling that you weren't that interested in guys. You go out a lot, don't you?"

"Not anymore. You're right, I've never fallen for anybody. Most of the guys were all over me, which I never cared for."

"But Scott isn't," Verity observed, her eyes bright.

"No, and maybe that's the reason I like him. It's low stress. He's just an easy person."

"There has to be more than that," Verity said. "It's not enough to be low stress."

Mindy thought that Verity had put her finger on it. There had to be more.

"What about you and Cass?" Mindy asked. "You have been going out forever."

"I wouldn't necessarily call it *going out*," Verity said with a teasing smile. "He comes over to my apartment and we watch TV."

"And that's when the hands come out."

"Yes."

"Do you just put up with it? I would hate that."

A giggle. "I don't exactly hate it. I think I would hate it more if he were like Scott."

"Wait. Why?"

"Because then I wouldn't know if he was really attracted to me."

Mindy saw the point of that. She didn't want to arm wrestle, but Scott's politeness left her wondering what he felt.

"What about church?" Mindy asked. She remembered that Verity had met Cass when she started going to her Pentecostal church.

"What about it?"

"Well, are you and Cass still involved? I haven't heard you talk about it."

Verity was delighted to talk about her church. She said they were growing in prophecy now.

"Not miracles?"

"Of course, we still pray for miracles, but we're learning about prophecy. Cass has a prophecy gift, so he's really into it."

"What does that mean? Give me an example," Mindy said. When Verity hesitated, she added, "I don't really know what you mean by prophecy."

"What Cass and I do isn't prophecy, exactly; it's a word of knowledge. Kinda like prophecy, but more private. We pray and ask God to give us a word. It can be a lot of things. Sometimes we don't know what the word means, but later on we realize that the word was telling us something we needed to know."

"Like if somebody is embezzling from the church?"

Mindy meant it as a joke, but Verity seemed more confused than amused. "It's never been anything like that."

"Anyway..."

"Anyway, sometimes we know the situation and we ask God to give us a word. Like in your situation with Scott. We could ask God to give us a word about why Scott is so neutral."

"He's not neutral," Mindy said. "If he were neutral, he wouldn't keep calling. He's just not handsy."

"Well, okay. Anyway, we could ask. Do you want us to?"

Mindy was blank for a moment, then said, "Sure, why not?"

* *

For the Thanksgiving holidays, Mindy went to her parents' home in Modesto—a large, rangy suburban house with white carpets and drapes. To be in the family home gave her a sense of solidity that she otherwise rarely felt. One night she and her three siblings played Hearts and talked about their lives. She was fond of them all, though they were very different from her. When her brother asked if she was going out with anybody special, she told them about Scott but downplayed the seriousness. That wasn't dishonest; she didn't know whether it was serious. She had thought of inviting Scott for the holiday feast, but then she realized that it would be foolish to involve her family until she had a clearer idea of where their relationship was heading.

It was perhaps to avoid this topic that she raised another: a potential change of jobs. During the Tahoe weekend, Randy had sat beside her during one meal and asked politely about her work. That was unusual: people rarely asked questions after learning that she taught in a preschool. But Randy wanted to know what her day was like. Somewhat to her own surprise, she realized as she talked to him that she was tired of four-year-olds. For years, they had been her delight. Now, she felt restless.

Something in her outlook was changing. Her interest in Scott forced questions on her, such as where she wanted to find herself in five or ten years. And did she want to have children?

A full year after the Tahoe weekend, Randy called to ask whether she was interested in a job. He was involved with a biotechnology startup company that was opening an office in downtown Palo Alto. Would Mindy like to work there?

Mindy told him she didn't even know what biotechnology was. He said that didn't matter. They needed a competent person who could do whatever needed doing to keep the office functioning. "You'd probably have a different job every day," he said.

The pay he offered was a lot better than what she got teaching preschool. However, as Randy told her frankly, nobody could guarantee that the company would survive. "It's a gamble," Randy said. "I really believe we can make it work, and if we succeed, we're all going to be rich. I mean, really rich. But these things are risky."

She asked her siblings what they thought. Their responses surprised her. All their focus was on money and security; they didn't seem to see that she was contemplating a dramatic change in the activities that made up her day. As she understood it, Randy wanted her to work in the background, keeping the office functioning smoothly. She had met enough engineers to know that they thought and talked in a way quite unlike ordinary people. From preschool baby talk she would transition to engineering lingo. From the drudgery of cleaning up toys she would take on the drudgery of cleaning up the lunchroom. These were the factors that mattered to her, not the pay or the benefits. If she had wanted to make money, she could have gone to law school.

By raising the job question, she diverted her siblings from discussing her love life. She could not disguise from herself, however, that the Scott question was more important to her. If not Scott, who? Perhaps no one.

The week after Thanksgiving, Scott took her out to dinner, talked easily to her about her family, encouraged her to take the job with Randy, but gave not one hint what his plans or hopes might be for their relationship. He kissed her goodnight, one kiss only, just holding her lightly in place with his hands on her back.

He was really an extremely nice person, she decided afterward, telling herself that she had no reason to be agitated. She was agitated, however. Should she ask him point-blank about his intentions? Should she make a scene? That did not suit her, but she thought perhaps it was logical. She wanted to know where she stood.

Verity, whom she called the next day, seemed muddled herself. She did not know whether Cass would ever want to marry her. And no, she had no word from the Lord. She had asked for one in the church prayer time but got no answer.

Tormented by uncertainty, Mindy tried to think what she would ask Scott when he next took her out. She never got the chance because he didn't call. It was almost Christmas, of course, and she knew he was close to his family; most likely he was busy. However, he didn't call after the New Year, either. He never called again. He disappeared from her life, and she wasn't sure whether she should be angry or thankful.

1990

23

WHERE IS THE WORD OF THE LORD?

To Verity, the case seemed clear: Mindy seeking direction for her life, she and Cass asking God for a word. They had learned how to do it at a retreat held at their church. Hearing from the Lord required paying close attention to the stray thoughts that traveled through your mind. Some of these might be messages from God, who spoke to his people just as he had in the Bible. The problem was that people didn't know to listen. They were like the little boy, Samuel, who heard God's voice but thought it was only the old priest. It was so important to listen! To expect! If you heard a word, you should tell God you were all ears. He would confirm his message with a strong mental impression.

For Mindy's case, though, no message came. Verity tried to clear her mind to minimize interference, but she never got a word she could hold on to; always, it was a gray smear that stayed below the level of intelligibility.

It was not as though words from the Lord were rare. Almost weekly, somebody in their church stood up to share one. Many were general, such as a warning that they should devote themselves to prayer, because Satan is a roaring lion threatening to destroy them. That message came just before Christmas, and who could question its truthfulness? It was a word for all seasons. Some words, though, were very specific. In late November a woman took the floor during their prayer time to say that the Lord was saying somebody had a cancerous tumor in her stomach. Nobody owned up to it, and perhaps that was because the indicated person didn't yet know anything was wrong. That was the kind of message Verity and Cass wanted for Mindy: yes or no—was Scott serious? No word came and then Scott dropped off the face of the planet. The whole thing proved unsatisfying.

Disappointed, Verity scoured her history for evidence that God had ever spoken to her. As a little girl she had enjoyed all kinds of fantastic ideas, making up stories in her head. Perhaps in that life of imagination

God had said something. But when she tried to think what, she drew a blank.

What did come back to her memory was the penumbra before a seizure. She recalled how the light would turn frosty and sound became brittle moments before she began to tremble. It was not painful but oddly beautiful. All her senses were engaged, and she was acutely aware of life, second by second. Many years had passed since she last experienced it. She took her medicine faithfully, and that had eliminated the problem. Or perhaps she had simply outgrown seizures. Or perhaps she had been healed when her peers at Mount of Olives prayed for her. She might never know for sure.

It dawned on her that her medications might be keeping her from hearing God's voice. Medications dull your senses. Maybe, Verity thought, they had killed her ability to hear God.

* *

Verity called her mother to talk about her seizures. She had no particular issue in mind but wanted to probe the topic, to test its salience. Perhaps something would emerge, something she had not known or considered.

Verity's mother had retired and moved to Arizona. This provided relief to Verity, who no longer had to feel guilty for not visiting. Perhaps she and her mother would never be close, but their conflicts had eased with the years.

Today her mother's voice on the phone sounded dry and clipped. "Are you going somewhere, Mom? Did I catch you at a bad time?"

"There is no bad time," her mother said. "I am always ready to talk to you. I am your mother."

"Yeah, I know that."

Her mother knew about Cass. She had told Verity that she was wasting time with a man who could not make up his mind; by now she should be married and have at least two children. Verity had not reacted well to this speech; it penetrated to her stomach. Falling into a sob, she hung up on her mother. Since then, neither one of them had mentioned Cass.

"Mom, can you tell me about my epilepsy?"

"Why are you asking? Has something happened?"

"No, Mom. Everything is fine. I was just wondering. When I got epilepsy I was just a girl. I don't remember much."

"I almost died," her mother said. "My only daughter. I took you to so many doctors, so many tests. I was very afraid."

"Was I afraid?"

"You didn't know what was happening to you. You couldn't remember anything after the attack was over, so what did you have to be afraid of?"

"Did I enjoy it?"

That stopped her mother for a moment. "Enjoy it? Why would you enjoy it? No, it was just something that happened to you, and you had no reaction. I protected you from all that."

* *

Verity called Mindy. "Guess what? My mom wants me to come visit her. In Arizona. You think I should go?"

"Well, she is your mom. I don't understand what you have against her."

"What would I do there?"

Mindy snorted into the phone. "Eat. Sleep. Talk. Go shopping. Go to the movies."

Verity arrived at her mother's front door unannounced, carrying a small backpack. Her mother knew she was coming, but Verity had kept back her schedule because she didn't want to give her mother control of her life. With a rental car she could come and go when she chose.

Her mother had bought new furniture and Verity was surprised at the difference it made. "It's nice," she said, stopping to look around. The stuff she had grown up with was part of her mother's identity, like the shell on a hermit crab. Verity looked at her mother more closely. She appeared the same: short, stocky, a helmet of orange-dyed hair.

"I'll show you where to go," her mother said, and led the way down a hallway.

She never said how much it meant to her for Verity to come, but the room was prepared, without piles of junk on the bed, and her mother had cooked pierogi. When Verity first smelled them, she wanted to cry. Her mother saw this but didn't comment.

When asked again about Verity's epilepsy, her mother at first responded with indifference, as though she were protecting a secret. Gradually, though, she yielded to conversation, describing the doctors they had visited and the coldness she had encountered in their waiting rooms.

"Dr. Boon had a receptionist who couldn't look at me. I was standing there in front of her, and she was talking to somebody else."

"Did you say anything?"

"I did, of course, but she couldn't understand me. She said 'What? What?' a hundred times."

"What about the doctor?"

"No point!" her mother said forcefully. "He wouldn't do anything about her."

"No, I mean, was he bad, too?"

"He was okay. Not good, but he was a doctor, he did his job."

Her mother had emigrated from Poland during the Cold War. She never said much about that experience; Verity knew nothing about her father, who had apparently disappeared from her life when she was just a baby. His name was on her birth certificate—she had seen that when she applied for a passport—but whenever she asked her mother about him, she waved the question away. "He's gone. He's not important."

But this wasn't true, Verity realized. She saw what a shadow her father cast.

"Mom, can you tell me about my dad?"

Her mother glowered unhappily. "Why do you want to know about him? He never showed any interest. I don't know where he is."

"I don't want to see him. I just want to know my background. Do you know anything about his health record?"

Her mother was instantly alarmed. "Are you sick? What is the matter?"

"I'm fine, Mom, but I started wondering about my epilepsy. Did I get it from him? Or did he have any other problems like that?"

"Like what? You don't have any problem now, do you? You take your medicine; you're fine."

The conversation reminded Verity of the reasons she avoided her mother. "Yes, I'm fine. I'm just curious. It's good to know as much as possible about yourself, don't you think?"

Her mother relented. "You don't have to know everything. Are you worried about passing it on to your child? You aren't pregnant, are you?"

"No, Mom." Verity almost giggled.

"Well, how would I know? You have this man Cass. I have never met him. I don't know what kind he is. He is a man; they have a sex drive. I don't know what you do."

"Thank you for that information."

Her mother leaned forward, a storm cloud of intensity. "I want you to get married and have children. I will come and help you take care of them."

"Is that a promise or a warning?"

"A promise."

"Mom, you are getting ahead of yourself. Cass is just a good friend."

That night, however, while she lay in bed, the idea of marriage reared up like a mountain. The truth was that she had never really considered it a possibility. Out of long-established habit, she had treated Cass as a friend, not a suitor.

Now the idea filled her, making her toss and turn. Verity contemplated domesticity, a home with a child. All her loneliness rushed into her heart and settled on these possibilities.

A more disturbing thought also came to her. Her interest in Pentecostalism was drifting away. For years it had filled her soul, but now it seemed almost beside the point. She didn't care so much about grasping a word from the Lord. She wanted a baby.

24

THE TRUTH ABOUT SCOTT

Late on a Saturday afternoon, one of Mindy's housemates called her to answer a phone call. It was a late spring day, breezy and cool, and Mindy was in the yard planting some tomato plants she had picked up at CVS. Brushing the dirt off her hands as she came inside, she asked who was calling. "I don't know," Brianne said. "Some lady."

"Is this the Mindy who was friends with my son Scott?" The woman's voice was low and slow, with a faint Southern accent.

"Scott from Seattle?" Mindy asked, curious but cautious.

"Yes. I'm Scott's mom."

The flatness of the statement made Mindy grip the phone. "Is he all right?"

The silence that met her question was absolute, seeming to last for minutes. "No," his mother said. "Scott died. I'm sorry. I thought you knew."

"What? No. How would I know? Where are you calling from?"

After another pause, the voice went on, a dry, low voice touched by weariness. "I'm in Seattle. I don't think we've met, have we? My name is Maude. I'm sorry to bring sad news."

If she really was Scott's mother, sad would hardly do justice, Mindy thought. "I'm so sorry. When did he die?"

"A month ago," Maude said. "No, it's been five weeks now." Mindy noticed Maude's tongue was slightly tangled, that fatigue clotted her matter-of-fact words. "It's all muddled for me. He was in the hospital for weeks before that. I thought he might have told you."

"No." It came to her that Scott's unexpected absence had been because he was sick. "What kind of illness?"

"He died of pneumonia."

Mindy heard a jerk in Maude's breathing. Was she crying? "I'm so sorry," Mindy said. "I had no idea."

Maude sighed deeply. "I called you because I thought you might know where he would want to give his money. He didn't leave a will, and it's not a lot of money, but I thought Scott would want to give it to a charity."

"But why would I know that?"

Another sigh. "I don't have much to work with. Your picture was on his mirror, and he had written your phone number on the edge. I thought you must be a good friend. Aren't you? How did you know him?"

"We met at a camp when we were in college. We were both counselors one summer. Yes, Scott has been a good friend, but I haven't heard from him in quite a long time. I had no idea he was sick."

"Can you think where he would want his money to go?"

Mindy tried to remember whether she had heard Scott refer to a charity or a cause. The effort made her realize how little Scott had told her of himself. He was so good at drawing her out, she hadn't thought about the lack of reciprocation. What information he gave had been superficial, never anything about what moved him. Staring into his death, she realized he had told her hardly anything that mattered. She was talking with the grief-stricken mother of a man she barely knew, though she had flirted with the possibility of marrying him, had he asked.

"No," Mindy said, "I can't remember him referring to anything. I'm sorry." Then a glimmer came to her. "You could give it to the camp. Mount of Olives."

"He had positive feelings about it?"

"Yes, I think so. We all did. It was a marvelous summer. Scott was very much a part of that."

When Maude hung up, Mindy walked back outside and continued with her tomatoes. She lost concentration and found herself staring at a plant, smelling its peculiar herbal smell, while having no idea what she was meant to do with it. Death was so strange. If she had never heard from Scott again, she would have forgotten him, but now she would always think of this day when she realized that he had not quit her. He had become sick. Sick to death.

She really might have married him. Now that possibility, unfulfilled and unfulfillable, would mark her life with a blue dot of tragedy—a sad Victorian-spinster story that she would not mention to anybody, not even her mother. Scott would forever be the path she could not follow.

Mindy lay down on the lawn, spreading herself on her back to think more fully of this moment. She wished that she had asked Maude about Scott's last days, the course of the disease, who had been beside him, what his state had been. Perhaps she could get Maude's phone number and call her back. She would not do that, she knew. It would be too awkward. Maude had sounded exhausted and fragile. What good would the answers do?

The sky was a clear and bright blue. She rarely looked at it, but now she examined it closely—a translucent bowl of light stretching from rim to rim, without a scratch of contrail or a smudge of cloud. How very beautiful was its color, how simple. Its calm accentuated how agitated she felt. She had never lost a friend. Scott had been and remained largely unknown, so she did not feel much heartbreak, really; but she felt deserted, stranded on her solitary path.

She would have to let the others know. They would be startled and full of questions, as she was. For the time being, however, she could hold the sparse facts to herself.

She did want to tell Verity, however. In those days they talked often, weekly or more.

When Mindy reached her, Verity couldn't grasp the news. Scott's death seemed unbelievable, like something she heard on the news. She switched to telling about the new church she was attending. Mindy didn't pay close attention until she realized it was an Orthodox church.

"Verity," she said, "I thought you were a Pentecostal."

"Well, I am. But I got curious about this church near my apartment. It doesn't look like any other church. It has a dome. I just felt I should learn about it, so I stopped by, and I met the priest. He showed me around and explained the icons and all that, and he invited me to come to a service. So I did."

"What does Cass think?"

"He likes it, too. It's so holy, it overwhelms you. And they pray for miracles, only the prayers are written out, and they sort of sing them. I'm really all caught up in it."

"Verity, you are amazing," Mindy said.

* *

A month later, Randy gestured to Mindy across the open-office space at his company, where she had, as expected, become a well-paid den mother. "Can I talk to you?" he asked when she joined him. "Let's go for a walk."

They went for a walk because the office left no place for privacy. Out on University Avenue, Randy was in no hurry to bring up whatever had prompted him. As they dodged their way down the sidewalk, past suits and skateboarders, he asked casually how she was liking her job, which she had started in February. She told him she liked it a lot and thanked him. She rarely saw him in the office; he spent most of his time with his real estate business.

Randy turned down Ramona Street, where there was much less pedestrian traffic. "I didn't want people listening in," he said quietly, then gathered himself and launched into his news. "You know we do business in Seattle. I was up there earlier in the week and got talking to some people who worked with Scott. They told me he died of AIDS."

Mindy was glad that they were alone, for instantly, before the words even registered, she had tears in her eyes. "That can't be!" she exclaimed. "How would he get it?" She knew that some people contracted the disease through blood transfusions, but Scott wasn't a hemophiliac, she was almost sure. Randy didn't say anything, so she went on. "Scott was so wholesome. That was practically his middle name. I don't believe it."

She glanced over at Randy, who was walking with his eyes down. His shoulders gave an almost invisible shrug. "I know, Mindy. But the people I was talking to said Scott had a secret life."

"How would they know, if it was secret?"

He said nothing for a few strides. His legs effortlessly ate up distance. "One of the men is involved in the gay lifestyle," he said. "I guess he encountered Scott."

When they got back to the office, Mindy tried to do her work. After an hour or so, she asked permission to leave early. Her boss barely looked up. "Sure," he said. "Go ahead."

Her house was empty. She sat on the sofa and stretched out her long legs. The news she had just heard was too awful to consider, but she knew that she had to. It would not go away and leave her in peace.

Mindy rarely got angry, but now she felt possessed by fury. Scott must have been testing himself when he took her out, sent flowers, and kissed her goodnight. She could have been a blow-up doll. Mindy burned when she thought of the time she'd spent thinking of him, the pleasure she felt anticipating their dates, and especially the care involved in trying to discern her feelings because she thought he might ask her to marry him. She had even asked Verity to find a word from the Lord. She wasn't especially bothered by his homosexuality; that seemed abstract and theoretical, miles from anything she knew. It was her sense of being exploited. What had he really thought of her? She would never know. He went from politely kissing her to having sex with other men.

This was such an ugly train of thought that she sought to escape it. Maybe she had failed him. Maybe he had longed to unburden himself of his secrets, and she had missed his cues. He asked all the questions and she let him. She had thought he was genuinely curious about her life, when all that time he had been avoiding talking about himself. It must have been hell for him. And she had allowed it to be.

He probably ended his life in misery, sure that he would horrify his friends if they knew the truth about him. He had not called any of them to tell them he was sick. Now that she thought it over, it wasn't clear that his own mother had known his condition or been with him at the end. What a lonely life. And he had left her lonely, too.

25

VERITY AND CASS

That fall, Verity and Cass finally married. It came as a relief to their friends, who didn't understand why they had waited so long. They weren't living together, or even sleeping together, so shouldn't the pressures of desire, if nothing else, have impelled them to get moving?

The truth was that religious experience had taken all their attention. Both Verity and Cass spoke in tongues, an experience so wonderful and life-changing they wanted every one of their friends to share it. (Mindy finally told Verity that she should talk about something else.) Cass was slain in the Spirit before Verity; she took longer because it reminded her of epileptic seizures. It was nothing like that, she found when she experienced it: like falling out of an airplane and landing on a feather bed. It brought complete spiritual nakedness—all that she had hoped would come from fully yielding herself to the Lord.

At the same time, Verity was experimenting with Orthodoxy, attending an extra set of services and reading endlessly about eternity.

What with all that, neither she nor Cass had time to think about getting married. But finally, they did. Verity's mother, anxious for grandchildren, pushed on Verity, which tipped her toward doing what she wanted to do anyway.

"Cass," she asked one day when they were on their way to church. "Do you think we could get married?" Her voice quavered because she feared rejection.

"It's okay with me," he said, as though she had asked about purchasing a new sofa.

Both ceremony and reception took place in their Pentecostal church. Verity had asked the Orthodox priest if they could marry in his church, but as soon as he understood the request, he became stiff and mannered and said the Orthodox wouldn't marry someone outside their faith. Cass was offended, but Verity saw that it was actually a benefit: everything would be less complicated in the flexible Pentecostal environment, and they wanted a simple wedding.

It was meant to be a small event for family members. Verity's mom and one aunt were her only family in attendance—and Mindy, of course, who counted as family. Cass issued an open invitation to his extended family and was surprised when twenty-five members appeared, including a cousin with a wife and four children whom Cass hadn't seen in decades, if ever—he wasn't sure.

The service was brief and would have been briefer had not the pastor lost his place twice and compensated both times by preaching a short evangelistic sermon. He was old; their regular pastor was booked and had sent him as his replacement.

Several of Cass's family members spent the first twenty minutes of the reception looking for the alcohol and then spent the next hour marveling over a wedding that featured non-alcoholic punch only. There wasn't enough food, either.

Verity and Cass seemed not to notice. They looked content, their faces soft in smiles, gazing toward each other as though they had eyes for nothing else. "Dude, do you know where we are going for our honeymoon?" Cass asked everyone. "Hawaii!"

"Really! Which island?" Mindy inquired, because that is what she heard people ask about Hawaiian vacations.

Cass didn't know. One of his workmates had recommended a resort, and he had been impressed by the video that showed young people on surfboards.

When they arrived in Hawaii late that night, coated with a thin film of dried perspiration, they wandered through the tropical luxuriance of their hotel: elephant's ear, palm trees, bougainvillea. "Oh my God," Cass kept saying. "Is this real?" Swimming pools and waterfalls; strings of colored light wrapping the trees; soft, warm breezes. Verity was nervous and tried to hold Cass's hand every chance she got. She wondered how they could afford such luxury and fretted over how it would be to sleep with Cass.

The resort was perfect for them. They enjoyed the buffets and the evening shows featuring, inevitably, hula dancers. Verity had brought several science fiction novels. She could have been happy simply reading all week, but Cass needed more stimulation, which the resort provided in plenty. He rented a Jet Ski and spent hours on it. He also pulled Verity along on hikes and snorkeling expeditions.

The honeymoon would have been perfect if not for the sex. They tried and failed to consummate their marriage. A great deal of sometimes painful grinding and a number of embarrassing accidents occurred, but no penetration. The experience was so frustrating that they stopped talking. Their meals, which they had already paid for, they ate in silence. Verity disappeared for long periods without saying where she was going, and Cass watched TV and hardly looked up when she came back. Neither one knew whom to blame. It was like being angry that you can't do a pull-up. If you can't, you can't.

"This is ridiculous!" Cass shouted on their third night's failure. He slammed his fist into the pillow. "You need to see a doctor."

"Where are we going to find a doctor?" Verity was on the edge of tears.

"I'm sure the hotel must have one."

Verity didn't see how a doctor could help. "What would he do?" she asked pleadingly. Asking a doctor to poke and prod like a plumber was too awful. She couldn't.

"You have to!" Cass shouted. His vehemence terrified her. Normally gentle and unflappable, he acted frantic.

The flight home seemed extraordinarily long to Verity. Cass was his usual bouncy self. He had never flown in an airplane before this week, and he looked around him with undiminished interest. Experimenting with opening and closing the air vents, fiddling with the audio controls, he seemed unaware of his new wife's misery. Verity was in the bleakest of moods. She wondered about an annulment and how she would explain it to her mother. The shame would be unbearable.

She was praying, of course; she had been praying since the very first night. "Dear God, I need a miracle," she pleaded silently, reverting to fervent Pentecostalism. "Please." What a strange miracle it would be! She thought of the water parting at the Red Sea. She remembered the temple curtain torn in two. She even considered Moses striking the rock with his staff so water flowed out. They needed their pastor to pray for them, she knew—their Pentecostal pastor. She could picture his face: a middle-aged man with graying mutton chops. She couldn't. It would be hideous to tell him what they were going through; when she thought about it, when she considered the actual words that would need to be spoken, she realized it was impossible.

They arrived home after midnight. Cass had moved his things in before the wedding, though the place was hardly big enough for two. As

Verity entered, pulling her suitcase, she saw the living room as a stranger might, shabby and crowded. Cass was already brushing his teeth while she sat on the sofa, staring into space.

When they got into bed, Cass went promptly to sleep, tired from the trip, but Verity thrashed and agonized. She couldn't even think, let alone pray. Where could she turn? Not to anybody at church; this was not a suitable prayer request. Her mother? Impossible. Verity did not have a regular doctor, and the thought of going to the clinic and describing her woes to a strange man was beyond awful.

For hours these phantom figures paraded up and down—pastor, mother, doctor. She felt hideously abnormal, a feeling that carried back her whole life. One reason she had fallen for Cass was that he made her feel normal. He was so unprepossessing, so unrushed. Even now he wasn't pressuring her, really; any man would be at least as persistent, she felt sure, from what she knew about men. Yet just the touch of his hand created a feeling of panic.

Verity got out of bed, careful not to wake Cass. She fumbled in the dark until she found her Bible, then tiptoed out the door and sat on her one-step concrete porch. In the cool night air, charged with moisture from the ocean fog, she felt calmer. She could imagine mist streaming down in long flying buttresses from the Santa Cruz mountains. It was a comfort to think of that huge and silent movement.

The porch light was just enough to read by. Opening her Bible, she found the Psalms and mumbled one after another. She did not really take in any meaning, but the ancient words released her from her torment, reminding her that she was only one person in an immense and deep universe. Under her feet the spinning globe propelled her through space at unthinkable speed, yet she felt no movement. How, she wondered, can we be so unaware?

1991

26

VIRGIN BIRTH

Cass worked as line foreman at a printer assembly plant, which kept him on his feet and moving all day. He liked the work, since sitting still was never his forte; and he was making good money, as he was quick to tell. The better his career possibilities, the less he thought about church.

It was not true that Cass liked St. Chrysostom, the Orthodox church that Verity had begun to attend. He went with her twice, but its "mumbo jumbo," as he called it, made no sense to him. Not wanting to attend their old church without Verity, he quit going to church at all. He still believed in God, he told Verity, but he admitted that disappointment with the miracle life had robbed his enthusiasm.

"What about the prayers that we've seen answered?" she asked him. They were side by side, watching TV together.

"I guess," he said. "But nothing spectacular."

"What do you mean, 'spectacular'?"

"I thought for sure we would see somebody come back from the dead. Or at least get their eyesight back, or have a limb restored. Stuff like that."

"Bethany's eyes got better. Remember? We prayed for her to pass the driver's test and she did."

He shrugged.

Verity's faith was much less transactional. She couldn't argue against Cass's conclusions, but she felt they were beside the point in a way. God was a mystery, and his ways were a mystery, and she felt she was paddling in a shallow inlet of a very deep ocean.

Cass worked long hours, with last-minute calls that summoned him early or kept him late. Verity could never be sure when he would be home.

For her, love was wrapped up in the details of Cass's life. She would be happy for him to reveal every mundane moment, and every thought. But Cass craved independence. He didn't like having to answer for his schedule, and he hated feeling that she kept track of him.

"I wish you would let me know when you're going to be late," she told him after he came in post-midnight. Verity had risen from bed when she heard him in the kitchen. He had microwaved some leftover Chinese food and was eating it, poking a fork into the Styrofoam container.

"You don't seem to get that I'm in charge there," he said. "If something goes wrong, I have to stay."

"I just want to know what you are doing."

"I'm working, okay? You get that?"

His tone grieved Verity, but she was not confrontational. When Cass avoided her eyes or dodged her questions, she let the moment pass. Without the church connection, she felt herself drifting away from him.

They still had, in any case, an unconsummated marriage. No one else knew, not even Mindy. Verity had promised herself she would go to a doctor but could not bring herself to do it. Periodically, Cass would try again. They both learned to dread the encounters. Afterward, Cass would stew on his disgrace, growing angrier day after day until he determined on another try. He never said anything to invite Verity into the process—he just went at it. Verity did not resist; she felt responsible for their troubles.

She compensated through her new church.

In the beginning, she knew no one there. The Orthodox seemed to harbor no compulsion to greet visitors; they let her come and go. She loved the solitude that she experienced in the services, which would not have been possible in an overly friendly congregation.

The building itself drew her. It stood out in a neighborhood of flat-roofed houses on small lots. From the exterior, tall, gray, blank plaster walls imposed a fortress. One entered the building through a set of brick stairs leading into a small courtyard. That was not beautiful—closed-in, planted sparsely—but it had an old-world ambiance that charmed Verity. She found herself wandering by it often when she had time.

One Saturday, she took a seat on a concrete bench there. She was alone with no plans for the day. Cass was out. He had left early without telling her where he was going.

She heard steps and looked up to recognize the priest. He had exchanged his robes for a soft wool jacket and a blue shirt. "Can I help you?" he asked in a tone that suggested no help. He obviously did not remember her.

It took all Verity's courage to look at him and introduce herself. She said she had been going to church there, and they had met before when he showed her around the sanctuary.

"Are you Orthodox?" he asked.

"No," she said. "I don't really know what that is." She paused and glanced at the priest's face. He was young, maybe 35 or 40. "I am a Christian, though," she added, though she was unsure whether that would make any difference. She expected to be expelled from the courtyard at any moment. In her current state of woe, that promised to leave her even more wretched.

The priest's face softened. "I wasn't Orthodox either," he said. "I came to the faith in college." To Verity's surprise, he sat down gently on the bench beside her. "Can I tell you how?" he asked.

Could he tell her? She wanted nothing more.

"I was lost," he said. "Utterly lost in the wilderness of sex, of alcohol, of selfishness. I didn't know what life was, or what it was supposed to be. I went to church—I had grown up in a church—but all I heard were harsh voices braying about something that made no sense. They were talking, but I couldn't understand. It seemed to be in a different language.

"Then this girl I knew, who saw how lost I was, invited me to an Orthodox Easter. Before I even got in the door, I sensed that I had entered a different world."

"That's what I felt," Verity said.

The priest turned to look at her, then held out a hand, inviting her to put her hand into his. She did. His skin was dry and cool.

"Come," he said, standing up and lifting her hand as though it were a string to pull her by. "I'll show you around the church."

"You already did that," she said.

"Did I? It won't hurt to do it again. The church building is like a book; it explains our faith. If you learn the building and all its parts, you begin to understand Orthodoxy."

He let go of her hand as he led her inside, shepherding her with a hand on her shoulder to stand in a specific spot. He did this repeatedly as they went through the small building, explaining things.

"Think of the church as a ship," he said. "An ark, actually, in which God's children are saved from the flood." He explained the narthex, the nave, the iconostasis with its glistening, gilded surfaces and its icons. He pointed out the Pantokrator under the dome and carefully named the icons, introducing each one as though the saint were present and listening. The Beautiful Gate and the Angel Doors were identified. They peeked in one of them to see the altar inside the sanctuary.

"Can I go in?" Verity asked.

The priest hesitated. "Are those leather shoes?" he asked.

She had to look to see what she had on. "I don't know. Maybe."

"No animal products are allowed in the sanctuary." He did not explain, and Verity did not ask. It elated her to learn that the church was ruled by mysterious decrees.

Verity remembered what she had felt from her previous tour: the hush, the palpable holiness. It would never have occurred to her that a building—walls and roof—could be set apart by God, yet here centuries of godliness seemed embedded, like an ointment rubbed deep into the plaster. She remembered feeling it before, but this time it was stronger. Perhaps it would only grow stronger year upon year, just as the knowledge of the icons and the furniture and the ritual could only grow deeper.

Verity walked home slowly. The San Jose sunlight washed everything in its brightness, but she tried to hold on to the softness and the colors that had occupied her mind. In their empty apartment she sat still for a long time, not even tempted to watch TV or to read, her usual activities. Her life had changed, she thought. It could never be the same.

When she got hungry, she heated a frozen lasagna. She hardly tasted it. After that she watched some television, though afterward she could not have told you what she saw.

In the middle of the night, Cass came in. She heard him unlock the door and saw the light come on in the bathroom. She had been sleeping, but his presence made her very awake. Sadness swept through her, dragging her back into the fact of a non-functioning marriage. Perhaps she could have asked the priest for help. That had not seemed relevant at the time. In fact, all her worries had been swept aside during her visit to the church.

Cass came to bed and immediately turned her toward him and began to fondle her. Verity did not resist. Her sadness only grew as she anticipated another failure. She was right: it came to that, messily. After Cass was done, she got up and brought a towel. Cass swore, loudly. Verity got back into bed and Cass turned on his side, away from her. Surprisingly soon, he was breathing deeply. For a very long time Verity listened. Could he be pretending? Could he really sleep after such a sad experience? She could not. It occurred to her that maybe he had been drinking. Cass was not a drinker, but she had read in some of her novels how alcohol affects men.

In the morning it was Sunday, and she made ready for church. Cass was reading the *Mercury News* and did not look up.

"Would you like to come to St. Chrysostom's?" she asked when she was almost ready to go. The question was not a practical one; she knew what he would say.

"No," Cass said, looking up from the newspaper. "You go, and I'll try to be out of here by the time you get back."

"You're going out?" she asked.

"I'm moving out," he said. "This is a joke."

"What do you mean?"

He did not answer. She knew what he meant.

"Let's talk it over when I get back," she said. "There must be something we can do."

She thought about that all through the service. The liturgy pulsed along but she had no mind for it, not even the curiosity that had sustained her so far. The building's mystery had evaporated. *What can I do?* she thought again and again. She knew one thing: she could go to the doctor. But that was impossible. She had thought through it a thousand times.

Anyway, it was too late. They had spoiled it already. She had spoiled it.

When she got back to the apartment, Cass was gone and all his clothes with him, plus his sound system. Nearly everything else in the apartment belonged to her. The few things he had overlooked, she knew he didn't care about.

Going through the apartment, she found no note. In a moment of panic, she realized she had no idea where he was. He had left no address, no phone number. She was able to calm herself when she remembered she could reach him at work. Supposedly that was against corporate rules, but in an emergency it was possible. Then she realized that she really had no reason to contact him. She had nothing to say. The emergency had already come and gone.

Exactly three weeks later, on another Sunday morning, she woke up with a violent nausea and threw up everything before she could make it to the toilet. She was miserably dizzy and sick all day. The next day was not much better, and she could not go to work. The third day she dragged herself to the office but had to vomit approximately every hour.

After those three days she felt slightly better, but her breasts were swollen and sore. Her whole body felt tender.

She suffered for three whole weeks, sometimes sick, sometimes recovering, then sick again, before she gave up and went to the clinic. Doing so made her very anxious, since it was exactly what she had avoided doing for Cass's sake. However, going to a doctor for the flu was very different than what that would have required. She remembered her doctor's visits when she was a girl with epilepsy. Her temperature would be taken, and her symptoms listed, then she would be given a prescription. She might not have to talk to anybody. Perhaps nobody would touch her.

The clinic was located less than a mile from her apartment. She parked in front of a one-story plaster building in a pinkish coral color.

To her utter surprise, the doctor was a woman. After hearing Verity's symptoms, which she offered in a low, faltering voice, the doctor handed her a folded robe and asked her to undress. Verity did not know how to refuse. The doctor very gently and wordlessly examined Verity, who was stiff with fear. It only took a minute; then she told Verity she could dress and left the room. When she knocked and entered again, the doctor looked at Verity with a quizzical half-smile. "You're a virgin?" she said.

Verity, who was already terrified, sick, and humiliated, nodded miserably.

"Then you must be the Virgin Mary, because I'm fairly sure you're pregnant."

1993

27
HOWARD IS DYING

Howard first noticed a shortness of breath while playing tennis at the city courts. The sunshine was sweet on his head and back, the air off the ocean suffused with salt, and he was enjoying beating his opponent soundly. The man claimed to have played tennis in college, but his backhand was vulnerable. Howard repeatedly hit into it and rushed the net, whereupon his opponent fell back on his heels and sliced a lollypop, which Howard destroyed. However, those three or four quick steps to the forecourt left Howard sucking wind. He was slow to recover, still panting when he went to serve.

Playing at public courts instead of a club made him feel ashamed, like he didn't have the proper clothes to wear to a concert. He worried that the man he played with, an agent, might think less of him. Howard also suffered from a feeling that Julie, his wife, was unhappy with him. All their married life she had been devoted, practically adoring. Lately, she was terse, almost unfriendly.

When he got home, he threw himself onto the sofa, feeling dizzy.

"What's wrong?" Julie asked, coming into the room from the backyard, where she had been gardening.

"That's the way you say hello?" He was annoyed.

"Sorry, but you sounded all out of breath."

He was perspiring, his armpits were slimy, and he really couldn't catch his breath—not fully. This he didn't understand.

"How did your game go?" she asked without much real interest.

"Great. He wasn't much of a player."

"Did he like your pitch?" Howard had planned to talk about a treatment.

"It wasn't a pitch. Just an idea."

"What did he think?"

"He said he'd get back to me."

Howard had moved on from that. His mind was now occupied by his health—a worry blooming like a puffball, threatening to split open and spill spores everywhere. He didn't want to go to the doctor. He hated medicine, and besides, they didn't have the money.

The problem persisted, however, and soon he could think of nothing else as he closely monitored his breathing, day and night. When he finally admitted to Julie that he was worried, her cynicism folded. "Oh, Howard," she said with tears peeking into the corners of her eyes. He found that gratifying.

He gave in to her urging and went to the clinic. Dr. Patel had a calm, reassuring manner as she checked his breathing with her stethoscope. Her unflappability caused him to hope that his problems amounted to nothing. Howard thought surely she would take him from the tiny examining room into an office, to sit behind a desk for a calm and supportive discussion. But no, she sat down on a stool in that sterile, inhuman environment and said, "I'm going to send you to a specialist—a pulmonologist. His office will call you and arrange for an appointment."

He had not expected that. "What's wrong?" he blurted out.

"I'm hearing something in your lungs," she said. "Don't worry, Dr. Frank is very good, very experienced. You'll be in good hands." She stood up to end the conversation.

It took him two weeks to get into Dr. Frank's office. Until then, he spent all his waking hours in the living room, usually in his robe, listening to his own breathing. Occasionally he asked Julie to listen to it with him. She had reverted to skepticism but did her best to show patience. For all she knew, he really was sick. It felt to her more like hypochondria.

Wanting comfort, he asked her to bring him things—a cup of tea, a book—which she did, but silently.

"You seem unhappy with me," he said. "I can't help the way I feel."

"I can't either," she said.

When the day for his office visit came, Howard asked Julie to go with him. "I have to work," she said, but he fussed so much about going alone that she gave in and took a sick day. She planned to sit in the waiting room and grade papers, but Howard wanted her to see the doctor with him. Dr. Frank was a tall, bony man with enormous ears; he took his time listening to Howard's lungs. Howard sat up straight and tense, anxious to be a good patient. Dr. Frank said nothing except to instruct Howard on how to breathe in and out and then to blow into a spirometer.

He sat for a moment, looking off into space. "Let's get an X-ray, shall we?" he said. "You can put your shirt back on, and Carlotta will show you where to go." He nodded at Howard, then at Julie, and left them.

Howard thought he had anticipated every possible outcome. Not so. He found with the doctor's departure that his fears took shape as terrible ogres, nighttime phantoms creaking on the stairs. Something was happening to him, something unknown, and it terrified him.

A nurse came in and asked perkily, "Are we all set?" Leading them down a long hallway, she opened the door on a room crowded with equipment. A technician positioned Howard on a table and took pictures. Back in the examining room, Howard thought of himself lying on that cold table as though laid out in a mortuary.

When Dr. Frank came in, he took his time attaching the freshly developed X-rays to a light table. For several minutes, he studied the film wordlessly. Then he came over toward Howard and Julie, who sat in small, sturdy metal chairs. He looked at them both and sat down.

"You have progressive pulmonary fibrosis," he said while joining his hands together and flexing them, a nervous habit. "What that means is that your lungs are scarred and hardened and unable to function as well as they should. That's why you have shortness of breath. You aren't getting enough oxygen. Nobody knows why people get it, and there is no cure."

Howard's first reaction was an immediate squib of relief. He had been right. Nobody had believed him, but he was sick. The news caught Julie completely off guard. She was accustomed to rounding off Howard's extremes, discounting his worries as well as his certainties. Now she realized Howard had been genuinely suffering. It alarmed and shamed her.

"So he'll always be short of breath?" Julie asked.

"Yes, I think he will."

"Will he have to quit tennis?"

"I'd encourage Howard to play for as long as he can. Sometimes the disease gives you a long period of stability."

They were slowly unpeeling an awful reality. "You make it sound like it's all downhill," Julie said.

"Well, as I said, there's no cure."

"He's going to die?" Julie asked, a squeak in her voice. "Is that what you're saying? This is a fatal disease?"

Dr. Frank seemed to shudder slightly at the plainness of her words. "It's not possible to generalize," he said. "Every case is different. But this is a very serious disease."

"How long?" Howard choked out. His initial pleasure in vindication had been turned upside down. "How long do I have?"

"Howard!" Julie said reprovingly. "He just said that every case is different."

"I know that, but on average. I want to know. How long?"

"It's a reasonable question," Dr. Frank said. "Even though your wife is right, every case is different, and it's dangerous to generalize. But let me try to give you a sense of the averages. You're a healthy young man. We've caught this early. That's to the good. I would hope for five years."

"Hope for?" Julie said.

"Yes."

"What are we looking at? Can you tell us about treatment and what the symptoms are? And the different stages?"

The doctor showed by his shifting posture that he was ready to move on. "The symptoms are what you are already experiencing. You don't get enough oxygen. That puts stress on other organs, like the heart. Every case is different, as I said. Sometimes the disease stabilizes for quite some time. Other times it moves quickly. I'm sorry to say there is no treatment. You should eat healthily, and get exercise, and stay as strong as you can."

"When do I come back?" Howard asked.

"Come back?"

"For another visit."

Dr. Frank looked blank. "That's up to you," he said. "I would recommend that you consult Dr. Patel if you have any particular concerns."

The doctor finally escaped and so did they, walking slowly to the car. Inexplicably, the day was fresh and sunny. "Let me drive," Julie said, and Howard gave her the keys without a word. All the way home he said nothing, though Julie tried to prompt him. She herself could not find anything to say. She had never been afraid, not even when Howard ran up credit card bills, but now her stomach felt tight with fear.

The next day she stopped at the library on her way home from school and read everything she could find on pulmonary fibrosis. It was not encouraging. The medical jargon was hard to penetrate, but as best she could understand, Dr. Frank had summed up the situation fairly. Howard was very sick, the disease would get worse, and ultimately, he would die of it. He was on a downward slope; the question was how steep and when he would reach the bottom.

Remembering what the doctor had said, Julie tried to get Howard to go out walking, and she tempted him to eat by making his favorite meals. That was ineffective. He stopped dressing; he almost never showered. Sometimes he turned on the TV, but never for long. She went to school and came home to find that he had not moved out of his living room chair.

"What are you thinking about?" Julie pleaded. "You have to tell me."

"I'm not thinking," he said. "I'm trying not to think."

"Can't you think about God?" she said. "What about, 'To live is Christ, to die is gain.' Where is that?"

She looked away to keep him from seeing her eyes. Howard, however, gave no answer. He had always overflowed with words, but now he was a cipher, which terrified her more than screaming or crying.

He did not tell her that he was screaming internally. Howard had never given any thought to death, and now that thief was standing over him. In one stroke, God would make the entire cosmos vanish. It was unfair. He had barely gotten started. He, Howard, would shout like Job that God was unjust, and shake his fist at the Almighty, but that, too, frightened him. Also, for the first time in his life, he wasn't sure anybody was listening. The universe beyond his skin seemed empty. He said none of this to Julie.

He couldn't help thinking that he deserved this fate. Hollywood had gotten into his head and lured him from faith. His lust for fame had stolen his soul. He knew it, and knew he needed to return to God, but he could not bring himself to it. Not when he was dying. He still had too much dignity to let the threat of death control him.

* *

The phone rang only a few times in the first weeks, which surprised Julie; she had not realized how isolated they had become. In any case, she did not answer. She did not want to talk to anyone. She did not want to pretend to be fine.

For the present, they could get by. They could manage the expense of the oxygen that Dr. Patel ordered up, especially since Howard had stopped doing lunch and they saved on restaurant meals. Julie worried how she would manage when Howard got truly sick, needing hospital care. For the present, he didn't seem that different. If she had not heard a doctor give his diagnosis, she would not have believed it.

One day the phone gave a single ring, then after a short silence rang again. In Julie's youth her family had used a signal like that to say that you had arrived safely at some long-distance location. It made Julie think that somebody was signaling to them, so she answered.

"Oh, hi," Verity said. "It's me."

"Who is 'me'?" Julie said cheerily, though she knew perfectly well. She found it annoying when people assumed that you recognized their voice.

"Oh, it's Verity. Hi."

"Hi, Verity. It's Julie. Were you sending us a signal?"

It took a confused exchange to establish that Verity had not been signaling. She had hung up the first time because she thought she misdialed.

Julie was not particularly fond of Verity. She had never entirely forgiven her for stealing Howard when they were teenagers at camp. Ordinarily, she would quickly turn the telephone over to Howard, who enjoyed Verity. But Howard had ordered her not to answer the phone. She didn't want to explain this to Verity, so for some minutes she kept up small talk while wondering furiously what she should do. Finally, exasperated by Verity's directionless conversation, she decided to see what Howard would say. To her surprise, he got up and came to the phone. Julie didn't listen in, but she assumed that he told her about his illness, because he was on the line for a good half hour.

"How did that go?" Julie asked, thinking that he seemed marginally brighter.

"It was good," he said in a distracted way. "Just fine."

"You told her about your health?"

He looked up with a sharp hawk gaze. "Of course. She's our friend."

Verity spread the word to their camp friends, who began to call, gently and sensitively pumping Julie for information. At first Julie tried to fend them off, but she gave that up when Howard told her he would love to talk to them.

In the face of their friends' concentrated attention, Howard revived. He still did nothing but sit in his bathrobe all day, but he was undisguisedly cheerier. All that interest in him was like a magic pill.

Leslie sent a box of cheeses from Wisconsin. Randy sent a book on heaven, which Julie found in the trash. Sam called to ask whether he could visit. He arrived on a Monday while Julie was at school.

Sam had never talked to Howard about his visit years ago, when Howard stormed off from the beach restaurant. At the Tahoe reunion, they had avoided each other. Under these circumstances, however, Sam knew that their relationship had to be restored.

Howard opened the door and seized him in a bear hug, swaying slightly and wordlessly. When he let go, Sam held him at arm's length.

"I wasn't sure you'd want to see me," Sam said.

"I wasn't sure you'd want to see *me*," Howard said. And that was all they said in the way of making up. They sank into conversation, going to work on the events that dominated their lives: Sam's lost church, Howard's lost life. When Julie got home, she found the two men sprawled on the living room furniture, deep in conversation. Their talking continued uninterrupted while she cooked dinner. Much of it was theological talk. Julie heard mentions of Augustine and Kierkegaard and Barth.

Over dinner Julie tried to shift the conversation, asking Sam what kind of work he was doing. He told her that he had started a tile company. Then he and Howard went on talking as though they hardly knew she was there. They said "existential" and "absurd" multiple times.

"Are you talking about death?" she asked.

Sam looked up, startled, then smiled. "No," he said. "Life." He didn't elaborate.

"Are you still following that guy?" she asked. "The one you were so excited about when you came out here for that conference?"

"John Casey?" He shook his head. "No. Not really."

"That's too bad. You were really excited about him."

"Yeah. My life has changed a lot since then." He paused and started to go on but stopped short.

Sam left the next morning—it was a lightning visit, he said, just to see Howard. When Julie got home that night, she asked Howard about their time. He smiled. "One man has lost his church, the other is losing his life." Howard chortled. It was a strange reaction. "We talked about the meaning of it all, of course."

"What did you decide?"

28

CONNECTION

On a November day, when the first rain of the season splashed the streets and traffic snarled the freeway, Julie came home to discover Howard in his office, hunched over his computer keyboard. "What are you doing?" she asked, somewhat alarmed. To her knowledge, he had not looked at his computer since his diagnosis.

He didn't even look up. "I'm writing a treatment."

"Of what?"

"Of my life. Of my battle with pulmonary disease. Of the comforts that friends bring. Of faith in the darkness. It's a movie."

It was pure inspiration, he believed: pathos, tragedy, humanity. Everybody who called had to hear about his script. He was very sure he had found the project he had so long searched for. Julie was happy for him. At one level she knew perfectly well that Howard's hunches were fallible. She also knew that he was brilliant. He was writing. He was producing pages. It had been years. His work made him cheerful again.

He was so sure of himself he showed the script to her. He had never done that, presumably because he saw no point. She had never resented being left out; Howard needed professional counsel, not her cheery enthusiasm. Now, though, he wasn't looking for counsel at all—he knew what he had. He only wanted her to share his delight.

Julie handled the fifty-page script with the greatest reverence. Only on the dining room table did she read, turning over pages and moving them from one neat pile to another. What she read checked her hopes. The script seemed flabby and lacking in direction, but what did she know? She gave Howard what little enthusiasm she could muster, and he didn't seem to notice.

An entire day went into agitating over who should see the script first. Walking up and down in the living room, Howard kept asking Julie about people she didn't know. Really, he was talking to himself. At length he decided on a top producer, somebody who had the power to turn wheels and make decisions fast. "I don't really know him; I've just met him, but Norah can get the script to him, and that's all I need."

Norah was one of those assistants who rule the universe. Howard had met her at church, where she told him she wanted to help Christians in the industry. He took the script to her personally, almost the first time he had gone out of the house since his diagnosis. He looked pale and shaky when he got home, but Julie could see he was pleased with himself. Norah told him she would get the script to Richard that very day.

Howard sat in his chair like a deflated beach ball, his skin pale, his eyes unfocused. Eventually he got up and went to bed, and he didn't get up for dinner. Next day Julie went off to work while he was still asleep, and when she came home, he was sitting in the living room with a book he did not seem to be reading. "I'm not feeling well," he volunteered.

"Why don't you go back to bed?" she asked.

Howard shook his head. "I want to get the phone when Richard calls."

"Please lie down," she said. "You can take the portable phone to bed with you."

Richard didn't call. Howard thought of various excuses. After a week had gone by, he called Norah. She said Richard had the script; no, she didn't think she could ask about it. It wouldn't help, she said. Richard made up his mind in his own way and in his own time.

Howard fretted for another week, hearing nothing, and then called Norah again. This time she spoke with a slight edge of impatience. If Richard hadn't responded, he probably wasn't interested. He read dozens of unsolicited manuscripts each week.

"Is there anything I can do? Can I write him a letter?"

"It won't get to him. You would have to be somebody well known."

"Can you give me his phone number? I could leave him a message."

"No, he doesn't give out his phone number."

That conversation left Howard angry and desperate. The assumption that his name wouldn't get past a secretary choked him. He had won the Newbery. Probably not thirty people alive could say that. Hollywood, he remembered, is a cultural wasteland.

He would be sure to remind Richard that he had been given first crack at the script when somebody else produced it and won an Oscar.

Making a list of the five best remaining options, he took it to the first one the next day. He could have mailed the script, but he always preferred a personal presentation, even if he only saw an assistant. After he did that, he felt better. He had wasted two weeks with Richard, but now he would move forward.

After another week of lost time, he got a rejection in the mail—standard boilerplate. He still had the list, so he sent the script on, hand-delivering it to an assistant who made him feel small, as though he were delivering sandwiches. He heard nothing. Should he call? Remembering the assistant's nastiness, Howard decided to send the script to everybody else on the list. That was a questionable strategy—he would look bad if two of them decided to take it—but he was impatient. Anxiety filled his heart; he had begun to doubt.

Julie assured him with all the certainty she could summon that he had written a compelling story. Surely, he would find the right place; he only had to keep trying. Howard sulked, unwilling to be encouraged.

* *

Julie watched with alarm. He was dying, she knew, and his colleagues were rejecting the story of his life. He might keep sulking until he sank into a depression and never emerged.

Yet one day he woke up with a new interest in life. Julie recognized it right away. Having spent her adult life anticipating his moods, she felt a new energy in the way he carried himself.

Not until Sunday, when Howard declared that he wanted to go to church, did she recognize it as a revival of faith. By this time, he was carrying oxygen assistance with him. It was an unwieldy device, a miniature bomb on wheels. Leaving the house was a challenge. Nevertheless, Julie got him to the service. Afterward he spoke warmly with the pastor and had exchanges with several acquaintances. People asked about the oxygen, and he bravely told them he was dying. He said facing death made the meaning of life powerfully real to him.

It was the first time Julie had heard him talk that plainly. On the drive home, she told him so.

"I think it's my message," he said, "with whatever time I have left. I see life in a new way."

Something in his tone made her think of their days at Mount of Olives, sitting on the picnic tables late at night while he expounded. She was glad; she loved that part of him.

"Howard, it makes me happy to hear you say it," she said. "What happened?"

He seemed surprised. "What do you mean?"

"Howard, you've been so down. You didn't want to talk to anybody. What made you change? Was it something Sam said?"

He shook his head, as though the question dazed him. "No, it just came. I figured it out for myself."

"But figured out what?"

"If I'm going to die, I've got to make something of it."

Monday, when she got home from school, he was at the computer again. "Another movie idea?" she asked.

Howard shook his head. "A Christmas letter. To let all our friends know."

"We never send a Christmas letter."

"I've never died."

The letter began with a short paragraph relating to the holiday season, but after that it launched into three single-spaced pages detailing Howard's journey toward the grave—medical, psychological, and spiritual. The prose was novelistic in detail. Julie spent a week of evenings plus the weekend making copies, addressing envelopes, stuffing and stamping them, then taking bundles to the post office. From his living room chair, Howard directed her in finding every address possible.

Their friends responded. They called with their voices catching. Lengthy, confessional reactions came in the mail. Howard had planned just the one letter, but very soon he saw that he had found an audience. Another missive—four and a half pages—combined detailed medical information with his personal spiritual grappling. He told in absorbing fashion how the news of his disease had laid him low, how he had threatened to curse God, how his anger at the unfairness had dominated him until he gained deeper perspective and saw the goodness of God and the sweetness of life—even life that has not long to go.

This letter drew more responses, which Howard answered individually. In the new year, he wrote general letters at least every six weeks, detailing his health challenges, faith responses, his doubts, and his personal crises. Postage alone became a significant item in their budget. Julie spent a large share of her free time addressing and stamping envelopes.

Then a woman in a small church in Silver Lake called to ask Howard to come talk to their Sunday morning adult education class. Julie answered the phone and almost turned her down, but something told her to check with Howard first. He was on the line with the woman for twenty minutes, and afterward said he had agreed to come to the church in two weeks.

The gathering was small—twenty-five or so—but he put on an intense, dramatic performance. He talked of life as a candle flame, shining in the dark. "What is the mystery of life?" he asked in a hushed voice. "What does it mean? Where does it go when the candle goes out?" He painted a portrait of a single, guttering flame, staring into it as though it were real. Describing his diagnosis and the shock that came with it, he gave a poetic, dramatic, engrossing performance that captivated his audience and left him completely played out.

Other invitations came, sometimes to bigger audiences. He gave essentially the same talk every time, always with full energy and rigor. The audiences lifted him, and then he collapsed. Julie was twisted in an emotional bind. Howard was living the life she had always thought he would, pouring his gifts into words and capturing people's imagination. But he was dying.

It took a lot to get Howard to these engagements. He tended to over-prepare and make himself frantic, and when the moment arrived, he was afflicted with doubt and woe. Julie worked behind the scenes, getting his clothes ready, calming him, and making sure she could get him where he needed to go. When they returned home, she still had cooking, cleaning, and paying bills. Plus, she had a full-time teaching job. It wore her down, but she was determined not to complain.

The year unfolded, and Howard still lived. He had crises, times when he was so depleted he slept for days, his chest heaving, his breath rasping. It looked like he might die. Then one day he would wake up and come for breakfast.

Another year, and he still crept forward. His strength was feeble, he was desperately sick, and he talked about facing the end. In that second year, the invitations stopped coming. People responded much less to his letters. If he noticed, it didn't show.

2001

29

ENVY

"Surprise," he said. "It's Sam."

Leslie, holding a glass of ice water, looked at him blankly. Then her face changed, and she moved smoothly through the doorway, embracing him. Saying not a word, she clinched for some time before backing away and looking him in the face. "Where on earth did you come from?" she asked in a throaty voice, and laughed.

"From Kansas City," he said, laughing as well. "I hope you don't mind that I dropped by."

"Mind? Heavens, no. How did you find me?"

"I knew you bought the place from Howard and Julie. I wasn't sure I could still find it, but I thought it was worth a try."

"Well, come in," she said. "Can you stay? Let me get you something to drink."

They sat in the living room, a spacious and sunny room that included Leslie's studio—two easels, a square dining-room-size table scattered with pens and other implements, a light table, and a huge blockbuster office chair, all under a framed print of Picasso's Don Quixote. The rest of the room was elegantly figured with brocade and leather furniture, Oriental carpets, brass lamps.

"Wow, this place is really different," he commented.

"How do you mean?"

"Howard and Julie had it very Scandinavian, if I remember. I like this better."

Inevitably, they talked about Mount of Olives friends. Leslie was in touch with Mindy and Randy, who she said were rich now thanks to the start-up.

"What does that start-up do?" Sam asked. "I've never been able to get that clear in my head."

"Me neither," Leslie said, getting to her feet. "It's some kind of bio-technology, like making drugs with bacteria. I've never understood it. But they are worth a mint. Some big drug company bought them out."

She offered him another drink, but he was only a few sips into his beer. "Well, I'm going to freshen this up," she said, and disappeared into the kitchen. What Sam had taken for ice water was vodka on the rocks. Leslie had become a drinker, it seemed; she refreshed her drink several times while they talked. It didn't appear to affect her unless it was to loosen her tongue.

"I hope you're not driving anywhere this afternoon," he said with a grin, and she smiled back beatifically. She still had that silky air.

"Don't worry about me," she said. "I've been working like the devil and you're helping me to relax."

Leslie remained a very attractive woman, small, slim, beautifully if casually dressed, and naturally charming. She had done something with her hair—Cynthia would know exactly what—that made her more Santa Monica. He thought he remembered her as a dark brunette, but now her hair was the color of silvery straw, and it looked as though it had fallen into place after being stirred by a breeze.

"So, what brings you to LA?" she asked.

He hesitated. "I guess it's a sort of vacation. I needed to get away, so I jumped on a plane."

"No Cynthia?"

He shook his head. "She was tied up. Anyway, I don't think she would enjoy this kind of trip."

"What kind of trip? What have you been doing?"

"Nothing," he said. "I literally just got here. You're the first person I've seen."

"I'm flattered. We should go out to dinner. Do you have time?"

"I have to get out to Redlands," he said. "I plan to see Julie and Howard tomorrow. Or at least go to their church. I don't know whether they'll be free."

She pursed her lips. "You know he's a big deal now."

"I know he has a pretty big church. Does that make him a big deal?"

She propped her chin on one fist. "He helped me a lot when I first moved out here. Sold me his condo, as you see. I didn't know a soul and he introduced me to Hollywood people. Gave me advice. He was very supportive. I haven't seen him much in the last couple of years, probably because I don't need his help anymore and he has lots to do with his church. But I ran into him at a gallery about three weeks ago. Here in Santa Monica. A really high-end gallery that sells very expensive abstracts."

Sam raised an inquisitive eyebrow.

"He was buying," she continued. "He didn't see me when I came in, so I just waited and watched. The price of these paintings..." She stood up again, hesitated for a fraction of a second, then went off to the kitchen again. When she came back, she said in utter solemnity, "He is a big deal."

Sam wanted to laugh. "That's what does it? He buys expensive pictures?"

Leslie took a deep swallow. She must be sloshing in the stuff. "Maybe you have to see the gallery to understand what I'm saying." She paused and looked hard at him. "What would make him a big deal for you?"

He gave a short, acrid snort. "I guess for me, it would have more to do with his church."

She shook her head. "Do you still think like that? I'd heard you got out of the pastorate."

"I did," he said. "But I still believe."

"Same as ever?"

"Maybe not the same." He felt put off by her skepticism, but he recognized that he was standing on mushy ground himself.

"Hey, I know," she said suddenly, getting to her feet again. "I've got a video of Howard preaching. Want to see it?" She was already striding to a bookshelf, where she began flipping through volumes. "Here it is," she said. "A friend gave this to me because I said I knew him. I haven't watched it. It's old—a couple of years old. Want to see it?"

In a minute Howard's face appeared on the screen, a foot high. His eyes alight, his lips moving, he was singing along to a gospel group. As the camera backed away, you could see that he was clapping, too. Leslie let out a shriek. "Oh, my!" she exclaimed. "Look at him. Look at him!" She found it hilarious.

She quickly got bored, however, and advanced the tape. Antic figures bounced around the screen. Howard was singing, Howard was praying, a teenage girl did an interpretive dance. Finally, they got to the sermon, and Leslie set the player for regular playback. They watched in silence. Once, Leslie got up to get another drink, but before she could turn her back on the TV, she stopped and sat back down. The production was professional, with multiple cameras. No doubt that contributed to the fascination, but mostly it was Howard. Sam realized that he had been exactly right in his intuitions when they were nineteen-year-olds: you couldn't take your eyes off him. He spoke in a way that caught your throat.

Leslie punched it off and they sat in silence for a few seconds. After a visit to the kitchen, she came back with more vodka. "You sure you don't want anything?" she asked. He held up his beer to show he still had some.

"Can you believe how religious we were?" she asked. "At camp, I mean. Absolutely sincerely, too. I was, anyway. We didn't have any idea of what life was like."

"No," he said.

"It took me about a year to realize it," she said. "After college, I mean. Then life caught up with me. You think Howard still believes all that? Because that was the old-time religion, wasn't it? Is that a performance?"

"I don't know," Sam said.

* *

It was painful to say "I don't know" to his friend's sincerity. He nursed it like a sore tooth as he drove out toward Redlands, inching through traffic. Sam wasn't cynical like Leslie, but he knew he had drifted. Against his convictions, he didn't attend church anymore. He still believed, but he wouldn't plant his flag.

He sometimes joked about it, saying, with a laugh, that he had pastor's PTSD. Even now, so many years later, he would fall back into rehearsing those awful meetings that ended with his being fired by the church he had started. Anger wasn't precisely what he felt, though there was some of that. Death was more like it.

He should shrug it off, he thought for the hundred and first time. Everything had worked out for the best. He made good money as a tile contractor. Four installers worked for him, and he owned his own showroom on the east side of town. With good employees, the business practically ran itself.

Sometimes people from his old church wandered into the showroom and were surprised and embarrassed to find him there. He made a special point to be friendly with them. Most people, he knew, were innocent of malice. They just got in over their heads. Sam thought that as a pastor, he had failed to prepare them for an encounter with evil, even evil in the church. He could hardly blame himself for that, however; nobody had prepared him, either.

He tried to shoo that thought away as he continued down the freeway. If it was evil he had encountered, it made only a small dent in his life. He should count his blessings. His son Russ was a sophomore in college and had inherited his mother's talents as a distance runner. He competed in a division III program, was studying political science, and thought of going to law school like his mother.

Meanwhile, at work, Sam could cruise. He had to extinguish the occasional dumpster fire, but otherwise he found time for the rigors of golf. A regular roster of friends played with him. The swish of the club slicing the air and the click of the ball on its face were music to him.

How was it that he had inherited all this good luck without half trying? He did wonder about it. The one thing he really wanted, he had lost, but everything else swam along.

* *

Just last week, when Cynthia was out, he had gone searching for the old camp pictures. He ultimately found them tucked in a plastic storage bin.

Spreading the photos out on the white sofa, he knelt before them on the white carpet. The faces of those friends, so young and hopeful, moved him.

He was still in touch with some of them, most particularly Howard. Sam called him occasionally, checking in. They knew each other well enough to skip the small talk.

Three years or so after Howard's initial diagnosis came a big surprise: he called wanting to know what Sam thought of his becoming a pastor. A fledgling church meeting in a middle school gymnasium had approached him about it.

"If you asked Cynthia, she would tell you to forget it," Sam said, tiptoeing carefully in. The subject was emotionally complicated for him.

Howard interjected that he was amazed at the lift the idea gave him. "I might not live to see much," he said, "but I love the idea of doing what I can." Hearing that, Sam pulled back from giving advice. Howard already knew what he wanted to do; he just needed somebody to tell it to.

In the years since, Howard's church had grown to thousands. They had a new building in the San Gabriel foothills. Sam thought ruefully that Howard was doing what he always claimed he would never do: following in his father's footsteps.

It gave Sam complicated emotions to think of Howard's success. Was he jealous? He had never wanted a big church like the one Howard led. In fact, he had not wanted a church at all. He had wanted God.

He wasn't the only one who had wandered, he thought. Verity, dear starry-eyed Verity, had become Orthodox. He knew a little about Orthodoxy because of his reading in mysticism. It was as far away from evangelicalism as you could get on the family tree, farther than Catholicism. Brian had been so concerned he flew out to California to talk to her, Sam heard. He grinned to himself at the thought of that conversation. Brian still stopped in the showroom occasionally to say hi. He always wanted to talk about Sam's spiritual life, which worried him, and sometimes to argue again over what had gone wrong in the church. Sam dodged the conversation.

Then there was Scott. What pathway had he followed before he died? Apparently, he had remained in a big non-denominational church where nobody knew his secret. A tormented soul.

These thoughts dropped Sam into a deep well of sadness. Who knew *him*?

At one time he might have said that Howard knew him, but that day was long gone. The only person in contention for that title was Cynthia. Her knowledge was a little frightening. That she loved him, he knew completely. He would confidently trust his life to her. His emotions? That was another matter, he thought with a grim smile. Though she was the reason he had come on this trip.

"Cynthia, can I tell you something?" he had asked over dinner just two nights before.

"Of course you can."

Cynthia had lit their table with two candles. In the darkness surrounding them, her pale face shone as she waited to hear what he would say. He swallowed hard. "I miss you. I don't think we talk the way we used to."

He didn't even pause to let her respond; he made himself cough up his melancholy. Rather than meter his words and censor anything he wasn't sure of, he blurted out what he had been thinking regarding his own directionless life, his lack of friends, his nostalgia for Mount of Olives, and his sense of how many of those old companions had wandered off the path. Cynthia listened. She didn't open her mouth to ask a single question.

When his monologue ran dry, she asked kindly and calmly whether he wished he still had his church.

Sam felt his shoulders turning weak, like a sandcastle dissolving in a wave. He had not said a word about his church. "I really didn't want a church. I was seeking God, and what I got was a church. Which I loved. You know I loved it. It was never my ambition, though. What I can't understand is, why can't I stop thinking about being fired? Is that normal?"

"And the other question," Cynthia said dryly, "is why you stopped going to church."

"I stopped more than church. I stopped seeking. I haven't been to a conference. I have hardly read a spiritual book, and I don't want to. I thought I was a mystic. What happened to me?"

Cynthia was looking at him with her head tilted very slightly at an angle. Sam thought, *Here we go.* He was about to be undressed.

"Are you sure you didn't want to lead a church?" Cynthia asked. "It's odd, don't you think, that losing it caused you such sorrow? If you didn't want it."

That pried open a small cleft in his self-identification. Was he fooling himself, claiming to long for God only? Was he in fact ambitious?

"You think I'm like Howard?"

"Not at all. But maybe you have some things in common."

"Because I've always admired Howard, but I can't stand that ambition."

"What do you mean by that?"

"I mean, it's always about *him*. The world circles around Howard. He thinks like a four-year-old. He always has. And four-year-olds can be very charming and beautiful."

"But not very civilized."

"It's more than that. Civilization is manners. I'm talking about religion. Who the world centers on."

"Do you think it's possible," Cynthia asked, "that your way of leading people to God was also selfish? I'm wondering whether any of us really escapes thinking that the world is about us. In which case, God becomes a way to elevate ourselves. Or to soothe ourselves."

"Of course," Sam said. "That's almost the definition of sin. And sin is universal."

Cynthia, who had said more than usual, was quiet. That created another moment of anxiety in Sam. He would rather have her talking than simply thinking.

"Okay," Sam said. "I am ambitious, though I try to act otherwise. I'm more like Howard than I care to think. And when my ambition was thwarted and I lost the church, I couldn't handle it. Rather than falling back on God, I stopped pursuing God. Does that mean I never wanted to know God in the first place?"

"What do you think?" she asked. He thought he saw a glimmer of a smile on her lips.

"It's all mixed up," he said. "Ambition, God."

"Yes, I think so," she said. "Not just mixed up. Mixed together. But that doesn't mean your pursuit of God was a pose. I think it means that you only knew how to go about it in certain ways. Being a pastor was the context in which you were comfortable. It suited your ambition, and it suited your longing."

"So, if I want to pursue God, I need to find another context. I'm not sure where."

That was the moment he decided to go visit Howard, the only person other than Cynthia who would understand his jumbled-up thoughts. Howard represented just what he feared: ambition that would swallow him alive. But Howard was surprisingly self-aware. Howard would get what he was talking about.

It was weird that even after all these years, Howard remained a reference point. Sam had wanted Howard to approve of him when they first met as college students, and strangely, he still did.

30

DISGUST

From the outside, Howard's church looked like any modern Southern California church: an open, sun-splashed patio; multiple glass doors; minimalist desert plantings. It could as well be a bank as a church.

Inside the lobby, with its gray carpet and high windows, Sam played out that fantasy in his mind. *Where do I go to make a deposit?* He was deliberately a little late for the service, and the lobby was almost empty. Pushing open a door to the auditorium, Sam was surprised by the darkness. He could only see dim guide lights along the aisle; he could not see the seats, or whether they were occupied. His attention was riveted by the stage, which was itself dimly lit. A band was playing, each musician in a splash of colored spotlight, while a woman sang. She was extravagantly dressed in a gold, sequined, form-fitting jumpsuit; her long hair swung behind her head. The music was loud, with emphatic drumming. Sam watched for a while but found the singer minimally interesting. Wanting to sit, he could not see where to go, even after giving his eyes time to adjust.

Then, from behind him, the door opened and light spilled in. Before Sam had a chance to move, the door closed again, and darkness returned. Somebody bumped into him from behind, giving out an exclamation that was followed by shushing.

"Why are we standing here?" someone whispered.

"There's somebody in my way."

"Then go around!"

"I can't; I can't see anything."

Several people muscled past Sam, each one excusing themselves. The party stopped in front of him, facing the same dilemma he had. A flashlight beam came on and danced its way to an empty row of seats. Sam followed and managed to get the last seat on the aisle.

While this happened, the stage fell into darkness and the singer disappeared. Then a slight gray dawn came, and a wisp of early morning mist eddied in, at first a curling tendril like cigarette smoke, then rapidly thickening into fog. Surreptitiously a drum began pounding, softly at first but building into a loud, hot monotony over which came an announcer's voice, like a DJ at a wedding, "Ladies and gentlemen, I give you our pastor, our shepherd, our prophet, our leader...I give you Pastor Howard!" The invisible audience erupted in applause. In the back, a spotlight found its way through the fog, growing brighter and cleaner until it revealed Howard himself, standing quietly.

He was dressed in everyday clothes, a crewneck cashmere sweater over a white collared shirt, tailored blue jeans, simple suede shoes. It was a scene Sam could never forget: his friend dressed like Pat Boone, appearing from the mists like a zombie in an old horror movie. Howard held a small Bible in his right hand. He began to speak in quiet, ordinary tones.

Sam was ready to scorn the whole business but could not. Even as the fog continued to ebb and flow around Howard, even with the lighting shifting in intensity and color, even when music began accompanying his words like a movie score, Howard's gifts stood out. Funny, articulate, folksy, personal, practical, emotive: Howard had all the qualities that great speakers do. He used movie clips that magically appeared on a screen behind him, perfectly synced. Songs were referenced and clips from them played. All the elements conjoined in a simple but profound message. Despite himself, Sam was moved. The service seemed showy and artificial, the very opposite of what he longed for. But Howard was a great preacher.

When the service ended, Sam sat in his seat trying to take in what he had just experienced. He couldn't imagine anyone speaking more skillfully. Technique had disappeared before a wave of emotion and meaning. It was obvious why the church had grown.

It made him feel infinitely diminished. He was a tiny creature on a ridgetop looking over a vast, sweeping plain. Envy filled him—a galling, rapacious sensation of loss and failure. He didn't like Howard's church. The music and light and fog were gimmicks he despised. If the devil offered him that, Sam would laugh. He was not tempted! Yet for Howard's success as a preacher, he felt scalding envy. He sat paralyzed in his theater seat, almost unable to breathe, smothered in his own sickening ego.

Eventually he got up to go. He was surprised to find that everybody else had left, and he was completely alone. Walking slowly, weighed down by his own disgust, he made it to the lobby. The spell of the performance did not carry there; people clustered together drinking coffee from paper cups, chatting happily. Howard was nowhere to be seen.

Approaching a coffee table, he asked a server where he could find the pastor.

"Pastor Howard?" she asked. "He might still be in his office."

"Does he come out here after the service?"

"Not usually. We rarely see him afterward. The best thing is to call the church office tomorrow morning and make an appointment."

"I'm from out of town. I'm an old friend, and I just wanted to say hello. I'm leaving tomorrow morning. For Kansas City."

"Kansas City!" she said. "That's a long way. Well, I don't know, but I can ask if he is free." She walked briskly back into the auditorium.

While he waited, Sam felt his anxiety rising again. He dreaded seeing Howard in his current state, though he had come all this way.

Before he could decide whether to leave or stay, the woman re-entered the lobby and gestured for him. She led down a hallway and poked her head in a doorway, then motioned for him to enter. Howard was sitting at a table looking pale and exhausted. A clear plastic tube funneled oxygen to his nostrils from a small, wheeled tank. At the table with him a man and a woman were talking and pointing to a paper that lay on the table between them. Howard glanced up to see Sam but gave no sign of recognition.

Then Sam's attention was completely taken up by Julie's bright and happy face. "Howard!" she cried. "Howard, do you see who this is?" She took Sam's hand and led him to the table. "Howard, it's Sam! Can you believe it?"

Howard got out of his seat and carefully steered his way around the table. "Brother!" he cried and hugged accordingly. He smelled of nervous perspiration, but he was game to act his best.

"Were you here for the service?" Howard asked.

"Oh, yes."

"What did you think?"

"You were magnificent," Sam said. "You've become a great preacher."

"Really? You liked it?"

They agreed to have lunch together. First, however, Howard needed to sit down to catch his breath, and then he and Julie had a long back-and-forth about where to go. They settled on a nearby Denny's. Sam was not a fan of Denny's; he had hoped for some local cuisine, maybe Mexican, but nobody asked him. He followed them in his car.

At the restaurant, Howard studied the gigantic, plasticized menu, asking the waitress questions about ingredients, mulling over his options and asking Julie what she thought. Finally, they got lunch ordered and were left alone.

"Shall we make this Dutch?" Julie asked brightly.

Though it was a reasonable question, Sam found himself annoyed. He had come this long distance to see them; they had chosen the restaurant without consulting him. But the faint hint of exasperation that he allowed himself seemed not to register.

Howard leaned forward across the table, all business. "So what did you really think? Was it all right? How can it be improved?"

Before he could respond, Julie jumped in. "Howard, Charmante has to go. She acts like it's her show. Her taste is…. It's missing."

"Wait, Julie," Howard said. "I want to hear what Sam thinks. I want a real pastor's opinion."

"I'm not one anymore," Sam said drily.

"Once a pastor, always a pastor," Howard responded. "My dad was preaching sermons to the nurses the day he died."

"Honestly," Sam said, "I don't have any suggestions. It's a different style than I'm used to, but your sermon was extraordinary. Do you remember that we studied that passage the whole summer at camp?"

"That's true," Julie said. "I didn't think of that. What did you think of the drummer? This was our first time with him."

"He's very expensive," Howard said. "But good. At least, I think he is good. I'm just not sure he's worth what we're paying him."

"Let's not talk about money," Julie said.

"Why not talk about money?" Howard countered. "Sam understands. Any pastor understands."

Julie shook her head and looked pleadingly at Sam. "Everything is so difficult. We want it to be great, but we don't have the resources to pay for what we really need. Howard can't stand begging, and I don't blame him—it's so demeaning. I think we do a great job, but everything comes from asking for favors. We can't just go get a new microphone. No, we have to ask somebody to sponsor it. Or borrow one from the musicians. It's mortifying. But you understand this."

He didn't, but he wouldn't say so.

"You have to understand," Howard said, "we never asked for this situation. I became pastor of a dinky little failing Baptist church that was on the brink of disappearing. All I wanted was to preach and minister to a handful of people. It just exploded. We didn't plan any of it. God did everything. But at this size and scale, you've got momentum. People are coming full of hunger. You've got to keep it going, but you don't have the resources to feed the monster. Some of our friends have the money to make it easy for us. But will they? I guess that's why they have so much: they don't give it away. Not even to old friends who are doing ministry."

"Sometimes," Julie said with a scowl that didn't suit her, "it makes you think back on Mount of Olives and wonder whether any of it was real."

"Wait," Sam said. "Who are we talking about?" He wondered if he was one of the disappointing people, even though they had never asked him for anything.

"I don't want to get into names," Howard said. "But I'm sure you can think of Randy. He's worth millions. And Mindy, too. They both made a mint from that company he started."

"Really?" Sam said. "I knew Randy had some money, but Mindy?"

"Oh, she's loaded."

* *

Afterward, in the car, Sam blamed himself for not changing the tone. He had flown halfway across the continent hoping for the renewal of a friendship and a chance to explore his own frustrated psyche. But he didn't know how to break into the squalid dribble of unhappy ministry-as-business talk, all about money and equipment and feeling unappreciated.

He was on the freeway now—a colorless, frantic strip of wasteland, a hateful part of California. On impulse, Sam pulled off at the next exit and set out exploring, trying to escape the monotonous landscape. Mountains were nearby, revealing themselves as ghostly outlines through the smog. He went looking for a road that would take him to them, turning on ranch roads that led in the direction of the hills. One and then another reached a dead end.

His mind was stuck on his reactions. Why was he envious? When Howard's book had won a prize, he never felt envy. Why now?

He should have said something. He should have said that the gimmicks and the showbiz turned his stomach. Pretending everything was fine was unfair to Howard. The preaching was magnificent but encased in such flash it became a performance—nothing more.

Sam finally found a way into the mountains—a road that wound through horse ranches and elegant ranchettes. There was no shoulder to park on, so he didn't stop. The foothills were arid, covered with scrub, and it wasn't clear that the wandering road would reach anything note-worthy, but he kept going. It was good to explore. He couldn't remember the last time he had done so.

The road opened to a wide, sandy field with a horse corral and plenty of room for pickups and horse trailers. A couple of passenger cars were parked in the slim shade under two stumpy eucalyptus trees that had once been topped. Sam got out to look around. On the far side of the corral, he came to a sign identifying the Lost Ranch Recreation Zone; rules and regulations were posted (no fires, no alcoholic beverages after 6:00 pm) along with a simple map. Another, smaller sign read simply, "No Go Trail, 5.4 miles."

The trail ran along a dry stream: sand and rocks and oaks and alders. A profusion of small yellow flowers flourished in the gravel. It was pretty country. He had lucked into it. Yet he felt nothing.

He had gone a couple of miles when he heard a trickling of water and discovered that the stream had come to life. In algae-scummed pools, jet-black tadpoles swarmed away from him. Taking a seat on a log, he breathed in the scene while wondering whether he should turn back. This was, perhaps, as good as it would get on this trail.

Why the envy? he asked himself again. It revealed a deep dissatis-faction in him. He wanted something more. He wanted to be somebody more.

2005

31
MINDY IS RICH

Mindy arrived home from work on a Monday, dressed in jeans and a men's shirt just as she had dressed in college in 1975. She still shared a small house with three young women who were her friends. But she was rich now.

She had sat in on a job interview today that made her reflect on it. The young man recognized Mindy's name when they were introduced. If he was as smart as he thought he was, he would have kept it to himself. It just popped out: he was incredulous that she was still working. "But you don't need to work," he said, "do you?"

The stock options she had received as part of her compensation at Randy's company, bits of ownership in a theoretical future, turned into tens of millions of dollars when the company was bought by a Swiss bio-chemical company. Until then, she had barely paid attention to those stocks. Gradually and then suddenly they turned into numbers she could hardly grasp. She could do anything now—vacation in Italy, wear designer clothes, or learn how to pilot her own airplane.

People treated her as though she had become something different. Sometimes they seemed attracted by her wealth, and sometimes repelled. Ridiculous either way, Mindy thought.

She poured a glass of water from the pitcher in the refrigerator and went outside to sit on the back patio. She could do anything, but she did not want to. The idea of moving into a bigger house alarmed her. That would throw her life into the air for no good reason. It was the same with her car, a Camry, which never broke down. She knew exactly where all the knobs and buttons were. What would be the advantage in a Mercedes?

She did worry sometimes about becoming reclusive. Here she was, all by herself, and perfectly happy.

Over the years she had worked her way up from office den mother to head of HR. That sounded impressive, but in her mind, it was still den mother except with more memos. She was the oldest woman in the office. The young employees tended to move on.

She didn't go out anymore. After Scott died it took her a year or more to find an equilibrium, and when she did, she found she didn't miss dating at all. She told Verity that if somebody could arrange a good marriage with guaranteed results, she would be interested, but that getting matched up with unknown men was exhausting to her as well as unproductive. Randy, who entertained quite a lot, sometimes tried to matchmake for her. Mindy took it in good humor. She went to the parties and talked to the engineers and divorced executives Randy introduced. Nothing stuck.

She should call Verity, she thought. Like clockwork every Friday, the two of them had a long talk on the telephone, and they often talked during the week as well.

Verity's appeal as a friend lay partly in the fact that she was always passionate about something. They discussed her daughter, Ivy, who had reached adolescence and considered her mother a complete idiot. Surely Verity would have some new outrage to tell her about Ivy, who had a boyfriend four years older than she and resisted the idea of coming home before midnight.

Another passionate topic was Orthodoxy. Verity was deeply absorbed not just in the mysteries of icons and liturgies, but also in the community that she found at St. Chrysostom's. She liked to talk about it, and Mindy was interested. *I really should visit there*, she thought.

I should call, Mindy thought, but the afternoon was very pleasant for sitting in the sun, and she didn't want to get up and go into the house.

So it came about that Mindy was completely unprepared when a co-worker rapped on her office door on Thursday morning and stuck his head in. He was a vice president for marketing, and at forty-two, he was one of the older managers in the company. Holding out a newspaper, he asked, "Did you see this?"

There was Verity's obit, as ordinary as mud. The picture looked to be a snapshot, and Mindy had to stare at it to be sure it was Verity. The rest of the obit, however, left her in no doubt that it described her friend. She had graduated from UC Berkeley and worked at SRV. She was survived by a daughter, Ivy. A service would be held at St. Chrysostom's.

"No, I didn't know," she said calmly while her life fell away from under her feet.

"That's your friend, isn't it?" the vice president asked. Mindy remembered, foggily, that she had told him about Verity at one of Randy's parties. He had been a good listener.

"Yes," she said. Mindy wanted to howl.

"Well, sorry to be the bearer of bad news," he said.

The obit, which he left behind, said nothing about cause of death. Mindy had talked to Verity last Friday, hadn't she? Or was it the week before? Had they missed each other last week? She couldn't remember. If Verity had been sick, she would remember that.

Mindy was thankful now that they had moved offices to a place where she could close her door. She called Verity's number and got the answering machine, with Verity's voice inviting her to leave a message. That made her cry. She dialed again, just so she could hear Verity's familiar, hesitating voice.

She laid her forehead on the cool glass of her desk. *Verity is dead.* It made no sense to her. How could Verity be dead? She felt sure that if she could dial the right number, her voice would come on the line.

She desperately wanted to talk to someone, but along with that strong impulse came the powerful realization that the person she yearned for was Verity. She could not go forward; she could see nothing.

Verity's death must have been sudden and unexpected, because otherwise she would surely have warned Mindy. But even that was uncertain. It seemed possible Verity had censored parts of her existence, not wanting the attention, not wanting to bother anyone. When Mindy pondered that, it seemed to her to be the most offensive possibility of Verity's death: that she had excluded Mindy, keeping her from sharing in whatever grief she was living. Thinking of that made her angry until she realized she was fantasizing and told herself to stop.

The obituary, cold and factual, read with all the emotion of a train timetable. It bore no fingerprint of a person who loved Verity. Who could have written it? Not Verity's mother, who was in a nursing home with dementia. Mindy craved knowledge, understanding. She would call Ivy if she knew how. Cass? Verity had told her more than once that she had very little communication with him. Mindy had no idea how to reach him anyway.

It was hallucinatory to sit at her desk, a rational, orderly space in an office dedicated to the control of nature, and to find that death had arrived unannounced and unregulated, finalizing, totalizing in its stopping of time. Life went on but not for Verity; her pendulum no longer swung. Mindy had not yet cried, and she felt no urge to do so. She had the stuffing knocked out of her and wanted to catch her breath.

It would not help to know what had happened. It would change nothing. Nevertheless.

It came to her that she could call the church. It had become the center of Verity's existence, and the service was to be there. Surely, they would know. She dialed information and was given a number, then dialed and got a female voice.

"Ah, Verity!" the woman said sadly. Mindy imagined her as elderly, plump, kindly. "Are you a friend? Or a relative?"

Verity had died of a sudden infection, she said. A small cut had become infected, and staph got into her bloodstream. "Nobody even knew that she was sick. The first we heard of anything, she had already gone."

"Was she in the hospital?" Mindy asked.

"Yes; apparently she called 911, but by the time they got her to emergency, the infection was raging and they couldn't pull her back. It happened very fast."

The words buried themselves in Mindy's heart. Yes, that was it: it happened very fast.

32

POISON IVY

The morning after Verity's funeral, Mindy went to church as she always did. She had attended this large, wealthy church for years, but today, looking around her, she saw its strangeness: choir in robes, organ, well-dressed people in pews, stained-glass windows.

Ordinarily, she listened to the well-crafted sermons intently. Today her thoughts wandered. With all that had happened the day of Verity's funeral, she was glad for a chance to think.

What had become clear, and what she was grateful for, was a better grasp of Verity. She had never taken Verity very seriously, she realized, and it appeared no one else had either. But Verity had been a very serious person.

That sounded stuffy, which Verity never was. It tore Mindy's heart that she would never again hear Verity dismiss herself with a laugh. She had found humor in many quirky corners, and most readily in herself. But Verity was serious because she had an aim. She wanted God, and she would bend heaven and earth for him.

I never saw that, Mindy thought. *I loved her for her simplicity, her humility, her humor, her lack of pretension, her willingness to ask any question. I barely noticed the center.*

* *

When Mindy got home, she found a note on the kitchen table: "Ivy" and a phone number.

She walked to her bedroom and changed out of her Sunday clothes, feeling intensely nervous, which annoyed her. Why should a fourteen-year-old girl affect her so? Then she went out to the kitchen and grimly dialed the number. Somebody answered with a grunt.

"Ivy?" she said. "I got a note that you called. This is Mindy, your mother's friend."

Whoever it was on the other end of the line said nothing.

"Ivy? Are you okay?"

"I'm fine. Do I sound sick?"

Mindy thought, *You buried your mother yesterday.* "No. I was just asking. What were you calling about?"

"Well, duh. You said if I needed anything."

"Yes. How can I help?" For the sake of Verity, she would persist; and she reminded herself that Ivy had reasons to be unhappy.

"I need a ride."

"Okay. I can help with that. When?"

"Oh, how about Christmas Eve."

"What?"

"I'm calling now. I don't need a ride next week."

"Okay, Ivy. I didn't know. Where do you need to go?"

"Walmart."

"Okay. I don't know where Walmart is, so you'll have to tell me how to go."

Mindy wrote down Ivy's address but didn't ask for directions; she felt that she held on to Ivy with only the slimmest of threads and it would be an impossible imposition to ask her to specify streets and freeways. Instead, Mindy found an old Thomas guide, located the address, and figured out how to get there.

The house was an undistinguished low-slung ranch, fronted by a scraggly lawn and a few starved bushes. Ivy sat on the front steps, dressed in black shorts with silver rivets, black fishnet stockings, high leather boots, and a black, tight-fitting pleather jacket. The day was cool, but she looked hot. When Mindy pulled up, Ivy got slowly to her feet, stretched, and strolled to the car. She was short and solidly built. Squatting down, she looked in the window as though inspecting Mindy. Her eyes appeared almost sealed shut with clumps of makeup.

"Let's go," Ivy said impatiently once she got in the passenger seat.

"Which direction?"

Ivy flipped her hand forward, and Mindy eased ahead.

"How are you doing?" she asked.

"I know you're my mom's friend and it's nice of you to give me a ride. You don't have to make conversation."

"But I want to. I want to make sure you're all right."

"And now you can see for yourself. Turn right."

Stung and puzzled, Mindy asked no more questions during the ten-minute drive to Walmart. "I'll wait in the car," she said after parking. "Do you need any money?"

Ivy hesitated, frowning. "Sure."

"How much?"

"Twenty?"

Ivy reminded her of some of her preschool four-year-olds who had to do it themselves. She needed a mother, even if she didn't want one. On her own at fourteen, she might be abused, offered drugs, or assaulted.

It is up to me, Mindy thought while staring into the bleakness of the parking lot. *But I will have to be very subtle. Ivy will spook.*

"What did you get?" she asked when Ivy returned.

"Just some stuff."

"What stuff?"

She pulled it out of the bag: Cheetos and a stick of deodorant.

Mindy lifted an eyebrow. "I can see why it was urgent." She was hoping for a smile but didn't get one.

"You said anything."

"I did. And I meant it. I still mean it. I loved your mom. I'm sure she would want me to help you out." Mindy almost said, "take care of you," but she caught herself in time.

When they got to the house, Ivy said, "I appreciate it," and began to get out of the car.

"You staying with friends?" Mindy asked. She knew she was at risk of going too far.

"Just some people," Ivy said and didn't look back on her way to the door.

Mindy leaned over to roll down the passenger window. "Hey, call again," she shouted, but couldn't be sure whether Ivy heard.

Several times that week she fingered the note with Ivy's phone number, considering calling, but she knew that pushing her way into Ivy's life could cut the thread. She had a bad feeling about Ivy's situation, but if she called the police, they would only make it worse. County social services might be a better bet, but they would want to know where the father was, and she didn't know if getting Cass involved was a good idea. For all she knew, he could be an abuser. It was too risky, until she knew more.

All she could think to do was to wait.

A week later the phone rang. Mindy answered but got no response to her hello. "Ivy?" she said, taking a guess. "Ivy?"

The voice was very faint. "Can you come get me?"

* *

She came into the house with nothing to say, as if in a daze. One cheek carried a four-inch purpling bruise, and her left arm hung by her side unused. Ivy had lost all her sass. "Can I take you to the doctor?" Mindy asked, but Ivy just shook her head. Similarly, she did not want to contact her dad. Mindy fed her some macaroni and cheese and tucked her into bed.

In the morning, Mindy tiptoed in and out of her bedroom getting ready for work. Ivy, flopped across her bed, did not stir. Rolling up her sleeping bag from the floor, Mindy quietly closed the door behind her. Sitting at the kitchen table with a bowl of Cheerios, she composed a long note listing all the food and drink that was available. "Call me if you need me and I'll come home."

She spent the day worrying about Ivy and what she would do with her. She need not have worried. Walking in the door after work, she found Ivy watching TV in her bedroom. Somehow, she had got a portable set and figured out how to hook it up to cable. All the lights were off in the room and the blinds were pulled. When Mindy asked Ivy if she needed anything, she said, "Do you have any beer?"

Mindy might have laughed but nothing was funny with Ivy. Mindy left her alone, hoping for some conversation over dinner.

She knocked on the door. "Dinner!" Ivy didn't come.

Mindy knocked again. "Not hungry!" Ivy shouted in a belligerent tone.

"I hope we get to meet her sometime," her housemate Bettina said.

"She just lost her mother," Mindy said. "She might need time."

After dinner she invited Ivy to watch TV with the rest of them in the living room, but all Ivy said was, "I'm fine." She was still watching her own TV when Mindy got ready for bed, so Mindy situated herself on the living room sofa with a blanket pulled over her. Sometime in the early hours she awoke to noises in the kitchen. The refrigerator opened and closed, and she heard the soft metallic chimes of the silverware drawer. She got up and stood in the doorway.

"You want some light?" she asked.

"No."

"Can I join you?"

"Be my guest."

Mindy filled a water glass from the kitchen sink and sat down across from Ivy. In the dim light, she saw that Ivy had a container of cottage cheese that she was eating with a fork.

"You want anything to drink?"

"Sure, I'll have a beer."

Mindy ignored that. "Ivy, do you want to stay here? Because you're welcome, but I need to get another bed."

Ivy didn't answer, and it took Mindy some time to realize that she was weeping. She put a hand to touch Ivy's, but Ivy snatched it away.

Mindy replenished her water glass. "Ivy, what about school? Do you want to go to school here?"

"No."

She sat down opposite Ivy and took her two slender hands. This time Ivy did not pull them back. "I'll do whatever I can, Ivy. Of course, I'll give you time to get through this. But sooner or later you have to meet me halfway. You think about it. I'm not going to hurry you, but like I said, sooner or later."

At the time that seemed like a good thing to say, but later Mindy realized she had no idea what Ivy was going through. What had bruised her? Who had hurt her? She might have been raped. She might be pregnant. Maybe she had nightmares about an assault. Mindy couldn't imagine. Her life had been so tame.

So, she gave Ivy space. She invited her to dinner every night but made the invitation once and once only. Ivy never came. Observing what food she ate from the refrigerator, Mindy bought more, principally cottage cheese. She asked Ivy what she wanted from the grocery store but got no answer.

One night as Mindy positioned herself for sleep on the sofa, an eerie comparison came out of nowhere, landing on her brain. In a strange way Ivy brought back the presence of Verity, who could also be moody and silent and often preferred isolation over chatter. Making the comparison touched Mindy in the heart; her breath caught, and she thought she might cry. Though Mindy had never lived with Verity, she knew that

Verity suffered through long periods of depression, and that during such times she stayed in her room reading science fiction or watching old movies. Verity could also be extremely stubborn, and sometimes she saw the world through a dark filter.

Seeing similarities between Verity and Ivy made it easier for Mindy to wait and be patient.

One evening, Mindy went into her room to change shoes and got caught up watching a John Wayne western that she remembered from childhood. She stood for five minutes watching it and eventually sat down. Ivy said nothing, and Mindy calculated that nothing needed to be said. The next night she went into her room just after eight, thinking that was when some old movies started. This time she watched Cary Grant and Audrey Hepburn. After that, she made a point of watching every night. Ivy never commented, and Mindy refrained from any attempt to make conversation. She thought that was what Verity would have wanted.

Whether this had any impact on Ivy, Mindy couldn't say, but she herself grew more comfortable with the silence. She fell into a rhythm of watching old movies with Ivy, and Ivy seemed more at ease, even if she gave no sign of meeting Mindy halfway.

Then one day, Mindy came home and discovered that Ivy had left. She called out for her and got no answer. When she went through the bedroom looking for a note, she realized that the TV was gone. So was the suitcase Ivy had been living out of, stuffed and overstuffed with black clothing. So, Mindy eventually discovered, was some of her jewelry—a diamond ring and some gold earrings along with silver bracelets and necklaces, stuff inherited from her grandmother.

She looked through the kitchen, still hoping for a note. She called Ivy, hoping against hope that Ivy would pick up, but instead got a recording saying her number was disconnected. More than she had realized, Mindy had appropriated a hopeful view of Ivy, believing that enough patience and kindness would surely win her over.

When she told her housemates what had happened, they expressed sympathy, but it was obvious they found Ivy's departure a relief. They didn't appreciate living with somebody who never said hello.

Their point of view was easy to understand, but Mindy found herself unable to let Ivy go. Ivy was just fourteen. Mindy felt she couldn't just release her dear friend's daughter to the forces of the world.

By calling Verity's church, Mindy got the phone number of a priest who knew both Cass and Verity. He didn't know them well—he didn't realize they had a fourteen-year-old child—but he had a phone number for Cass.

When she heard Cass's voice on the line, Mindy felt deep relief. At least here was somebody to share the burden.

"Hey, that's really nice of you," Cass said when he heard that Ivy had been staying with her. "I really didn't know where she was."

"But Cass, you still don't know, do you?"

"Well, no. She's very independent, you know." He gave a little chuckle.

Cass spoke easily and lightly about Ivy. Though perfectly friendly in a matter-of-fact way, he acted like Ivy was a distant connection, maybe a niece he had met at family gatherings.

"Do you know how to contact any of her friends?" Mindy asked. "If you give me a start, I'll try to follow up."

Cass sighed. "I kinda know them. There's a girl named Anna. Another one who's older named Carolina." But when Mindy questioned him, he didn't know their last names; he didn't even know what school they attended. He was, in fact, vague about what school Ivy attended.

"Oh, yeah, that school of hers, I don't think they get her. I mean, Ivy is hard to handle. I don't think they clicked, you know what I mean?"

"I'm glad you brought that up," Mindy said, trying to keep her impatience at bay. "Is there a counselor or a vice principal or anybody I could talk to? Somebody who knows Ivy?"

"Oh, no, I don't think anybody in particular. You can just call the school and they'll direct you."

"Okay, I'll do that. What's the name of her school? I don't think I've ever heard."

There was a long silence, of a kind that, coming from chattering Cass, was ominous. "It's in the San Jose school district," he said. "I'm certain of that. I'm sure if you call them, they'll connect you."

Mindy hung up with a sinking heart. It made her feel greater pity for Ivy, whose own father had no idea where she went to school. She had lost her mother and was alone in the world.

As a last resort, Mindy drove to San Jose, to the house where she'd first met Ivy. She had long since forgotten the directions, so she found it only after several false tries—a shabby, non-descript house. Even from across the street, it looked empty.

On the front porch, she found flyers from yard-work companies offering their services. One purple flyer stuck in the screen door had been there long enough for its color to fade. Mindy knocked nevertheless. She knocked again. Then she went back to her car, feeling desperate and frustrated.

2006

33
HOWARD IN THE BIG TIME

Howard sprawled inert in a reclining chair in the living room, where Julie refreshed his water glass and brought him snacks. He wanted chips but rarely got them; Julie favored carrot strips, sometimes with a small dish of ranch dressing to dip them in.

He had preached three services on Sunday, investing his whole heart. Monday was dedicated to his recovery. Julie knew to baby Howard on Mondays.

Howard had recently been featured in *Spirit Magazine*, touted as "Southern California's most innovative megachurch pastor." Several publishers had approached him, asking whether he planned to write a book. One had taken him to lunch at an expensive restaurant and offered a dynamic writer to work with him. That made Howard laugh: did they think he didn't know how to write?

Even though it all went swimmingly, Julie felt wary. The more success Howard experienced, she noticed, the more uneasy he felt. When he first took up the church he had been relaxed and casual, but now he was paranoid about criticism, and he jumped all over anyone who made a mistake. It worried Julie, who was carefully attuned to his emotional state.

Late that morning the phone rang, and she let Howard answer it. From the kitchen she could hear an unusual attentiveness in his voice. He didn't say much, other than "Yes," and "That sounds great."

When he hung up, Howard promptly called her into the living room. "Julie," he said. "That was the 650 Club. They want me to come out to be on the show."

The 650 Club was a cable television program. The host, Harvey Cold-field, was famous for putting religious broadcasting on the map and keeping it there. Julie was familiar with Coldfield from walking through the room when Howard was watching. Howard, she knew, got a kick out of him. He said he watched the show for research purposes, but she wasn't sure whether he was joking.

"Are you going to do it?" Julie asked.

"Of course!" His eyes seemed strangely besotted. "Julie, this is the most popular show in the world."

She knew that wasn't true. Howard was exaggerating.

"When do they want you to come?"

"This week! Thursday. We'll have to fly on Wednesday, won't we?"

"You want me to go?"

"Julie, of course! You can't miss this. It's our chance."

She sat down, still slender and graceful. "Our chance for what, Howard? You aren't selling a book." She genuinely wanted to know why he found this so thrilling. In his excitement, he could barely enunciate his words.

Howard stared at her. "If you don't understand, I don't know how to explain it to you. Julie, this is the biggest show in America. Millions of people watch it."

"You said that. It sounds great. But you know, Howard, I'd just be in the way. Let's save the money. You go."

He wouldn't allow it. He insisted she get on the phone to their travel agent and buy two tickets, and then call the 650 Club to give their arrival time and ask whether someone would pick them up. It took some time to find the right person, but she was very nice and said their plane would be met.

"Do you have a hotel recommendation?" Julie asked.

The woman gave a little cough. "You can stay at the Foundation Inn unless you have another preference. It's complimentary."

Howard was jubilant when she told him that. He asked Julie to look at his navy-blue suit to make sure it was clean. Then he began discussing what shirt and tie he would wear. This was totally unlike Howard. Ordinarily, she put out his clothes for him and he barely seemed to notice. Now, however, he argued with himself about one color scheme or another and tried to involve Julie. She said she needed to make lunch and left him.

Over tuna fish sandwiches he told her—commanded her—to call all their friends and tell them what was happening.

"Why?" she said. "I doubt they watch the 650 Club."

"They'll want to see me," he said. "They won't want to miss it."

For two days, he was like that. She had his suitcase packed on Monday, but all day Tuesday he went over it, having her take out one item and replace it with another, then fussing over both choices. He kept a yellow legal pad by his chair, jotting down thoughts about what he wanted to say.

"I'm sure they want it to sound spontaneous," Julie said. "Just a regular conversation."

He exploded. "Of course! But you have to be prepared! Do you want me to get on there and just drool?"

"Howard, you're not going to drool."

"It's like stand-up," he said. "It sounds off-the-cuff but it's not."

"I'm sure you'll do fine."

Getting to the airport on Wednesday, he was so tense she thought he would blow apart. "Be careful, be careful!" he shouted in alarm when she changed lanes.

"Relax," she said. "It's called traffic. Perfectly normal."

"You don't understand; if we got in an accident and missed our flight, I don't know what I would do."

In the plane, Howard slept, for which Julie was grateful. The extra stress could aggravate his lung disease. She lived in constant fear that his health would deteriorate, that he would die. Howard thought of that possibility, too, she knew, but they rarely spoke of it to each other.

At the Charlotte airport, they were met by a blond young thing with a Deep South accent. She introduced herself as Kate and said, when asked, that she was a student at the university, studying media relations. She seemed awed by Howard, though it came out she didn't know who he was. She apologized for not doing her research. "I didn't know I was going to get to meet you until this morning," she said. "It's been so busy." The reason she revered Howard, apparently, was simply that he was a guest on the 650 Club.

The Foundation Inn was luxury accommodations with colonial pillars in front, hardwood floors, vast Persian carpets in the lounge, and a classic, sleek look to their room. It excited Howard to be indulged with such splendid surroundings. Kate escorted them and their luggage, including Howard's oxygen machine. She asked whether they would like a tour of the university and seemed relieved when Howard said no. "What time are we on tomorrow?" he asked, and Kate said she would pick them up at eight.

"You see?" Howard said as soon as they were alone. "You wouldn't want to miss this."

Julie thought to herself that she would gladly miss this, but she wasn't sure that Howard could manage without her. He was fragile, and she had to protect him.

* *

In the morning, Kate rang their room from the lobby five minutes early. Julie was still applying mascara and didn't move as quickly as Howard thought she should. He kept calling her as he stood in the door. "You go ahead," Julie said. "I'll be down in a minute." Howard said a few accusatory words, but he waited, steaming. It was tense and quiet in the elevator.

Kate seemed anxious on the short drive to the studio. Julie felt sorry for her, stuck with chauffeuring people she thought were important even though she had no idea why.

In the lobby they were asked to show ID and fill out a form. A phone call was made from the desk and in a few moments, two young men in sports coats and slacks arrived to take them inside. Kate gave Julie a kiss on the cheek, saying, "Good luck!" as though she were sending them off on a journey.

One of the men asked, "You're Julia?" as he led her through a hallway.

"Julie," she said.

"Well, you must be very proud."

"Oh, of course."

A door opened and she was led into a small room with a window looking onto the studio. That consisted of a fake living room with an overstuffed tan sofa, a matching chair, side tables and lamps, and deep-green leafy plants. In a half-circle around the furniture, men and women lounged by massive television cameras. Julie could hear them talking but the sound, coming through small speakers set overhead, was tinny.

"I'm soundproof?" she asked her guide, who had taken a seat on one of a row of black Naugahyde chairs.

He nodded. "You could have a crying baby in here and they wouldn't hear it."

Julie studied the room. "Where is Howard?" she asked. "My husband?"

"Oh, he's probably meeting Dr. Coldfield. Just a handshake, really. Then they'll put him in the green room until he's ready to come on."

The idea of Howard left alone troubled Julie. "I could sit in there with him," she said.

"It's better you're in here. Most people enjoy it. Have you ever seen a TV show?"

"No. Not really."

He pointed across the set. "See over on the other side—the glass? It looks like the window in a limo. You can't see in. You see? That's where the producer is, where they control the sound and the cameras. The Holy of Holies, we call it."

"And where is Dr. Coldfield?"

"He'd be in his office. Unless they're still working on the makeup."

"Will I get to meet him?"

He glanced over at her and gave a smile. "Probably not. He'll be gone before you get out of this room. You a big fan?"

"Not really. My husband is."

"He must be excited to meet him."

"Oh, he is."

They had run out of small talk and sat in silence. "You don't have to stay in here with me," Julie said, which drew another smile.

"It's fine," he said. "If you have any questions, I'll try to answer them."

Julie felt tightness in her abdomen, like a premonition of nausea. Ordinarily she felt very relaxed in situations that would make other people anxious, but for some reason, the studio produced a sense of dread. As though he read her mind, the man glanced at her and asked, "Can I get you something to drink?"

She shook her head. "I'm fine."

"Most people get nervous. Has your husband been on TV before?"

"I'm not sure. Not that I remember."

"It really gets to some people."

Julie gave her head a quick shake. "He loves an audience. He doesn't get stage fright."

The man shrugged. "Television is different. I don't know why."

They sat in silence, staring into the studio. Nothing was happening. Then Julie noticed a slight quickening of attention among the cameramen, and a short, graying man walked onto the set, accompanied by a very slender, very well-dressed woman in very high heels, who stood a foot or more over him. They were looking together at a clipboard. Suddenly Julie recognized the familiarity of the man's head.

"That's him!" she exclaimed. "Isn't that him?"

"That's the man."

"He's so short!"

For the first time her companion's face fell into what seemed like a genuine smile. "Don't let him hear you say that."

Their glassed-in room had a small TV monitor suspended from the ceiling, and it now blinked on with a picture of the set. Harvey Coldfield was escorted over to the chair. He sat talking, an ingratiating smile on his face, while the tall woman pulled at his suit lapel, picked something off his collar, and touched his tie. When she backed away, Coldfield was on the TV, his face taking its familiar shape, with puffy, pink cheeks and a smooth brush of graying hair. He was a handsome man, Julie thought, who could easily pose as a grandfather in a TV ad. Funny to think of him as short. On TV he looked full-size.

Theme music began, and a disembodied voice introduced the 650 Club and its host. On the TV screen, Coldfield's face grew larger. Disembodied applause covered the theme music, and Coldfield began to speak in professional, self-assured, rounded tones with a hint of a Southern accent. Julie was so caught up in simultaneously watching the TV screen and the stage that she didn't pay attention to what he was saying. She remembered that he began every show with a monologue about the day's news. Julie caught that he was talking about cow slaughter in India: apparently Muslims were persecuted because they ate beef. Cows were sacred in India, Julie remembered, but she had never heard that Muslims had anything to do with it.

Coldfield also said something about a big vote in the Senate on the defense bill, which would give our troops a salary boost. "If that concerns you, you just might want to let your congressman know. Or your senator, actually, since this is up to the Senate now."

Smoothly changing subjects, he stressed that he had a great treat in store for them: Jenny Stratnor! The disembodied applause came on at her name. Julie had never heard of Jenny Stratnor, but apparently that put her in the minority. Jenny was going to share her experiences raising an autistic son. "It's quite a story," Coldfield said. "You won't want to miss it. We'll also hear from a young pastor in Southern California who is experiencing a huge revival. Thousands are coming to Jesus, and he'll explain why." They went to a commercial.

The TV screen was blank while the commercial played. Coldfield sipped something from a glass offered by the woman in high heels. She said a few inaudible words. Julie felt let down that Howard had second billing and his name was not mentioned, but nevertheless, she watched with great interest. Jenny Stratnor came on to great fanfare, kissed Coldfield on the cheek, and proceeded to sing, accompanied by her own guitar. She had on a filmy lime-green dress with spaghetti straps, and she moved about with grace and confidence. Her talent was obvious. She was a professional. After one song, she took a seat on the sofa and proceeded to share about her son Ryan. Tears came when she described his diagnosis.

"And Jenny, I have to ask you—did you pray?"

She blinked her eyes. "Oh, Harvey, we prayed and prayed. Our hearts just broke."

"But no miracle?"

"Harvey, we saw so many miracles! I could talk to you all day about how God answered our prayers. He just drew us into his love. It was so powerful, I don't know how to describe it. To me, that's the true miracle. And I *know* that Ryan will be healed. I'm still praying for complete healing. I *know* it will come. I just hope it comes while I'm still here."

"But you'll see it in heaven," Coldfield said.

"Oh, I will. I know I will."

She had written a book, which Coldfield held up to the camera. You could order it at the 800 number or make a gift to the 650 Club and get it free. They went to a commercial.

Now Julie felt her nerves, the tightening of her throat. It was completely unlike her to worry about Howard this way. She was desperately nervous for him, and she feared that he might be so too, given how tense he had been.

He came on like a movie star—relaxed, golden. To her surprise, Julie teared up. He was, at last, getting his due. She felt glad that she had come to see this.

The rapport with Coldfield was immediate; the two men seemed so comfortable together. Coldfield said he understood they were seeing a revival in their church and asked Howard to what he attributed it.

Howard shook his head as though in wonder. "There's such a hunger for Jesus. People hear that something is happening at our little church, and they come out of curiosity, but when they hear us talking about Jesus, they're overcome by it. We don't have to stoke their hunger. All we do is put out the food."

"Ah, that's so good to hear," Coldfield said, leaning back and almost chortling. "A hunger for Jesus. Is this young people?"

"Young people, yes, but all ages. They just come because they hear that something is happening."

"Well, what do they hear? Do they hear of miracles?"

"Miracles, of course. Jesus is a miracle worker, and that's what we see him doing."

"Howard, I think you have experienced miracles yourself. You were telling me something backstage before the show began. Can you share that?"

Howard smiled so broadly. "I'm a walking miracle, Harvey. Ten years ago, I was diagnosed with a terrible lung disease. The doctors said I had less than a year to live, and there was nothing they could do to help me. I was popping pills, and I had to carry oxygen with me everywhere. I thought my time had come, and I was at peace with that. I was ready to see Jesus! But then the Lord spoke to me and said, 'Just pray.' I prayed. The elders of my church came and prayed. And I was healed! Just healed!"

"You're completely well?"

"Completely! As good as new. That was eight years ago. It happened just when I was first joining my church. It was just a small church, almost ready to dissolve, and they asked me if I could help them. I thought I didn't have much time to live, but I might as well do what I could for as long as I had. Since then, thanks be to God, we've grown and grown. It's a miracle church."

Coldfield took this in with easy enthusiasm. "That is just so very exciting, Howard. It's something we see all the time on the 650 Club, isn't it? Can you share any more? I'm sure you're not the only one to experience Jesus' miracle power."

"You want the truth?" Howard asked. "We are overrun with sick people. They come because they are desperate, looking for Jesus, looking for healing. We had a virgin birth. A young woman who got married in our church, but she and her new husband couldn't consummate the marriage. They tried, they really tried."

"I hope this is okay for a family show," Coldfield said with a chuckle.

"Oh, sure," Howard said. "We don't need to go into any details. They came to me for counseling, and truthfully, I didn't know how to help them. I told them to go to a doctor. They said they had already done that. It just wasn't happening. So, I prayed for them, and I asked God to miraculously help them. I laid hands on them and anointed them with oil and then sent them home. Next thing I knew, she was pregnant. When I heard the news, I felt great. I assumed they had finally managed to have a normal marital relation. But she came and told me no. The doctor who told her she was pregnant was extremely puzzled. He said, 'I don't know how this happened. You're still a virgin.' She said, 'I don't know how it happened either.' She came to see me, and I said, 'It's a miracle. Praise God.'"

Coldfield loved that story. He could hardly believe it. "And where is the young lady today?"

"Oh, she's in church every Sunday, with her husband and her little boy. She'll be there this Sunday when I get back."

"And the other members of the church know?"

"Some do. But I don't publicize it. A thing like that, you want to keep it private. Imagine how the little boy would feel when he got older."

Coldfield laughed and laughed. "People would think he was Jesus!" he sputtered.

* *

Initially, when Howard started talking about miracles, it made Julie happy. Howard sometimes lapsed into intellectualism when he was trying to impress people, and Julie knew that wouldn't work on this show. If Howard came off as some kind of professor, Coldfield would lose interest. When they began to talk about Jesus and miracles, she knew that wasn't going to happen.

Her comfort soon fell apart. Unsettled by Howard's exaggerations about his own health, she could hardly believe it when he launched into Verity's pregnancy. She had known him to exaggerate, but this was outright lying. She found herself longing for the show to end, for the lying to stop.

Finally, it did. And what was she going to say to him?

Howard would be a case. His guilt could make him nasty and offensive. It could plunge him into despair.

Or, it was possible he might be invigorated that he had so pleased Harvey Coldfield.

* *

Mindy was watching. She had never seen the 650 Club, but Julie had left a message saying that Howard was very anxious for her to see the show, so she had noted the time.

Initially, she thought she was factually out of touch, that she had not been told of Howard's return to full health. But then she recognized that Howard was telling Verity's story in a mutated form. She began to cry. Big, wet tears streaked down her cheeks. She was thinking of Verity, who had shown so much courage. All her life Verity had been overlooked and taken for granted, and now her story was being twisted into something very different from the truth. It felt like an assault.

Before Howard was done, Mindy rose blindly from her chair and found her way to the kitchen, where she got a glass of water from the tap. It was an instinctual reaction, born of a need to do something, anything. Leaning over the sink, she gathered herself.

What would make Howard do that? Did he harbor some resentment from long ago? Or did he do it just for the publicity? She had known Howard for a long time. *He is a show-off*, she thought, *very talented but narcissistic.*

But why should he do that? He had published a prize-winning book, and he pastored a booming church. Wasn't that enough?

Going back into the living room, she dumped herself onto the sofa, holding her water glass with both hands. What, she wondered, would Verity have made of Howard's misappropriation of her story? It was easy to picture her leaning forward, eager and shy, making gnomic remarks, then releasing a short giggle. Verity, she thought, would be bemused; she would shrug with her skinny shoulders and treat it as a bit of humor, an *amuse bouche* of the mind.

Did Verity even have an ego? She must have. She must have felt Cass's rejection, and then her daughter's. In fact, Mindy remembered with a jerk, Verity had called her once, miserable about Cass. But the next time they saw each other, the gripe had vanished. She didn't hold anything against him.

It floored Mindy, to consider that lack of pride. Or perhaps it was not a lack. Perhaps grace overflowed. If so, it was like nothing she had ever experienced.

* *

Sam was also watching, splayed out in a comfortable reclining leather seat in his living room. He had not really wanted to see Howard on this show, but almost against his own will, he switched it on.

The 650 Club was cheesy and manipulative, loud and bright. It was easy to see why people watched it. When Howard came on, Sam was pleased to see how easily he adapted to the ambiance. He didn't look nervous; he seemed happy and relaxed. Then Howard began talking about miracles, and as though a switch was flipped, Sam began to resent him. No, *no, no,* he thought, because he wanted to be over his jealousy, and he had thought that he was. This was a new provocation, making up miracle stories that skewered his friends.

The moment seemed so grievous, he had to pray—but how? With what words? "Lord Jesus Christ, Son of God, have mercy on me." He had heard it before; he had probably prayed it before. Now, it seemed the only prayer possible. Sitting in his armchair, he repeated it, then took a deep breath and repeated it again. Through the rest of the day, over dinner with his wife, while staring at a book, he silently continued the prayer, even in his bed, waiting for sleep.

34

THE TRUTH AND NOTHING
BUT THE TRUTH

Harvey Coldfield did not linger after the show was over. Howard had anticipated at least a short afterglow as he said farewell, but Coldfield was gone before Howard quite realized he was going. Someone in the production team gave a thanks and a firm handshake. While Howard waited for more affirmation, Kate appeared and asked brightly if he was ready to go. She led him outside the building to where Julie was waiting and went off to get the car.

"How about that?" Howard said jovially, willing himself to ignore Julie's stony face. "Did you get to see the whole thing?

She only nodded.

What on earth, Howard asked himself, had he done wrong?

The car pulled up and Howard opened the door for Julie, then went around to get in himself. During the short drive he concentrated on Kate, who wanted to know how he had felt meeting Coldfield. Julie did not speak, which was very unlike her.

In the elevator, he asked, "What's wrong?"

She looked at him with an expression he could not read. Anger? Pity? Contempt? It panicked him, because Julie was the foundation of his world, always supporting him.

"I don't get it. Why won't you talk to me?" She shook her head and pointed cryptically toward the door.

Neither one said anything as they made their way down the corridor to their room. Once inside, Julie turned on him with a savage look. "You lied, Howard. You lied to people all over America. All over the world, I suppose. And I told our friends to watch, and if they did, they all know that you lied. What is wrong with you?"

"What? What are you talking about?"

"Oh, come on. You know what."

"No, I don't. Really. I don't have any idea."

"You're completely healed. And we've had so many miracles in our church, we've even had a virgin birth."

"What?" Howard's thoughts swirled as he tried to grasp what Julie was saying. He slowly realized that she referenced his enthusiasm about miracles. He hadn't lied; he wanted Coldfield to know that God was doing amazing things. Of course it was impressionistic; that is how you talk on TV when you only have a few minutes to get your point across.

"I have been healed. That's no lie. The doctor said I had five years to live, and it's been ten. If that isn't a miracle, what is?"

She pursed her lips and shook her head. "And the completely healed man carries oxygen with him everywhere he goes."

"That's petty," he said. "The big truth is that I'm alive. I give God all the credit."

"And the virgin birth? To a woman in our church? You were telling Verity's story, weren't you? Unless I missed a second virgin birth."

"Well of course it was Verity. I had to change a few details."

"Why?"

"Julie, that's what you do. To protect people. You don't want strangers poking around in their lives. It's very sensitive subject matter."

"Howard, she's dead. Nobody can poke around in her life."

"Well, what about her daughter? What about her husband?"

"They're divorced. Anyway, I don't believe you. You needed some miracle stories and you just made it up. What do you think the people in our church will think?"

"They won't think anything. They'll be proud that their pastor was on the 650 Club."

"What about our friends? Who you wanted me to call so they could tune in! You think they'll be proud? When they heard you lying about the woman they all loved?"

"Look, I loved her too! More than you ever did." He was almost shouting now. He had never seen Julie like this.

Between his wounded innocence and her savage prosecution, they got nowhere. Howard flopped on the mini-sofa. He was aghast that on this, his most wonderful day, his own wife was attacking him.

He tried everything to allay her. Humor was a complete mistake; it only made her more furious. She wouldn't listen to his explanations. She didn't want to talk at all, really, because she had already made up her mind. Back she went, time and again, to her fundamental screed: you lied. Howard thought it was crazy, and as it went on, it began to scare him. He was used to floating along on his own self-confidence, with Julie cheering him on. What was she likely to do? She might sabotage him. It wouldn't take much. In his current state of health, he needed her very much, and it wasn't going to get any better.

They had to break it off when Kate called from the lobby saying she was ready to take them to the airport. Their argument had obliterated any sense of time, and they had forgotten all about their flight. Julie scurried to pull their suitcases together while Howard used the minutes to breathe some oxygen. Feeling shaky, he asked Julie if they could wait until tomorrow to fly.

"We can't afford that," she snapped. "Since you're completely healed, you can get on a plane."

He meekly went along. Neither one spoke during their trip to the airport, and not even Kate could find much to say. Julie managed their check-in while Howard sat numbly on a nearby bench; she led the way to their gate and found two adjacent seats in the waiting area.

"Are they going to feed us on this flight?" Howard asked. Julie shrugged. "Does that mean no?" Howard asked plaintively. Julie wouldn't even answer. "Look at me," he said. She refused.

The flight to Ontario required a change in Phoenix. Julie navigated them through the airport and onto the second plane without a word spoken. Trying hard, Howard made several pleasantries as they wound their way through the long, crowded concourse. "I like this airport," he said. "It feels airy." A short time later: "Ah! The scent of Cinnabon!" He got no response. All the walking wore him down, and he thought he was a very good sport to keep going uncomplainingly, but Julie didn't acknowledge him.

He couldn't understand it. She had never acted like this before. When they got settled in their narrow airplane seats, he made up his mind to go the second mile. Placing his hand on top of hers, he said, "I guess I need to apologize."

"For what?"

He was surprised by the response. "I've done something wrong, and I should apologize."

"Howard, what did you do wrong?"

He froze at her hostile tone. "I don't know. You say I lied, but I didn't. It's not lying to change a few details to preserve anonymity."

She stared at him like a snake ready to strike. He had never seen her that way.

"I don't know where this is coming from," Howard said. "Why are you behaving like this?"

Gently, she removed his hand from hers, then slowly raised her book and continued reading.

"Why won't you listen? I'm trying to apologize."

Without raising her eyes from her book, she said, "You can apologize when you find something you're sorry for."

After that, she would not engage him, not look at him, respond to his questions, or even tell him to be quiet. He tried to talk to her every half an hour or so; she would not answer. Just a few hours ago he had been on the 650 Club, trading stories with Harvey Coldfield, dazzling a gigantic watching audience. It seemed monumentally unfair, or beyond unfair, utterly irrational, inexplicable. Were others bizarrely angry at him? No, it was just Julie. She had singled him out.

The trouble was, he could not live without Julie. She was probably the only one reacting this way, but she was inescapable. Life without her was impossible. If she stayed hostile, who would take care of him?

Howard had a strong imagination, and he could picture himself wasting away and dying alone. *I don't have any income*, he reminded himself. What would he do for money if she left him? He would have to rely on the church, an idea he hated. He couldn't stand begging. And if his illness progressed so he couldn't preach?

He had no idea where her hostility came from. It had bounded up out of nowhere. Calm, placid water and then Jaws exploded into the air.

He could see himself declining, languishing, weakening. His fate took over his face, gripping his jaw in a paralysis of grief. Julie looked right at him. She certainly saw his agony, but she did not flinch.

* *

It was late at night by the time Julie unlocked the condo door. She paused on the doorstep, feeling the desert warmth. It was a great relief to be home. Howard was getting their suitcases out of the car, an act of penitence. She usually did such lifting for him, but tonight she padded onto the living room's plush carpet without looking back. When she thought of sitting next to him on the long flight and in the car ride home, she felt something like a spasm go through her gut. The man she had physically adored her entire adult life repelled her.

Howard staggered in with the suitcases, panting heavily, and she walked into the kitchen to water her houseplants. She had to clear him from her sight.

Six violets sat on her kitchen windowsill. She took her time filling the watering can at the sink and carefully dribbling water on each one. That Howard was self-centered was no new information. Further, she had known for many years that he had a loose understanding of truth, that his reality required a constant reshuffling according to his priorities. She admitted all that, so what was her problem? It was not simply that he had lied. The far deeper crime was that he had lied about Verity. All their Mount of Olives friends would feel it as a violation. They still shared some primitive, tribal bond forged that summer, and Verity was the epitome of their young, innocent former selves. He had screwed her. He had screwed her after she was dead.

Julie wanted to stop the world and think. What was she going to do?

Stuck in misery, she looked in the cupboard and found some pasta. They hadn't eaten since breakfast, and she was ravenous. The water boiled, and she dumped in the noodles. While she waited Howard came into the room.

"You're cooking?" he asked.

She grunted in reply. There was enough for both of them, but he would have to figure that out.

When the pasta was done and drained, she sprinkled parmesan on it and took her bowl into the living room to eat.

"What about me?" Howard asked. She made no answer. Eventually, the sounds of Howard making his own meal came through the door. Howard must have eaten at the kitchen table because he didn't join her. When Julie finished eating, she carried her bowl into the kitchen to rinse it in the sink. Howard was crouched over a bowl, stuffing noodles into his mouth. He didn't look up; Julie didn't say anything but went to bed.

In the morning, she woke up from a heavy sleep and realized that Howard's side of the bed was undisturbed. Padding into the living room, she found him lying on the sofa, his neck crooked against the armrest, his breathing heavy. *Poor man,* she thought; she had scared him. For the first time, Julie felt regret. In his own limited way, he was suffering, unable to understand what he had done wrong. After she'd spent so many years idolizing him, pity came to her as a novelty.

The drama of a public life had always been Howard's core appeal for Julie. He had been the charismatic boy orator, the word magician, then the writing meteor arriving from nowhere, winning prizes. She had loved him when he aspired to Hollywood fame (he still did) and even when he was dying onstage, making notes on his performance as he did it. No longer could she suspend disbelief, however. It was all a show: cardboard scenery, wooden swords.

She let him sleep and went into the kitchen to get breakfast. Over a bowl of raisin bran, she considered how the world had changed—how *she* had changed. No longer was she the vain, silly girl who had wanted Howard with the subtlety of a child demanding candy. Probably Howard's lust for fame was similar, only he had never outgrown it. He was still clamoring for candy. That, Julie thought, was the way to think about him, even though it implied condescension.

She was not sure how to love and live with a man who, she saw so clearly, was childish—worse than childish. Her eyes were open now, and there was no closing them again.

What was she going to do? As she sat staring down at the gleaming tabletop, the answer became awfully clear: she was going to forgive him. She had to. For a long time, perhaps fifteen minutes, Julie sat posed in her seat, thinking of that.

Then she got up and went into the living room. It was necessary to move quickly while she had the nerve; otherwise, she might not be able to stomach it. Howard was still fast asleep, breathing heavily. Julie sat down in an upholstered chair and watched him. This was the man she had committed her life to. It had proven an imperfect bargain. He was not the sterling character she had thought, and he had not committed to her with anything like the same acuity. Most likely he was incapable of that. Perhaps he did the best he could.

Falling forward onto her hands and knees, she crawled across the room and poked him. Waking slowly, he opened his eyes.

"Howard?" she said. "Are you awake? Can you listen?"

His eyes did not immediately focus. She could not tell whether he saw her or just stared.

"Howard? I want to talk to you, and it's important, so I need to know whether you can take it in."

"Yes," he said.

"You hear me."

"I hear you."

Gathering herself, she put out a hand to touch his arm. "Howard, I'm going to forgive you. I realize you don't understand what you did wrong, and I'm not entirely sure you can understand. I'm going to forgive you anyway, out of love. Grace, you know. Unmerited favor." She smiled at using the phrases that Howard knew so well. Did he understand them? She thought not.

She took a deep breath, blew it out, and went on, leaning toward him and patting his arm. "You don't have to do anything to earn my forgiveness. It's done. However, I am going to insist on some things. These are non-negotiable. You hear?"

Howard did not respond. It was hard to be sure that he understood her words. She decided she wouldn't badger him, though. If he didn't get it, she could repeat herself later.

"You can't ever go on the 650 Club again. Or any television show. Or any big conference. You stick to our church, where people know you. When you get away from that, you forget yourself.

"Also, you don't tell stories about people you know. Not unless you get permission first. You can't get permission from Verity, so you aren't ever going to tell stories about her. But it's the rule for everybody. You preach from the Bible, which you do marvelously, and skip the stories. You aren't going to talk about people unless they are characters in the Bible. Not ever.

"Howard." She gripped his forearm, pinching hard. "Those are my requirements. Do you hear me?"

35

FINDING IVY

The apartment building was gray stucco with a concrete porch that ran straight and flat before six front doors. There were parking spaces separated from the porch by a miserable weed-infested bed of juniper. Mindy had stopped by many times to pick up Verity or drop her off. The place reminded her viscerally of her friend, so absolutely disinterested in appearances.

From the street, she could see the eviction notice taped to the front door. She parked anyway, got out, and rang the doorbell. When she rang a second time, she thought she heard it reverberate in an empty room. But who could have emptied it? Maybe Cass, though it seemed unlike him to take such trouble.

Howard's TV appearance had shocked Mindy into thinking about Verity. That led her to wonder whether she had tried hard enough with Ivy. In the middle of the night, she had woken up thinking about it, and she couldn't get back to sleep. There had to be some way to find her. Of course, she had disappeared of her own free will, and most likely she wanted to keep it that way. But what if she didn't? What if she were sick, or hurt, or hungry? What if she thought she couldn't ask for help because she had stolen Mindy's jewelry?

It came to Mindy that she should look for Ivy at Verity's old apartment. Why had she not thought of that before? Ivy had spent most of her life there. It was logical to think she might return.

Immediately, the possibility expanded into conviction. She felt sure it was so. Nevertheless, lying in the dark, her mind wandered to other possibilities. A photo of Ivy, even an old one, might help; she could take it to stores near Verity's apartment to see whether they had any leads. She could even make a flyer to post on bulletin boards and telephone poles.

But then, in the morning, she hadn't taken time to make any flyers or find any photos. She had just come. For nothing, it seemed.

Before giving up, she rang one more time. As a parting gesture, she tried the door. To her surprise, the handle turned. The door stuck a little but swung open when she gave it a shove. "Hello?" she called. It looked like an accident, a door left open.

Mindy stood for a few moments in front of the open door. Looking in, she could see some furnishings: a chair, a TV. "Hello?" she called again. No one is here, she thought, but if she didn't check, she would spend the next week wondering what she had overlooked. Treading softly, she entered.

She had never actually been inside Verity's place. It looked very ordinary in the dim light, with plain wooden furniture padded with foam cushions. There were no pictures on the walls. She moved forward, knowing that she had no right to be there at all, and feeling the creepiness of invading the space of her dear dead friend.

Glancing in the kitchen, she found its cramped space as tidy as a motel kitchenette. How could that be? Was it possible that Verity had known she would not come back?

When Mindy entered the front bedroom, she immediately sensed the presence of someone. A chill ran through her. The blinds had been drawn, so she could not make out anything, but she stopped in the doorway and cleared her throat. "Hello?" she said. When a response came, a low, guttural sound, she almost jumped out of her skin.

For just an instant, she imagined that Verity lay in the bed. That frightened and elated her in equal portions, until she got a grip on her thoughts. Verity was dead.

"Ivy?" she said. "Is that you?"

"What do you want?" It was Ivy, all right. Mindy recognized the voice. She also recognized the sour, metallic smell of sickness in the room.

"I came to check on you. To see if you are okay."

There was no response.

"Can I take you home with me now?"

* *

Ivy was sick and depleted—probably dehydrated. Mindy nursed her, bringing meals and checking her fever while not saying much or asking any questions. Within a few days, Ivy seemed better, but she still declined to talk or to join in house meals. She did come out for television shows, since the portable set she had used in the bedroom never reappeared.

Mindy's housemates politely attempted to connect, but Ivy scowled and said nothing. They had returned to the earlier stalemate.

The next week, a heavy storm blew in off the Pacific, chilly with soaking rain. Mindy always felt the cold penetrating her bones, especially with the first rain. She turned on the heat in their little house and still felt the weather looming like a hostile guest. It triggered memories of her childhood, of wet shoes and a trail of moisture streaking the tiles at the doorway of every classroom. She had not yet asked Ivy about going to school, a fact that was beginning to trouble her. Ivy was like a snappy dog that she watched warily, afraid of its bite.

Their situation couldn't go on like this forever. Most likely Ivy would leave again—a possibility Mindy dreaded. If she stayed, they would have to find a more realistic way to coexist. Mindy had not yet mentioned the stolen jewelry. The stuff didn't matter, but she couldn't pretend that nothing had happened.

Yet she did. Another week passed. Mindy went to work every day and came home to find her charge unmoved. Ivy lived and slept in sweats, which did not lend themselves to Goth. When Mindy looked at her, she saw a child, vulnerable as a peach. Her preschoolers had been like that; you could see right through them even when they threw a tantrum.

In that liminal space, uncertain of everything, Mindy found herself thinking of Verity quite often—not only because Ivy was her daughter, but because in some poetic way, Verity's life rhymed with this uncertainty. Verity didn't plan; she responded. Her reactions were instinctive and emotional, despite her work as a programmer. Mindy missed Verity. She tried to imagine what Verity would say about Ivy, what she would do. But Ivy had moved out on Verity, too; she brought no answers.

It hurt to think what Howard had done to Verity. Some people might brush the offense aside. He couldn't hurt Verity in the grave. But it was a heartless act nevertheless. Mindy wondered what part of Howard's heart was missing, to think that he should use somebody so incapable of using anyone. The more she thought of it, the more it stung.

Here, right in her home, was the real fleshly proof of what had happened between Verity and Cass. Ivy was not a story that could be twisted for one's purposes, but a human being.

The next morning, a Saturday, Mindy decided to make cookies—oatmeal cookies, the humblest. There being no oatmeal in the house, she had to go to the market. While there, she bought a carton of vanilla ice cream. It had been years since she'd last made cookies, but the very tactile experience of smashing butter, oatmeal, sugar, and flour together connected her to her childhood, when her mother had given her the run of the kitchen and stood aside while she made a mess. The ticking oven warmed the room, and soon the delicious smell of baking cookies filled the house. One of her housemates wandered in and asked who she was baking for, and Mindy shrugged. "Nobody," she said with a smile. "Or anybody."

She meant what she said, but when the cookies were done and cooling on a rack, it came to her that Ivy was her target. She had not come out of her bedroom, though it was now late morning. Mindy read the newspaper in the living room, but she kept glancing up to see whether Ivy had appeared. Eventually she got up and knocked softly on the bedroom door.

"Yeah," Ivy said, and Mindy went in. The room was dark, but Ivy was propped up in bed with a book lit by a chrome gooseneck lamp. She didn't look up.

"Hey, I made some cookies," Mindy said. "Do you want some?"

"Sure."

"Come out to the kitchen. I'll make us some coffee."

It was a gamble, and for a long, paralyzed moment she watched Ivy to see whether she would move. When she rolled over and sat up, Mindy withdrew from the door so as not to appear to track her too closely. Halfway through making coffee she looked up and saw Ivy standing in the doorway, dressed in sweats that had apparently been laundered with bleach into a blotchy brown-gray. Ivy was quite short, Mindy remarked to herself; she left a bigger impression.

"Do you take milk or sugar?"

"Both," Ivy said.

"Have a seat," Mindy said. "Grab a cookie."

When the coffee was made, she poured a cup for them both and sat down opposite, wrapping her hands around the mug, enjoying its warmth. "Your mom didn't drink coffee," she said. "At least not that I ever saw. What about your dad?"

Ivy merely shrugged, and Mindy let the moment pass in silence. She had placed a plate of cookies between them, and now she took one up and nibbled on it. "She liked cookies, though."

"Ice cream," Ivy said.

"Yes." Conscious of not reacting, Mindy looked down. "Anything sweet, wouldn't you say?" But Ivy did not respond.

With an internal rush, Mindy realized that it was time to play her cards. She had waited long enough. "I really loved your mom," she said. "I knew her for years and years, but it wasn't until she died that I realized how much she meant to me. I miss her. Terribly."

She let the cards lie on the table, hoping for a response, but Ivy remained silent. She had taken a cookie and seemed to concentrate on examining its surface. Mindy plunged forward. "I'm not going to pretend that I know you or that I've fallen in love with you, Ivy. I don't think you'd want me to pretend. And that's not what I do, anyway. I'll tell you the truth, and I hope you'll always do the same to me. Even if it's unpleasant."

She thought of bringing up the stolen jewelry, but she knew that would take over the conversation and she didn't want that. "I'd like to offer you something," she said. "We're in kind of a temporary arrangement, and it's fine, but it's not really a good solution for me to sleep in the living room and bother you every time I need some clothes. So I'm wondering whether you want to stay with me for good. If you wanted to do that, I'd figure out a different living situation. Either we stay here and we each get our own room, or we move to a different house where there is more space. I don't want to do either one unless you tell me you want to stay long term."

For the first time, Ivy looked at her: a doubting, skeptical look. "How long is long term?" she asked.

Mindy didn't have a ready answer. "I don't know," she said. "We could talk about that. It needs to be long enough to make a change worthwhile. It's a big deal buying a house and moving, you know. Until you finished high school?"

Ivy seemed to be considering what she offered, a fact that elated Mindy. Ivy put a whole cookie in her mouth followed by a swig of coffee. She ate like a feral animal, Mindy thought. *She is a feral animal.* Living with her would prove unpleasant, at least sometimes. How did it come to be that gentle Verity raised such a creature? The prospect of sharing a house with her for years—of acting as her parent, essentially—was not attractive.

"Of course, it would depend on your dad. I think he'd be fine with it, but you'd have to ask him."

Ivy made a grimace.

"He's your dad, you know. He's responsible for you."

"He doesn't care."

"Whether he does or not, he's legally responsible for you. And as long as I'm bringing up unpleasant facts, I should say that if you're living with me, you have to go to school. And you have to help out with dishes and things. Do your part."

"You want me to be a slave."

Mindy had to smile. "No, Ivy, that's not slavery. It's called sharing. When we work together."

Ivy said nothing, but an angry look had taken over her face.

"You think about it," Mindy said. "There's no rush. Think about what you want to do for yourself. We can make it work, but it's up to you."

* *

For the rest of the weekend, they said nothing to each other. Mindy read a book while stretched out on the sofa, making no attempt to engage Ivy. She did not want to scare her off by trying too hard. Ivy teetered on the edge, she felt; she reacted to whatever frightened her.

Ivy stayed in her room. She didn't appear for meals and didn't join them to watch their favorite shows, even though Mindy asked her. On Sunday morning, Mindy invited her to church—something of a *pro forma* invitation since Ivy was still in bed—but Ivy didn't even bother to answer.

At the service, Mindy sat alone in the stained-glass light, taking in music and prayers and preaching, feeling herself uncoil. After the service, she stood outside in the sun feeling like a turtle coming out of hibernation.

An old friend approached her, holding a coffee cup and asking how she was. Without intending to, Mindy found herself explaining about Ivy. The friend kept asking questions and Mindy explained more and more about her dilemma.

"Maybe it was not so bright an idea to invite her to live with you," the friend said. "It's taking on a lot."

"That's true," Mindy said. "I'm doing it for her mom. I feel like I owe it to her. And truthfully, Ivy is in a bad place. She needs a mom."

"But you're not her mom. She's never going to accept you as her mom. She'll just resent you."

"Why?" Mindy asked.

"Because she'll think you are trying to control her. She does not want to be controlled. I think that's clear."

It was clear, and her friend's admonitions echoed in her head as she walked toward her car. Everything grew more complicated the more she thought of it. Truthfully, it seemed unlikely that Ivy would accept her offer of a bargain. She could easily imagine, however, that Ivy would stay on and avoid making any commitment. Then what would she do? How did you keep your balance with somebody constantly dodging into the shadows whenever you tried to touch? It felt hopeless.

She drove home slowly, trying to think of a way forward. Perhaps she should try again to talk to Ivy, but what would she say? She had already put everything she had to offer on the table.

The house was quiet when she let herself in. Her housemates had gone off to their own churches, and Ivy had the bedroom door closed. Mindy wasn't ready to talk to Ivy and felt relieved she didn't have to; but the closed door represented Ivy's surliness. It was a child's pose, Mindy knew. Nevertheless, it was strangely powerful.

Mindy took her time making herself a sandwich. Just when she was ready to sit down to it, she relented. Ivy might be hungry enough to come out. Knocking softly on the bedroom door, Mindy steeled herself for a rebuff, but when she cautiously opened the door, she found no one inside. Ivy had gone once again. Her clothes were gone.

Mindy's immediate response was relief. If Ivy was gone for good, Mindy could say she had done what she could. It was almost unbelievable how light that made her feel. Released from responsibility for Ivy's troubles, she was free.

However, she had not eaten half her sandwich before that sense of release was honeycombed with sadness. Dear Verity had left nothing behind except this daughter. Mindy had tried, and maybe she could say she had tried her best, but it amounted to failure. What would happen to Ivy was anybody's guess, but it couldn't be good. She wasn't going to finish high school. Miserable companions would find her; sex and drugs would follow. They probably already had. She might end up sick and addicted and a tool for men with no more sense of responsibility than she had. She might end up dead. It was awful to contemplate. Mindy had no idea whether Verity could see what carried forward on Earth, or whether she even lived in a form that would care. Perhaps the bliss of the presence of God made such troubles seem incidental. That seemed unlikely to Mindy, however; how could that be if God so loved the world? She hoped that Verity could not see. Surely it would crush her.

That thought made a miserable companion to Mindy all day, one that was renewed every time she entered the bedroom and felt its emptiness. In an odd way, she found that she was missing Ivy. Ivy's absence was like a tooth that had been pulled. The pain was gone, but the empty slot drew her tongue.

Just in case Ivy returned, Mindy did not sleep in the room but stayed on the sofa.

Her housemates hardly noticed that Ivy had left, and when Mindy said she didn't know where Ivy was, they didn't seem to mind. Ivy could disappear and hardly be remembered by them. For Mindy, Ivy's absence meant that she had no way to show love for her dearest friend, who had herself disappeared without warning.

Going to work on Monday gave her a distraction. She applied herself single-mindedly to the tasks of the day, keeping her melancholy at bay.

She was unprepared, therefore, for the pile of jewelry she found on the kitchen table when she reached home. It made a bright hoard of red and gold and silver, with glints of diamond. She did not at first recognize it as hers, but when she did, she saw in a flash that Ivy must have dumped it there. This angered her, to think that Ivy could just leave the stuff without even a note. Perhaps it was her way of clearing herself from the smallest tie—a way of closing accounts. *Here's how much I care about your stupid jewels. You can have them; they aren't even worth stealing.*

Then she heard the dumb sound of canned laughter. A TV was on. It wasn't playing in the living room; Mindy had walked through there. Her bedroom door was closed, and she walked cautiously toward it. Opening, she found Ivy scrunched up on the bed, watching a small portable TV— apparently the same set as before. Ivy didn't look up.

"What a mess you are," Mindy said, and began to laugh.

ACKNOWLEDGEMENTS

Friends and family members were kind enough to read this book in various stages of its long development. I owe them a lot for their criticisms and comments. I want to thank Dan Baumgartner, Kathy Sutherland, Katie Stafford, Silas Stafford, Joyce Denham, Cari Dreesmann, Wally Kroeker, Carol Andersen, Joy Fargo, and Mike Fargo. Also, memories of camp were shared by Doug McGlashan, Nate and Cari Dreesmann, and Carl Vanden Heuvel. Most of all, my wife Popie Stafford was a tireless reader and encourager; I am forever grateful.

Made in the USA
Las Vegas, NV
23 July 2023

74866669R00136